SHARKING

Anchor

SHARKING

Sophie Stewart

Anchor

TRANSWORLD PUBLISHERS LTD
61–63 Uxbridge Road, London W5 5SA

TRANSWORLD PUBLISHERS (AUSTRALIA) PTY LTD
15–25 Helles Avenue, Moorebank, NSW 2170

TRANSWORLD PUBLISHERS (NZ) LTD
3 William Pickering Drive, Albany, Auckland

Published by Anchor – a division of Transworld Publishers Ltd

First published in Great Britain by Anchor, 1999

A catalogue record for this book is available from the British Library

ISBN 1862 300585

Typeset in 11½/15pt Adobe Caslon by Kestrel Data, Exeter

Reproduced, printed and bound in Great Britain by
Mackays of Chatham plc, Chatham, Kent.

To Rachel

'I can't let go'

from 'Your Love' by Frankie Knuckles

Contents

1. The Mid-Twenties Skunk Crisis

'My life's a sham,' said Lilly.

I looked up from the orchid spliff I was lighting and tried to appear interested.

'All I do is spliff and fry chips. I feel like Michelle from *EastEnders*. And I think I'm becoming a man. I can't stop masturbating and I'm gonna have to get a lawnmower for my bikini-line.'

'It's just mid-twenties life crisis,' I comforted. 'Everyone's got it at the moment. Ben says his life disgusts him.'

Lilly fixed me with a nasty glare. 'Mid-twenties life crisis my arse. Mid-twenties skunk crisis, more like.'

'D'you want a toke?' I asked, proffering the joint.

'Jesus, don't you listen to anything I say?' Lilly threw herself back on my sofa and hit her head with the palm of her hand. 'I've had enough.'

I wondered if Lil's bad temper was to do with her stomach. She'd gone to see the doctor that morning because she reckoned her belly was distended and she had ovarian cancer. The doc said it wasn't cancer and that she was suffering from 'obesity of the stomach'.

'I just don't fucking COUNT any more,' Lilly ranted on.

'What?'

'In my house. Now I'm not in the band I don't fit in. At least you dance, I'm just a kitchen porter.'

'Oh, Lil.' I couldn't understand why Lilly wanted to fit in with the bunch of bohemian wankers in her house. They were the sort of people who talked loudly on the phone about auditions and gigs and exhibitions. Several of them were writing Generation X novels.

'This summer's been the worst I've ever had. That animal's ruined my life.'

'Come on, Lilly, it's not that bad. You know, sometimes I feel like Anne Frank, like locked up in sordid conditions.'

Lilly grimaced. 'Whatever.' She stood up and paced over to the window, playing with her ratted dreadlocks. 'Anyway, it's all right for you. You've got a sort of depression lifestyle but I . . . I need COLOUR.'

Lilly's mind was made up. She would take on extra shifts at the café and concentrate on sit-ups. She'd been through a bad stage, what with the animal and the band splitting up. She wanted to get it back together again. Obviously, I wasn't involved. I listened to Lilly clomping down the stairs and felt the paranoia rising inside me again. It would be a week, tops, before Lilly started getting up to her old tricks. I knew I was fucked.

Lilly shouldn't even have been in London that summer. Normally she travelled in the brighter months, her aim that year having been to go to a leper's ashram near Pakistan. But then the punk band she was in, Vaginal Discharge, became surprisingly successful in the spring, actually playing several gigs that didn't result in police intervention. An A&R man even attended one of their sessions, so Lilly decided to stay in London in case VD were signed. Of course, there was never really any chance of this but, where bands were concerned, Lilly lived in a world of fantasy. She certainly had all the ego of a pop star but sadly she possessed no talent whatsoever. Her singing was so bad Sarah had called hers 'the voice that launched a thousand suicides'. And the other squatter-smack-head members of her group were just as hopeless. It wasn't even so much that they were punk bands, but that they were so bad they just ended up sounding that way, delighting in being shunned whilst simultaneously craving the public recognition they so obviously didn't deserve. I'd only ever been to one of Lilly's gigs and that had been enough. The bedraggled audience had consisted entirely of slam-dancing anarchists, mental patients and neo-Nazis. Lilly had not sung a word and just danced around like a demented chicken whilst screaming, 'I Have No Shame,' into the microphone. Anyway, in June the band split up and Lilly was left working as a kitchen porter in between signing on. No band, no travelling. So she started shop-lifting.

Now Lilly had always been a bit of a klepto, calling her lifting 'liberation' and justifying it with a spurious kind of socialism. But that summer, pissed off and with nothing to do, her lifting went from 'buy one, get one free' to grand robbery. We'd be walking down the King's Road when she'd suddenly spy a dress in the window, say, 'Mine,' and emerge with it stuffed under her arm. She started to carry bags lined with tin foil wherever she went (thus avoiding setting off the alarms –

her 'simple but radical' method was simply to cut the alarm cord). Bored of lurking in south-west London, Lilly then began to target not just individual shops but entire counties (she even did one of those day trips from Dover and went lifting in strange French provincial towns). Getting done didn't concern her.

'I'm not singing any more,' she said. 'And a girl's gotta have a talent.' Besides, she was a natural and had been in training all her life (her gypsy mother was a heroin addict and prolific criminal – apart from when she was in bins or clinics or gaol). I thought Lilly's optimism misplaced. It seemed to me that it was more a matter of odds. The more Lilly lifted (and her lifting was obviously completely out of control – she'd even been stealing smoked salmon and she didn't eat fish) the more chance she had of getting arrested. And if Lilly got arrested, what would happen to me?

We know so little of people, even those that are closest to us, my mother once told me. And Lilly and I weren't even that close. We'd only met two years previously whilst working in Nippers topless cocktail bar. She'd found me cowering in the loos on my first night, going, 'I can't do it, I can't do it,' and had given me half a gram of speed. I did it. Lilly became my protector at Nippers, telling the blokes to treat me right as I was a Class Bird and introducing me to a judge who paid me seventy pounds to spank my bottom. We'd stayed friends ever since. After I left, I used to visit Lilly in her various disgusting squats (there was one where they shat in pizza boxes and another where a prostitute lived in a skip outside) and she would torture me with some of the grotesque 'songs' she had written. I admired the perverse bravery with which Lilly conducted her life – she'd once been found wandering round Thailand wearing nothing but a bathing cap with

CUNT written on it – but I also found her totally unpredictable. The truth was that I had no idea how Lilly would react if she discovered my 'mistake'.

It was fortunate for me, but perhaps not for Lilly, that the animal got loose that summer. Ben, our dealer, had been sold an enormous amount of skunk weed freshly imported from the Dam. Whilst admiring his new stock one night (stoned, of course) he'd fallen over and burst two of the vacuum-packed bags with a spliff. Despite wrapping the bags in duvets and using potentially lethal amounts of air freshener, Ben was still unable to cover up the sickly-sweet stench. Paranoid at the best of times, Ben had lost it and (according to my sister, Jinty, who was going out with him) had spent the rest of the night locked in the bathroom with the skunk and a baseball bat. By the following afternoon, the word was out: the black-and-white furry animal was on the loose and at vastly reduced prices for large quantities. Already ravaged with apathy and paranoia, I thought I might as well pick up a couple of eighths. I was totally stoned when Lilly happened to visit. She'd only been wanting to take a lunch-break from her criminal activities but she didn't make it out again that afternoon. The next day we didn't leave my flat at all, calling a cab to come over with extra fags, Rizla and cream cakes. I realized that I had accidentally hit on a cunning plan to control Lil's kleptomania: all I had to do was to keep her too stoned to walk to the shops.

Don't think ruining Lilly's summer was easy for me. It cost me, big time. By mid-August, Lily and I had been fucked for a month and I was struggling to keep up with my ludicrously large puff bills. I'd been intending to save money for dance college; actually all I was doing was working nights to pay Ben. Lilly herself rarely forked out for the animal. She was the sort of person who said she didn't like drugs but could never resist them when they were free. I felt guilty but it wasn't as if Lilly was the only victim of the animal. Most of Fulham had been savaged; lives mutilated by herb worship. Touchy-Feely had been chucked by his girlfriend and not even noticed. Cassie had jumped London when she'd blown a month's rent on skunk. Lacking pride, futures and self-respect, we were easy – some might say willing – victims. Even Ben was said by Jinty to have become a wibbling idiot (then again, she cheerfully called him 'loser' to his face even when he was straight).

I remember going round to Ben's one afternoon that summer, panicked into picking up another quarter when Lilly admitted to window shopping – i.e. stalking premises.

Jinty greeted me enthusiastically, yawning and saying, 'Oh God, another of the addicts.' My sister was one of those rare hypocrites who, whilst going out with a drug dealer and living off his money, despised the trade. She didn't even drink and preferred to spend her spare time reading *Women Who Run With Wolves* whilst listening to ambient whale music.

'Ben's in the garden with that loser Hardcore.' Jinty walked towards the bedroom and Budweiser, Ben's manky parrot, made a grab for her ankles. 'Christ, this parrot's ruining my life!' she screeched.

It seemed that everyone had an excuse.

Ben was lying in a hammock puffing on a huge one whilst Dave Hardcore sat beside him reading *The Big Anal*.

'Fuck, not another of the frigid whores,' said Ben, picking some dried mud off his Stussy T-shirt.

'All right.' I nodded at Dave.

'Righteous,' said Hardcore, giving me a creepy wink.

I'd been at sixth form college with Hardcore and somehow

he'd managed to meet Ben through me and become involved in Ben's Bolivian Posse. I think Ben liked Hardcore since, unlike most of us, Hardcore was a genuine cockney and gave Ben much-needed street cred points. Ben was no hard-man; just a middle-class boy gone bad. He'd once been sent to a posh reform school where the other boys in the dorm had tied his ankles to the rafters. The master had found Ben, cut him down and lectured, 'I said keep him quiet, not hang him.'

Hardcore, though, was the sort of boy who was bad by nature, psychotic by choice.

'You caught us avin a break,' said Hardcore, putting down his magazine and stretching in the sun.

'Surely you mean wank,' I said, catching a feature heading on Dave's mag ('Married Women and their Impotent Husbands – Uncensored!').

'Nah. Ben was tryin to bury the animal under a rosebush.' Hardcore pointed to a discarded shovel and an inch of displaced soil. 'And I'm writin a novel.'

'Really.' Dave was under a dangerous misapprehension that he was 'artistic'.

'Yeah. It's about me being a casual and football hooligan when I was younger and then me becoming a right raver and me Mission.' Dave's 'Mission' was to be the Fuck of the Century. 'It's called *Casual Sex*.' He pointed to a scrap of scrawled-on A4 lying beside him. I caught the first words, *My Mum always said . . .*

'Looks good.' I felt inexplicably overcome by futility. 'Look, Ben, I was wondering if like—'

'Yeah, yeah.' Ben hauled himself out of his hammock and lazily handed me two eighths. I promised to pay him 'soon'.

'Oy, Parrot!' screamed Dave, who had dragged his lardy body into a vertical position and was dancing by the garden sprinkler. 'Your mum walks around Fulham with a mattress nailed to her back.'

Ben rushed out and the two of them wrestled around in the water-spray. They still acted like teenagers but protruding between their shorts and T-shirts were beer-bellies that shook up and down every time they moved. Somehow, those bellies seemed to symbolize my summer.

Lilly seemed, if not content, then pretty resigned to being stoned with me. We spent August rolling in between the fag-butts, papers and roaches that soon made up the bloated ashtray that became my flat. Sometimes, we'd read magazines featuring successful twenty-somethings, bitterly demanding what they had that we didn't. The answer – an ability to get through the day without getting wasted – depressed us, so we puffed more. We'd watch videos (never getting to the end as we always passed out before then) or just lie on the floor dreaming. I fantasized about setting up a hydro-ponic skunk-growing system but I worried about thermo-nuclear helicopters. Lilly thought about becoming a social worker. She was such a good person. She told me that when she was younger her favourite game had been Running a Battered Women's Refuge and she still often talked to tramps. When I wasn't working at night, we'd head out to satisfy our skunk-induced eating disorders. Crazed with munchies, we were without culinary shame. I used to hoard Tooty Fruities and Lilly was obsessed with pork pies. Maybe it was the munchies and Lilly's subsequent distended stomach problem that sparked her back into action. Or maybe it was just her understandable boredom with me. Personally, though, I blame Seb.

*   *   *

It was on yet another of Lil's and my feeding frenzies, swaying back from 7-11 through hordes of drunks, that we saw the portly figure of Sebastian on Fulham Broadway. I'd been avoiding Seb for a few months due to his growing obsessions with collecting Third Reich paraphernalia and the French. It would be hard to encapsulate Seb's hatred for Frogs. His rants could go on for hours (his particular favourite being the Channel Tunnel. Why build a tunnel to France when *it was obvious that the French were bound to start using it themselves*? Seb thought they should have built the Chunnel to the Falklands). You couldn't go anywhere with him in case he heard a French accent; his jaw would become tense and then his eyes would start to pop. More than two and he would become psychotic.

'UDA! NO SURRENDER!' he greeted us.

'All right,' I said.

'I've got a job,' he suddenly gloated.

'Don't be ridiculous.'

Seb was both rich and provocatively lazy. He could spend an entire day reading *Horse and Hound*. I'd first met him during my six-month stay at uni. I'd staggered into the Student's Union bar on my second night, pissed after necking a bottle of cider in my room. I spied a lone figure wobbling round the bar ranting 'Deutschland! Deutschland!' whilst doing Nazi salutes. 'Where's your pass, boy?' he shouted, looking at me. '*Das ist ein haus*,' I said, quoting the only sentence of German I knew. By the end of the night we had devised a cunning plan to become drug dealers so Seb could finance an Oswald Mosley fan club and I could buy great clothes. The following day, we both emptied our bank accounts and bought a load of draw off one of Seb's school acquaintances. I never even sold a sixteenth. I hated my redbrick prison and Seb never had any friends due to his bizarre right-wing libertarianism. So we just puffed ('I haven't the heart to touch breakfast, Jeeves,' Seb would say, 'you'll have to smoke it yourself,') and went for ambling walks where Seb would cackhandedly try to rape me over bridges. We once entertained a private Smokers' Olympics, holding events like Rolling a Spliff in Under Thirty Seconds and Not Coughing for Two Minutes. It had been a great relief when I'd finally been asked to leave college owing to my attendance being so bad they didn't even know I was there. Seb, though, had stuck it out, relying on a mixture of cheating, doctors' notes and swapping personalities. Since he'd come down to London, he'd continued with his Fascist Fogey personality, spending his days penning letters to the *Spectator* and visiting obscure private museums.

'It's true,' he went on, now. 'I'm a wage slave, a graduate trainee merchant banker.'

'Bastard.' The world had gone insane. I'd always longed to be a merchant banker.

'My Uncle Eddie sorted it for me.'

'But why?' Seb had always sworn he'd never get a job.

'I have come to believe,' Seb mused, putting on a self-important face, 'that counter-culture is a con. That by our non-participation in everyday life we will end up with non-lives.'

'You mean you're broke,' sighed Lilly in an I've-heard-this-all-before sort of way. She looked down at the pavement and stubbed her rank trainers on the concrete.

'Well, yes, I do have a private investigator after me . . . but no, it's more than that. I just can't seem to accept the ludicrousness of my lifestyle any more.'

'It stops being fun,' I agreed, watching exhaust smoke curl lazily in the twilight like a thousand late-night spliffs.

'You've thought about getting a career?'

'Occasionally. I don't want to spend my entire life scream-ing "Fuck this shit" in a relaxation tank. You know what I mean?'

'You scare me sometimes,' said Seb, shaking his head. He grinned.

'Anyway, must dash. Don't forget, South Africa, Land of the Free!'

Lilly and I went back to her place and stuffed ourselves stupid. Despite more puffing, neither of us could seem to relax. I guess we both felt like we'd been had. Seb was now a merchant banker and what were we . . . ? Maybe everyone else was just pretending to be fucked up, knowing that it didn't matter much what they did or didn't do as they knew they'd eventually be bailed out. I'd sometimes walk round Fulham and look at all the stoned Sloanes and want to machine-gun them out of envy. Why should they have so much and me so little? My parents were practically bankrupt and Lilly actually supported her mother.

'We're getting behind,' Lilly said sadly. 'Other people our age have endowment morgages, not small-scale drug problems.'

The next day was when Lilly told me her life was a sham and she didn't want to see me any more. And all because Seb had become a merchant banker.

You would have thought that now I didn't have to keep Lilly stoned to stop her shoplifting, I would have cut down on the skunk. Hah! I was puffing more than ever. Sometimes I even shocked myself with the level of my abuse. But if I wasn't stoned, I thought, and I couldn't bear my thoughts. In fact, I might as well have been banged up as all I did was puff and pace and think about the horrors of prison showers. I knew that Lilly would soon be bored with kitchen portering and sit-ups and start casing Fulham again. The likelihood was she'd be caught. My only hope was she might get into another band but with Lilly's singing there was more chance of her getting muff-dived by the Pope. I knew I should tell Lilly, give warning, and my fingers permanently edged the phone. But, as usual, I said nothing. I couldn't justify my previous actions, it was as if another recklessly deranged person had done them. Of course, I knew that by saying nothing . . . fuck it. I sat back and let it happen.

Sarah called me, demanding an ounze of skunk.

'But you don't puff,' I said (Sarah was too snobbish to do Class B drugs).

'I've no choice, darling,' she sighed. 'My nose has been surfing the crimson wave for months and the doc basically said if I don't cut down I'll lose it. Jonny said he'd buy me a new nose if I needed one but you know how unreliable men are.'

Sarah's plan to save her nose was simple: she would get so stoned she'd be unable to toot.

It was funny, as if I could have asked anyone's advice, it would have been Sarah's. Her life was littered with victims, people she'd casually discarded when they were no longer of use to her. But I was scared of Sarah; afraid she might blackmail me or something. Sarah was a hard bitch. Even Lilly hated her. Lilly thought Sarah a Sloaney Cunt and Sarah thought Lilly the Creature Whom Style Forgot. To be honest, Sarah was a bit of a Sloaney cunt but we were related. She was a second cousin of mine whom I had been forced to visit occasionally as a child. We'd loathed each other. Sarah had been the sort of kid who had all the Sindy doll stuff but wouldn't let me touch it. We'd drifted back into contact after I'd been in London a couple of years. I used to meet Sarah around town as she was dashing off on shopping trips and sometimes I dropped in on her impossibly smart flat in Chelsea. Sarah never showed much interest in me as I went to unfashionable nightclubs. We'd only really become friends when I happened to visit her after she'd just returned from a four-day coke spree on a yacht in St-Tropez. She began babbling confessions at me in between cries of, 'No-one must ever know!' – one of which was that she supported her lifestyle by being a high-class escort. She said she didn't really have sex with the customers, it was more just a social thing (as I'd been working in Nippers at the time and knew something of the world of escorting, I took Sarah's 'just a social' line for the lie it undoubtedly was). Since then Sarah had given up literal prostitution and now lived in Notting Hill Gate supported by her club-owning boyfriend, Jonny, probably the slimiest man in London.

Sarah's and my days were simple but sad. I'd stay in bed until I ran out of cigarettes and then amble round to her fraud palace. Sarah would then get up, telephone Jonny for a fight about maintenance ('tight git', 'freeloading cunt') and then we'd head down the White Horse and start whoring around for free drinks. Sarah termed men who didn't buy us drinks as 'bastards' and those that did as 'idiots'. I would have liked to have contradicted her but unfortunately the evidence seemed overwhelming. Actually, Sarah's favourite song was a transvestite country and western tune called 'No Dick's as Hard as My Life'. She took shameless advantage of men's wallets but the more they gave her, the more she seemed to despise them. Thing was, Sarah didn't like girls much either, thinking them fools and saps. She even disliked my old friend

Cassie Lunchtime, saying she'd rather be friends with a skinhead than a hippie.

After a couple of vodders, Sarah and I would lie down on Parsons Green and spliff ourselves silly. Despite being September, the weather was still good.

'I could almost forget about *Ambition*,' said Sarah one day, sunning herself in a stylish bikini top. *Ambition* by Julie Burchill was Sarah's fave book and she treated it as some kind of sick Bible. I wondered if Lilly was at work or if she was out prowling the shops.

'Tim at the club,' I said finally. 'He said that he'd been thinking about *The Wizard of Oz*.'

'What?' Sarah gave me a familiar patronizing look.

'You know, about making a wish. He said that he'd wish for ambition.'

'Desperate . . .' Sarah lit a spliff. 'Hardcore once told me that his only ambition in life was to live opposite a brothel with no curtains.'

'He became obsessed with sex-cabinets in Germany,' I admitted. I wondered if I was ambitious. I was too stoned to work it out. I'd had an awful nightmare the night before in which I'd married an unemployed welder from Tufnell Park. I'd ended up fifteen stone and munching Whopper burgers as I wheeled my three educationally sub-normal, incontinent children down the Holloway Road.

'It's funny,' I said eventually, 'but sometimes I feel as if I'm waiting for my life to begin.'

'That this can't be it.'

'You feel it too?' I'd always assumed Sarah was too good-looking to really feel discontent. I used to watch her body bronze and glisten in the sun whilst my own skin stayed a remarkably resilient shade of grey.

'You know, I spend so much time regretting my past and

worrying about my future that I've no time for the present.' Sarah adjusted her sun-specs. 'I must get an orange T-shirt. You know, orange is the new black.'

It was after one of Sarah's and my sunny, lazy afternoons on Parsons Green that Lilly turned up round my place. I hazily opened the front door and she rushed inside, red-faced and panting.

'I've got done,' she said simply.

'What happened?'

'What the fuck do you mean what happened?'

A cold, freezing feeling spread through my body. I started to run up the stairs.

'WHAT D'YOU THINK HAPPENED?' I reached my flat door but Lilly was too quick. She forced her way inside and slammed the door shut. 'I thought some guy was eyeing me up and then I walk out of the shop and he nicks me.' Lilly's face was hard with rage, even her eyes were spasming with hate.

'Did they call the police?' I felt like I was going to be sick.

'Oh, they did.' Lil picked up a glass of Diet Coke and threw it against the wall. 'And then I went down the station.' A book hit the floor. 'And they were just about to caution me – first offence and all – ' I attempted a lunge for the bathroom door but Lilly was too quick for me. She grabbed my arm and I ended up sprawled on the sofa. 'And you'll never guess what.' With one flick of her arm, Lilly wiped off an entire table-contents. 'Turns out I'm a wanted criminal. Possession of Class A substances. Luckily for me I was in Thailand at the time of the "alleged offence".' She hurled her bobbly hat at me. 'I don't even fucking use coke.'

'I'm sorry.' I cowered pathetically on the sofa. Lilly was far bigger than me and wasn't scared of using her fists. 'It wasn't my fault.'

'You know, they couldn't believe I hadn't already been picked up. I was lucky, they said. Lucky.' Lilly lit a cigarette, her hands shaking with anger. 'Five fucking hours I spent being interviewed by CID when all I should have got was a five minute caution!'

'Did they charge you?'

'No, I told them.'

'Oh God.' I was going to prison and probably for a very long time. Tears began to well in my eyes. Lilly looked at me in disgust.

'I told them my drug addict mum must've given my name out. I didn't recognize the photo.'

'Thank God,' I sighed, putting my head in my hands.

'Jesus, you're the most selfish person I've ever known.' Lilly shook her head and sighed. When she spoke again her voice had changed from anger to bewilderment. 'I just couldn't believe it. That you'd shop me for your own crime. You did, didn't you?'

'Yes.'

'Why? What did I ever do to you?'

I couldn't explain. There was a limit to the amount of lies even I could tell.

After Lilly left, I tried to clear up my flat. She telephoned two hours later. To call me, after what I'd done, Lilly was the kindest person in the world.

'It's OK, I forgive you. I know you've had a lot of problems.' It struck me how much I got away with by being fucked up. I told Lilly I loved her. I wished I could have said it was a relief now she knew, but it wasn't. It just made me remember things that I'd forgotten I was trying not to remember.

'I'm a terrible person,' I blubbed.

'No you're not. That's what's so ridiculous about you. You're just thoughtless. I am SO fucking angry with you, but . . . oh, they only cautioned me and I kind of understand. It's like with my mum. You've got no fucking respect for yourself. You just don't THINK, you're too fucking busy surviving.'

I had the weirdest feeling, almost as if there was a ghost in the room with me. I really had to cut down.

Of course, the inevitable happened: Sarah relapsed on the toot and Ben sold all the skunk. I don't know for how long Sarah had been nasal diving again but one day on the green I noticed that a side of her face was swollen. She said it was some kind of pollen allergy. An hour later, Sarah started getting a tick around one of her eyes. Then she had a fit in front of me. Mild. Not a lot of froth. Some Sloane offered to call an ambulance but Sarah recovered quickly and threatened to kill them.

'I feel like Leah Betts,' Sarah sighed. 'I wish someone would lock me up.' Then she lit a cigarette and went home. I trotted off to Ben's to pick up some more skunk but he told me he was just smoking the last of it. From now on he'd be back to pushing weed and coke. The skunk had ruined his life. He turned off the telly (he'd been watching videos of himself snowboarding) and calmly weighed me an eighth. No messin. No abuse.

'What's wrong?'

'Nothing.' Ben handed me the weed and lit the last of the skunk spliff. 'Hardcore got done.'

'Oh not again.' It was not for nothing that the Fulham police called Dave a 'one lad crime wave'.

'Just possession, but man he got one talking to down

the station. I never knew white boys got beaten so bad by the rozzers.' Ben threw a match at Bud. The parrot was obviously stoned and looked a total wreck. 'And man, I picked up a couple of kilos today.' Ben shook his head. 'My last deal, definitely. When everyone's carrying guns and walkie-talkies, you know you're outclassed.' Ben handed me the joint and I tried to look interested. I'd heard this 'last deal' crap one too many times before.

'I've peaked and now I'm falling. I've watched the best go down, hard men. My number's up. But what the fuck do I do? Twenty-six, no qualifications, never had a proper job. I could've been something. If it wasn't for the ankle injury, I could've been the don skateboarder.'

'At least you've got money,' I said, staring enviously around Ben's sitting-room.

'Yeah . . . but it's the paras I can't deal with; you know, Toby and shit.'

Toby had been Ben's brother. He'd been picked up with a load of hash and had hanged himself while on remand. Ben carried on in the family business, despite his practically sectionable paranoia, saying of the Establishment: 'I Do Not Accept Their Authority.' Whenever Ben got pissed he used to fantasize about going down Scotland Yard with a couple of Uzis slung over his shoulder, screaming, 'Go on, take me if you're hard enough!'

'I know,' I said slowly. 'People talk about the horrors of crime but they don't understand that what does you in is the paranoia.'

'You know it.'

'But it's the paranoia that protects you, that makes you careful.'

'It's a question of odds. My number's up, I know it.'

I wished I could have talked to Ben, asked him if there was

any way to be less paranoid. Whether the spliff helped or just made it worse.

'I'll miss the animal,' I said finally.

'You know it. This stuff's so fucking good it ought to be illegal.'

'It is illegal, Ben.'

'Oh, yeah.' Ben took a huge last toke. 'You know, sometimes I wonder what my life would've been like if I'd never puffed.'

A week later puffer-extraordinaire Cassie Lunchtime returned to London after three members of her commune were sectioned. She had nowhere to live, so I offered to put her up whilst she looked for a room and I waited for dance college to begin. Cassie wasn't exactly the Fulham scene's most dynamic member (Jinty called her the world's only living brain donor) but to be honest I was a bit lonely. Sarah had disappeared back to the club scene, obviously having given up giving up toot, and Lilly was still being a bit funny with me since she'd found out about her surprise cocaine conviction. Besides, Cassie wasn't that bad a tenant. Although my optimistically entitled 'studio' flat was tiny, Cassie hardly had any stuff apart from some tired seventies outfits and pots of E45 cream and she was never any hassle. Like Lilly, Cassie was a hippie type, but whereas Lilly travelled the world, Cass only thought about travelling the world. Mostly, she just melted into my sofa clutching comfort knickers against her face whilst reading *My Life as a Siamese Monk*. She was permanently surrounded by a haze of dope smoke and sometimes used to carry a piece of wood called Lulu around with her. Looking at Cassie, it was hard to believe that she'd once been a dancer (if a rather poor one). She was basically pretty, but somehow she managed to appear simultaneously overweight and terminally ill.

Cassie was living on a small allowance from her porn magnate father and it was with great difficulty that she even managed to get it together to sign on. Actually, I had to drive her down the dole office. I asked Cass what she was going to do with her life, but she was always vague to the point of vacuousness, reciting old hippie clichés like, 'Go travelling,' 'Set up a market stall,' or 'Join a Buddist monastery.' The closest I ever got to an answer was one night after we had been hot-knifing for three hours.

'You know, yesterday I realized that I'd been depressed for eight years. I mean, how am I supposed to make decisions about my life when I don't even know if I want to live or not?'

I wondered if all the times I thought Cass was stoned she was actually unhappy. She rarely bothered even getting dressed and lived in T-shirts stained with the E45 cream she applied to her weeping eczema.

'Have you thought about seeing a counsellor?' I asked finally.

'I did once, years ago. You know, Josh.'

'But you were going out with him.'

'Yeah, but he was a counsellor.'

'Did he help?'

'Not really. When I broke up with him, he said I was locked in an Abusive Cycle.'

Cass never even bothered looking for a room but luckily one of her ex-commune mates wangled a Housing Association place in Shepherd's Bush. We decided to celebrate. Cassie got an eighth and I got a bottle of wine. I was glad she was going, really. Cass was a bad influence on me. Even after a week of her company I was beginning to question why I bothered getting up. Cass's conviction that the outside world was a horrendous and demented hellhole to be avoided at all costs was strangely convincing. And there was the spooky fact that perhaps I almost enjoyed living with someone. My only ambition as a child had been to live on my own. Yet without other people around I would let both myself and my flat degenerate into medieval levels of squalor. And also Cass's snoring, scratching figure helped comfort me in the dark hours when my nightmares (Lilly, police stations, et cetera) wouldn't let me rest.

Anyway, Cass and I celebrated. Cass rolled spliffs and scratched her skin and I poured wine and dragged on my new inhaler. All the puffing had been wreaking havoc with my chest and the doc had forced an asthma pump on me. It had almost amused me to discover, on production of my new toy, that Cass had been using one for years. Apparently inhalers helped reduce the traditional puffer's cough. I wondered if Cass and I should watch a video but you can only watch bootleg copies of *Pipkins with Hartley Hare* so many times.

'Spliff's weird,' said Cass, easing herself down into my sofa. 'You know, I think being stoned is like lying under some huge feather duvet, kind of comforting but kind of claustrophobic.'

'Mostly it just makes me feel like I'm passing out,' I admitted. 'I never actually do anything when I'm stoned.'

'Yeah, but you can be like active in a passive way. You know, listening to music can be a really spiritual thing when you're stoned.'

Later the doorbell went and I meandered downstairs like some sleepwalker in a fog. To my amazement, I was greeted by my friend Susie from Essex. She looked just as ridiculous as ever, wearing red satin hotpants and her hair in a pineapple.

'Jesus-fuck, I've just been on a date with this disabled telly presenter. It was worse than Lagos. Let me in.' I did so. 'State of you. Too snobby for bath water, are yer?'

'Oh Susie . . .' I led Susie upstairs to my flat. I may have liked Cassie and Lilly and even Sarah but I RATED Susie. Yes, she looked like a satanic go-go dancer, but she had a quality that the rest of us lacked.

'Right, Cass,' she said, hopping inside and helping herself to a glass of wine. 'How're you two, then?'

'Bored,' I said.

'Depressed,' said Cassie.

Susie laughed. 'You posh ones are all the same. You sit in yer snobby flats goin on about how yer daddy didn't love you enough. Get a life.'

I suddenly thought how I wished I'd seen more of Susie that summer. She'd been grannie-bashing in Ilford and I'd been too stoned or too paranoid to make the track out there. It was typical of me, really. I always thought there were better, more interesting ways to live than the way I chose, but I could never think of any until it was too late.

'I need to go back to Chingford,' I said suddenly. In Chingford I'd been young, I'd been happy, I'd been on E.

'Gary still asks after you,' said Susie. 'In a bitter and sarcastic way, but e does ask.'

'I miss Chan's.'

'Yeah,' said Susie, her eyes misting over. 'I mean, no. Last summer was sick.' Our drug abuse had forced Susie into doing a runner to Israel. She'd returned with a deep tan and a dose of the clap. 'Oh, it was OK but it's all over. No-one goes down Chan's no more.'

'I was alive in Chingford.'

'Fucked, more like. Anyway, what, are you dead now?'

Last summer: I'd partied, I'd clubbed, I'd felt like a normal person. I thought, I even miss the come-downs.

'Got any new tunes?' Susie put on the stereo and jumped around the room whilst I puffed and Cassie picked at her eczema. 'I'm completely pissed and I'm round me mate's dancin like a maniac. I love my fuckin life!'

I remembered Lilly, unable to comprehend that me, her friend, had betrayed her. I started rolling my next joint.

2. The Chingford Years

The Chingford Years. Well, a summer, the year before the tragedy that was my skunk crisis occurred, before Lilly got done for lifting. Depending on my mood it was either a time of innocence, of rediscovering childhood with new toys, or just another sordid date with despair.

I was reminded of The Years when I met Gary in Covent Garden. I'd just come out of a ballet class at Pineapple where I'd been told that my plié in second looked like a constipated person on the lavatory. Then someone grabbed me.

'Tara!' said a bloke, letting go of my arm.

'?' I looked harder. 'Fuck, *Gary!*'

I couldn't believe it. The change was remarkable. Gary no longer looked as if he'd done three years down a mine-shaft. He looked fit, almost *healthy*.

'All right?' he said.

'Yeah,' I lied. I felt like shit and was still racked with guilt over Lilly. I was thinking of writing a book called *Hate For One: The Art of Self-Loathing.* 'How are you?'

'Sweet as. I'm seeing this don gel, Cherrie. We, like, go to the cinema and hold hands.'

'Christ.'

'No job, course, but Cherry's dad might get me to do a patio for him.' He looked at me with something like pity. 'What're you up to? Still clubbing?'

'Oh no, not really.'

'Funny, someone said they'd seen a picture of you in *i-D.*'

'Must have been someone else,' I lied.

'Nice day,' he said.

'Yeah.'

We stood there staring at each other and the sky fell open and collapsed on my head.

It had all started with Susie. I'd been behind the bar at the Escape reading *Do-It-Yourself Psychotherapy* when a strange girl, half-cut and half-dressed, staggered up to the counter, slurred, 'I'm fucked,' and fell over. I was quite relieved, really. I'd only been working at the club two months but I was already stupefied with boredom. The Escape Club was the sort of place that you only went to if you couldn't get in anywhere else. The punters weren't even losers, they were losters, people who'd never had anything to lose in the first place; a mixture of emotional incontinents and no-hopers. As barmaid, I had the pleasure of their moronic faces and hilarious jocularity all night ('Can I help you?' 'Only if you're a qualified psychiatrist! Haha, geddit?'). Which was why I'd taken to reading self-help books behind the bar.

'So what fucker's gonna buy me a drink then?' the girl

screamed, picking herself up off the floor. No-one was keen so eventually I put down my book and, grateful for any distraction, gave her a Margarita from the jug I was necking. She clambered clumsily onto the bar stool opposite me and raised her glass.

'Cheers, doll.' She downed it in one and I poured her another. Even in the dim light of the Escape, her make-up was quite the most lurid and comical I had ever seen. It looked as if it had been applied by someone with Alzheimer's.

'Are you all right?' I asked. She raised her eyebrows and appeared to think for a second.

'Yeah, I am. Beyond drunk, obviously, but all right. I've just split up with me boyfriend, see. We ad a fight cos he thought I was being unfaithful.'

'Men,' I said vaguely, not knowing much about them.

'Problem is, is that I am. I don't mean to be. I just get bored and next thing I know I'm in bed with some geezer and he sort of slips it in when I'm not looking. Is that so wrong?'

I shrugged.

'What kind of wank-stain is this anyway?' she asked, looking around her in disgust.

'The Escape Club. I'm Tara.'

'Susie.' She sighed. 'Pity about the police involvement and all that but sod it, I'm glad it's over. Boyfriends. You want fun and all you get is videos and take-away curries. Ave you got a ball n chain?'

'No.' Even the idea of me having a boyfriend seemed uproariously farcical. 'I mean, look at me.' I had recently been told that my appearance at work was 'unacceptable' and I had to make more effort.

'You're all right,' smiled Susie. 'You wanna get out a bit. Ave a laugh.'

'I know.' Another barmaid and I had recently started doing Tedium Charts behind the bar.

'You should come up Chingford with me. The blokes there, you gotta laugh.'

We swapped phone numbers and then Susie staggered out as she had to catch the last train. To my amazement, she called me the next night. Did I want to go down Chan's? Why not? And so began the Chingford Years.

I wish I could better describe that first night at Chan's. I'd driven down on a balmy Sunday evening through the spooky East London suburbs (I was a south-west London girl and didn't like leaving my territory). I found Charlie Chan's underneath Walthamstow Dog Tracks and walked to the club wondering what the hell I was doing going out with some lunatic I'd only met once before. Susie was at the door smoking a fag and fiddling with her ridiculous pineapple hairstyle.

'All right,' she said, seeing me.

'Hi.' I tried to smile but I think my face was frozen with shyness.

'Fuck, this is worse than a first date,' she laughed. We went inside and it was exactly what I'd expected an Essex club to be like: full of mirrors and cockneys drinking fluorescent cocktails. Susie took me to the loo and we crowded inside a cubicle. She gave me an E and then said, 'Oh why fuck about,' and handed me another one. We popped the pills and went outside and I hung around while Susie chatted to her mates.

Of course, I'd taken E before. Halves here and there. They'd never done much for me. I'd always been more of a coke baby; snorting, going to posy clubs, too worried about embarrassing myself to actually have any fun. So an hour later when, in a rare moment of musical experimentation, the DJ played a remix of Frankie Knuckles' 'Your Love', I couldn't believe what happened. I took Susie's hand and led her onto the dance floor, feeling an uncontrollable desire just to be my body. I danced until I was sweated through. I talked to everyone. One guy cartwheeled over to me, kisssed my hand and then disappeared back into the throng. I was so happy it scared me. I felt unique and yet part of a wonderful community. I told Susie I loved her. Then suddenly it was all over and we went round to someone's place and drank tea and smoked spliffs and I lay down on a sofa and stared softly at the smiling ceiling. I remembered how when I was a child I'd read the Narnia books and every evening I used to go and stand in my wardrobe and wait to be admitted to the fabulous world I'd been told about. It had taken me a month to realize that my wardrobe's only secrets were the skiddy knickers I hid there. That night at Chan's was my entry to Narnia and I was no longer the Ice Princess ('You're an alien, not a human being,' my mother had said. 'Why can't you be a normal teenager and row with me?'). Suddenly, after years of deadened emotions for both myself and all other members of humanity, I too was able to love. Powerfully, intensely, for entire evenings.

And so I became a part of Chingford. I spent night after night at Susie's house. She lived with her parents and bro in Barkingside (not Barking – apparently this was important). Her father was retired and sat all day playing an electric organ whilst wearing a gas mask because of his wife's incessant smoking. Her mother spent her days bird-watching and doing Callanetics half-cut. Her brother had Gone Odd and was training as a biology teacher. Susie herself claimed to be a hairdresser but was sacked with alarming regularity due to the amount of sickies she pulled. Her friends were pretty similar; all living at home, doing semi-skilled jobs and having large disposable incomes. They'd used to be football hooligans until they discovered E; now when they went down the terraces they just had a dance. The Chingford Faces were basically walking pharmacies with the brains of stoats who spent their lives getting lucky and quaffing Green Bastards (lager and blue curaçao). We got on.

Our top nitespots were Chan's, the Epping Forest Country Club 'Jungle', Maestro's wine bar and the Maypole pub. Susie and I would sit in the Maypole gossiping and waiting to come up and then head down Maestro's to dance and pull. All my Fulham friends thought I'd finally lost it ('I mean *Chingford*,' sneered Sarah. 'What on earth do you do there apart from shag random manual labourers?') but Chingford had something Fulham lost years ago: a sense of community. My friends were just a bunch of people who'd got together over the years for want of anything better to do; the Chingford lot had been born in the same hospitals, went to the same schools and would probably be buried in the same graveyards. Everyone knew everyone else, everyone shared their lives together, everyone was dedicated to following the same one-way path to oblivion. Unlike my cronies, Chingford people didn't sit around whining on about how their daddy didn't love them enough and why it would all have been different if they'd had trust funds. Instead, Susie's crowd just did drugs. Insane amounts of drugs. Now I'd thought my friends were drug addicts (and they were) but somehow the Essex lot were able to use huge doses but actually have fun rather than long stays in expensive clinics. They took Es to go down their dad's for Sunday lunch. They took Es to watch the footie. They took Es because there was nothing on telly. No-one ever seemed to get depressed. I realized what a drama queen I'd been becoming: hysterical because I didn't fit in at my new dance college (the other students still laughed about the day I'd taken my pointe-shoes to an improvisation class. They were all barefoot and displaying tatoos). In Chingford, even parental death was treated lightly.

'My mum's just popped it,' a bloke down the Maypole said to me one night.

'God you must feel awful,' I'd said.

'Nah, not really,' he'd shrugged. 'I've just dropped two Easies and I'm on a promise with this gel tonight.' Not for them counselling or aromatherapy, just immediate narcotic action. I liked this.

Inevitably, I got myself a Chingford Lad, Gary. He was a failed actor turned drug dealer. His last major role had been in a Walker's crisp advert. But he wasn't bad looking and had a nice haircut. That our two main lines of conversation were, 'Are you coming up yet?' and, 'I'm fucked', seemed irrelevant. Words were not important to us. We communicated by higher means: touch, gesture, snorting crushed Es. We would meet down Chan's where he'd be with his cronies, dancing like a psychopath and looking like a god.

'All right, gel?' he'd say, putting a sweaty arm around my shoulders. 'You on some then?'

'Yeah. You?'

'Yeah, two Es and a Valium.'

'Why the Valium?'

'It was free.'

Then we'd groove all night and afterwards head off to some dodgy joint where Gary would count his takings for the night (he always carried fifty Es stuffed behind his balls wherever he went).

'Fuck,' he'd say, examining the wads on the bathroom floor. 'I hate dealing drugs, me.' That was the funny thing about Gary. He had absolutely no sense of irony. I would watch him staring into the mirror for hours on end and when I joked that he was vain he'd say he wasn't, he was just insecure, see. Then, after Gary had finished his counting, he'd raise his eyebrows and say, 'You fancy doin it in the bathroom, gel?'

And, sad to say, I'd normally agree.

Everything began to go very fast and blurry here; like being on a merry-go-round. Together, Gary and I were disastrous. We simply couldn't stop taking E. Not that we ever actually tried to stop; out every night, edging round dancefloors, convincing each other to take Just One More because it was obviously Duff Stuff. It didn't get very deep. I don't think we ever really had a conversation. I don't even know where it went wrong; just that one minute I was going out to have a good time and the next I was going out to have a Sick One or Do a River (River Phoenix was Gary's hero). I suppose that I knew it had to stop, but I wasn't going to be the one to stop it. Gary occasionally mentioned staying in and watching a video but I took the suggestion for the joke it undoubtedly was. Then Gary and I went back to his flat one Monday after a really stupendous weekend binge. We were having sex when he started hallucinating about dinosaurs. I think we both knew it was all over then. When we woke the following afternoon, we were silent. This wasn't unusual. What was odd was the vague sense of disgust each of us felt for the other. After that we would occasionally bump into one another down Chan's and I would look at him and feel a confused mixture of uneasiness and embarrassment. He would just look horrified. Then Gary stopped going down Chan's altogether. Rumour was that he'd had an epileptic fit one night and had gone to recuperate at his aunt Doreen's.

I carried on regardless. I was having a good time and besides with E I didn't need men. In fact, I thought that by dropping three Es I'd discovered a way to have sex without the moist, infected miseries of the bedroom. Others weren't so impressed, though.

'It's not drugs you need,' my sister Jinty had told me when I begged her to dump Ben, her coke-dealing boyfriend, for one with a line in disco pills. 'More like emergency admission to a psychiatric institution. Jesus, as if we haven't got enough psychosis in the family.'

At work they weren't pleased with me either. I had been nicknamed 'bug-eyes' and used to collapse on the bar floor and go, 'S not my fault, I've got a heart condition.'

I didn't want to do anything but get off my head. What else did I have? My poky flat, washing up and pliés.

Annoyingly, Susie seemed to have had enough of me too. She said I was becoming even more boring than her other friends and accused me of not being able to string a sentence together or of actually possessing a head to get off. In fact, Susie herself didn't really have that much in common with the other Chingford Faces. She was viewed as eccentric for reading novels, shopping in Oxfam and being a socialist. I think she was always more interested in promiscuity than drugs. It was thus a surprise when one afternoon in the Maypole she claimed to be bored of sex.

'But you always said you were a nymphomaniac.'

'Nah. I just lie there and groan at appropriate moments.' Susie stared blankly at the warm pint in front of her. 'You know, I just don't enjoy it no more.'

'The sex?'

'Nah, not the sex – though I'm sick of that too. I asked Wayne to lick me out and he said there was only one time he'd tongued a woman and that'd been when he was being born . . . but it's not that. I'm gettin flashbacks and I can't even remember what I'm flashing back to. I just feel really, really . . .' Susie sighed. 'Dunno.'

'I've got a half from last night if you want it,' I said generously.

'No!' she almost screamed. 'I don't want it. You know when they played that "Can You Feel It" last night? All I could think was no, I couldn't fuckin feel it. I've decided to go and do cherry-picking on a kibbutz in Israel.'

I was about to laugh when I realized she was being serious. 'I'll leave next week.'

'Oh.' I didn't know what to say. In the short time I'd known Susie I'd really got to like her. She was so good-natured and easy-going and always willing to have a laugh. 'I guess this calls for a celebration,' I said eventually. I went and bought Susie and myself some more drinks.

'I've got it,' she said when I returned.

'Not AIDS?'

'Nah, what E makes me feel. It makes me realize what I aven't got. I feel . . . *empty*.'

Susie left and I continued travelling down to Chingford, but it wasn't the same. I'd go out and drop five Es, dance all night, love everyone, snog sexy guys and then go home and want to shoot myself. I never knew when to stop. I didn't really fit in in Chingford; I never really had, I'd just been on too many drugs to notice. To the Chan's crowd I was just some kind of deranged Sloane. They thought my cockney accent just as ludicrous as my Fulham friends did. Unopened bills littered my flat. Jinty was no longer on speaking terms with me. College was about to start again. I was sitting in my flat one afternoon chain-smoking and trying to find a piece of paper with my term dates on it when I discovered an old voucher I'd been given for Christmas. It was for a session in a relaxation tank (from Jinty, obviously). Bored and blank, I thought I might go. At least it would stop me smoking for an hour.

I arrived at the clinic and went into a small room where I undressed and applied Vaseline to some scars I had on my body. Then I opened a little door and crawled into a warm tank of salty water. I closed the door and lay there in the pitch black. I gulped down an initial feeling of panic (pathetically, I was still afraid of the dark) and splashed the water a little with my legs. I whistled. I yawned. I felt quite bored. Then I began to notice that my legs were no longer splashing but were kicking in the water. Some of the salty liquid went in my eye and I cried out in pain. Next thing I knew I was screaming and thrashing about in the tank. I shouted, 'Fuck This Shit!' over and over again. I felt like a total fool. I'd spent the last of my stock of money. If it wasn't for the fact that I'd paid my college fees earlier that summer then I'd have spunked that, too. It wasn't that I regretted using E, it was just that I hadn't done anything else that summer other than using, recovering from using and trying to score some more again. I couldn't go back to the blank cloud of nothingness that had been my life, but I was still incapable of any form of emotion without narcotic assistance. I felt as if I'd been watching the television without realizing the programmes were finished.

I thought I'd forgotten, that I was different now, but it was so strange seeing Gary again in Covent Garden. I'd had sex with this guy and I felt *nothing*.

'Well, gotta be goin,' he'd said awkwardly, the crowds on Floral Street pushing us apart. He started to turn and then suddenly whipped back around. 'D'you remember that tune we always used to listen to? You know, Nightcrawlers' "Push the Feeling On"?'

'Oh yeah.' It had been a Chan's favourite.

'And how we could never work out the lyrics?' I remembered: Gary and me in bed, 'It's "Eliza feels good",' 'Nah, "Life will be good",' et cetera, for hours. We were that obsessed we used to have a looped tape of it. 'Well a mate of mine called Kiss and would you believe it, it's Michael Jackson played backwards!'

'What?' I tried to get my head around this one. 'I don't fucking believe it. You mean there were no lyrics, it never meant anything in the first place?'

I would have said How Symbolic, but I doubted that Gary would know what symbolic meant. Lucky bastard.

3. Great Clothes

It was Lilly who, having decided her life was a sham, informed me in autumn that we were to become High-Maintenance Women. The only difference between us and good-looking girls was that they wore more lipstick. We would go down the gym every day, have our hair done, buy great clothes and hang out in beauty salons.

'I'd need a week in a beauty salon to remedy this disaster,' I said bitterly, picking a malignant spot on my chin. I'd dropped in at Lilly's on the way back from dance college and suspected my festering leotard might need to be surgically removed. I felt like someone from a BBC2 documentary. 'Anyway, I thought you thought you were becoming a man.'

'I was, I mean, I did . . . and that's exactly my point. It's part of being a woman, of being feminine, being obsessed with your appearance.'

I wondered if Lil's new concern over her appearance was to do with femininity or her band breaking up. She'd always seemed quite happy looking like a rough, overweight version of Courtney Love. Maybe she was just worried as now she wasn't in a band she wouldn't have groupies and thus would have to make an effort to score.

'And I saw that Nico last week.' Lilly fingered her dreadlocks. 'He always said that one day I'd be sorry I chucked him and that I'd realize he was the best I'd ever get. That day arrived yesterday.'

'Lilly, honestly.' Nico'd been so ugly I used to feel sick looking at him.

'I mean, how are we ever going to have relationships again if we carry on looking so rough?'

I shrugged my shoulders. I never really had 'relationships' anyway. It was more a question of taking hostages.

Lilly seemed to take my complete lack of interest in her beautification plans as some sort of challenge. I lay on her floor smoking whilst she bombarded me with 'evidence' ('I read it in a magazine,') about how blokes were 'visual' and ugly girls didn't stand a chance. We had to act fast as it was all getting too late. Our bodies were decaying as we spoke. When I pointed out that neither Lilly nor I had the money necessary to finance her plan, she claimed I had an attitude problem. We never did have any money, let's face it, we never would and she was in the same boat as me since she'd given up shoplifting (then again, even when Lil had been lifting, she'd had the most amazing ability to thief the kind of clothes that made you wonder how on earth someone could go into a shop and pay for them). If we were to be poor all our lives we should at least be good-looking and poor.

'I mean, I work as a kitchen porter, live in a hovel and have spots on my back. *But no-one need ever know.*' I thought this was lucky, looking at the state of Lilly's room. 'I've had enough of being a paranoid, self-loathing tramp. I need glamour, excitement, sexy boyfriends. I mean, d'you remember when we worked in Nippers and blokes would pay sixty quid to tweak my nipples? I want those days back.'

I remembered our topless cocktail waitressing as one of the worst periods of my life: hiding in the lavatory applying Dermablend to my scars and then having loads of cockney wankers laughing at my small tits and trying to make me give them hand-jobs.

'Look, if you want those days back, you're welcome to them. I can't be bothered. I don't see the point in pretending to be together when you're not.' I regretted the last line as soon as I had spoken it. The gleeful look on Lilly's face obviously meant I had stitched myself up.

'Ah, that's exactly my point. If you look together, you start acting together and suddenly you're together.'

I looked at some skiddy knickers of Lilly's steaming beside the ashtray. I wasn't totally convinced.

'You know when I went to America after Thailand? I worked in this shitty little bar with this girl Courtney. Five days a week she slaved her arse off doing a job she hated. But for the other two days she lived like a queen. She drank champagne, ate in the top restaurants, danced in the top clubs and wore fucking great clothes. When her credit card bills came through, she'd hold her clothes up and go, "I don't care, they can take me to court, anything. Cos whatever they do they can never take these away from me." ' Lilly looked at me in triumph. 'Know what I mean?'

To anyone else, Lill's logic would have sounded like the grotesque, drug-sodden ramblings of a care-in-the-community case. But the next morning I sat in Charing Cross hospital, skimming through a tattered copy of *Hello!*, and began to wonder if she was on to something. Clothes for me were a matter of disguise rather than adornment. I was actually at the hospital waiting to see whether I'd be granted plastic surgery to reduce some scars on my body. Despite being a dancer and thus a 'priority case' (it was perhaps ironic that I'd chosen one of the few professions where my scars would be a problem) I'd been hanging on for years. I sometimes felt like I'd spent most of my life in hospital waiting-rooms. Not just for the scars, as I'd also had long-term problems with my knees. I remembered when the first of my knee operations had gone wrong. I was continually trundling into the Charing Cross on crutches, waiting to see yet another doctor who didn't know why the knee wasn't getting better. I'd eventually given up and ended up lying in bed all day quaffing vodka n Valium, watching with detached disinterest as my body sagged and withered and wasted away. Maybe I was still trapped in that time. I rarely even bought clothes because of my What's the point? I repulse myself, theory, and comforted myself with the thought that as long as I didn't try to look OK, I was still left with the possibility that it was an option. Sometimes I'd try to large it, chipping to a club and reckoning I was cool. Then I'd go to the loo and see my reflection and think, Christ, I'd forgotten how ugly I am. I wanted to change. I wanted to be the type of person who'd inspire jealousy and envy in others rather than pity. The nurse told me that the consultant was ready to see me. For some reason, I thought of an item I'd seen on the news years ago. It'd been about Ethiopia after the famine and the reporter was saying you could tell things were getting better because the women had started beading their hair again. After I left the hospital, I went out and bought some new knickers from M&S.

It all started so sensibly. Lilly and I doing healthy diet plans and joining a gym. Lil cut down on her pork pies and took up kick-boxing. I tried not to eat in bed at night (for one thing, there were so many crumbs around my flat it'd been invaded by cockroaches). Lilly was serious about getting a boyfriend. She de-crustified herself, cutting off her dreadlocks and chucking away some of her more obscenely ripped jeans. I was even allowed to confiscate her bobbly hat collection.

'Thing was,' she said to me one day, heroically plucking stray hairs from her newly waxed bikini-line, 'I never thought I could be a babe. So I thought, sod it, I'll be a freak instead. But . . . I dunno, I want to be like other girls now.'

I think Lilly also had the sneaking idea that if she looked more glamorous she might have more luck with her singing 'career'. This was a fallacy, but at least it gave her hope.

True glamour, of course, resided in Sarah, who would emerge, from scenes of unimaginable domestic squalor, a scented and dazzling peacock. I met her one drizzly Saturday afternoon when I was malingering round the King's Road. I'd just been looking at all the gorgeous young things and wondering what it was like to be really good-looking. Then I saw Sarah, dressed in tight black leather and carrying what seemed like dozens of those square, shiny, horribly expensive bags.

'Tara!' she waved and walked over to me. I sighed, really not in the mood for another session of being patronized by my cousin. I was dressed in scuzzy jeans and hadn't bothered having a shower. That morning I'd opened my wardrobe to get a T-shirt and had seen myself naked in the door-mirror. I looked like someone after a shark attack. 'God, I'm exhausted,' said Sarah, flicking her hair around. She peered at me. 'You really ought to remove those blackheads. Where are you going?'

'Nowhere, really. I was just having a wander.'

'Let's get smashed.'

I was pretty hungover from getting pissed at work the night before and had sworn to spend a day detoxing.

'OK.'

We went into the Dôme and Sarah bullied her way into getting us a table. She sat down and removed her sun-specs. I saw that close up she actually looked (for her) fairly awful: heavy make-up over poor skin and puffy eyes.

'I know, I look frightful, don't I?' she said, rubbing one of her eyes. 'Like someone who's just had an abortion. And actually I have just had an abortion.'

'Oh *Sarah*, not again.' Poor Sarah. I always suspected Sarah wasn't as tough as she acted because surely no-one could be *that* hard.

'Yes, it's too dull. I had it on Monday. Excuse me!' She gave the waiter a threatening look. 'A bottle of Chablis, pronto.' Sarah really did have a talent for abortions. This must have been her third.

'Was it Jonny's?'

'Oh, fuck off, are you calling me a slut?'

'No.' I was far too scared of Sarah to do that.

'I think it was. It's hard to tell, you know.'

'How do you feel?'

'Fucking terrible.' Sarah put her sun-specs back on. 'Not the abortion so much as the Satan's scurf.'

'I thought you were cutting down.'

'I am, coke's a waste of time. I'm HIV negative, you know.' The waiter came back with our wine and Sarah pretended she'd dropped something under the table. 'I'm sure

I recognize that waiter,' she hissed. 'It's like I remember his face from a really funny angle; you know, as if I'd been giving him a blow-job.'

I knew I was supposed to say something like, I Know What You Mean.

'Yeah, I know what you mean. Anyway, how did you get preggers?'

Sarah shrugged her shoulders. 'Puking, I spose. It's so embarrassing. Bulimia is *so* old hat.' She stared at me. 'You're looking very thin. Rexic again?'

'Not really—'

'Men are such cunts,' Sarah carried on and then launched into another of her anti-man rants for fifteen minutes. She was permanently enraged by the male species: their sickness, their perversions, their lack of adequate financial support. 'I developed bulimia so I could be thin enough for Jonny and then I get pregnant. Men have it so easy. I've never heard a man worrying about wrinkles.' Sarah was one of those paranoids who wore factor 25 sunblock in December.

'Yeah,' I agreed, 'but they're all on hair vitamins to stop them going bald. And Ben went down Harley Street the other week to see if he could be stretched taller.'

'Fool.' Sarah looked down at her shopping. 'It's ridiculous, really. We wait to be beautiful enough for our lives to begin whilst being fully aware that beautiful people are not old.'

'But Sarah, you know you're really good-looking.' I thought: Imagine being me.

'It's just the biggest joke, really.' Sarah's fingers reached behind her sun-specs and I realized that Sarah, *Sarah*, was crying. She shook her head. 'All this effort to be attractive when . . . I remember when I was escorting and chaps would be fucking me and I'd stare at the ceiling, trying to work out what clothes I'd wear the next day. You know, sometimes I think I'd have slit my wrists years ago if it wasn't for the thought of someone finding me naked in the bath.'

I was trying to hold on to the hope that I would be given the plastic surgery. I knew they were about to hold my case conference at the hospital. Never a great sleeper and even worse since Lilly had found out I'd shopped her for my own crime, I used to sit up half the night smoking and watching adverts telling you not to smoke in bed or you'd die. I had this awful tension that made it difficult to eat. Just about the only thing I could swallow was mashed potato and I loathed mashed potato. Needless to say, I was losing weight fairly rapidly. You would have thought that dance college would have congratulated me. Instead, Tonty, my ballet tutor, actually took me aside after class one afternoon and lectured, 'Angel, dancing is not about *looking* like a dancer.'

I couldn't seem to do anything right. On Saturday Lilly and I went shopping in Oxford Street. At first, I was just keeping my eye on Lilly, checking that she didn't start liberating again. Then we entered Selfridges. I walked out of the grey drizzle into this bright scented land of possibilities. I thought: If I had the clothes, I could look like these people. I was so sick with envy that I actually wanted to throw up. I proceeded to shop, facialize and accessorize the rest of my overdraft. Every time I handed over my credit card, a nauseous cold fear swept through me.

'Tara, are you sure you need those silver sandals – Red or Dead hotpants?' Lilly would say, watching me with horror and admiration.

On Monday, I took everything back.

Lilly was soon back on form again. It wasn't easy for her, living an honest life, and I was desperately grateful that she seemed more content (not just for her sake, but so as I felt less guilty). She auditioned for a circus troop and started reading Anaïs Nin's diaries.

'I'm just so horny,' she would say, lying spread-eagled on her period-stained bed. 'All men have to do is say good morning to me and I just like wet myself, d'you know what I mean?'

'Not really.' I was too busy weighing myself. I'd decided that if I was going to be ugly all my life I might as well be ugly and thin.

'I have this fantasy that I'll meet this bloke on a bus and he'll have two trips on him and then we'll go for a walk in Battersea Park and end up shagging on the come-down.'

'That's beautiful, Lilly,' I said.

'D'you like my new Wonderbra?' Lilly shoved her pneumatic breasts at me. 'Watch I don't poke your eyes out with these.'

In my desperation to think about something other than my next hospital appointment, I even started forming a Composite Wardrobe (although I don't think matching manky leotards with foul tracksuit bottoms was quite what the magazines had in mind). I actually ironed something. But I felt so totally *drab*. I threw caution to the wind and decided to get my hair highlighted. Cassie came with me to ease my nerves. The hairdresser told us about her face-lift and I wondered if I was too young to get one. Whilst we waited for the bleach to work, Cassie turned towards me and looked at me in a serious manner.

'You're not going to lecture me about something,' I grimaced.

'You're losing too much weight,' said Cassie, eyeing me sadly.

'You puff too much, do I say anything?'

'That's not the point.' Cassie played with one of the foil-packets on my head. 'You should concentrate on loving yourself and not all this superficial shit.'

Yeah, yeah. 'But Cass, I would love myself if I was gorgeous. And Lilly's loads happier since she did her High Maintenance plan.'

'Tara . . . It's me, can't you even attempt to be honest?'

I lit a cigarette. 'God, this bleach stinks.'

'Tara, I'm not going to let this go again.' Cass took the cigarette from me. 'Lilly was just trying to give herself a kick-start cos she got so lax this summer when her band broke up. I don't notice her losing a stone and living on a diet of finely chopped mashed potato.'

I shrugged and looked in the mirror, noticing how fat my face was.

'I was reading something, you know,' said Lunchie quietly. This was amazing in itself as Cassie was generally too stoned for her eyes to be able to focus properly. 'It was saying about how some people have the habit of doing the same thing over and over again but expecting different results.'

'And?'

Cassie shrugged. 'Well, I don't really know what it meant but . . . you can't stop, you know that. You never could.' Cassie reached out and touched my arm. She was getting too close, as usual.

'That was just at school.'

'Tara, you don't need to lose any weight. I don't know what's started you off this time, but it's nothing to do with that High Maintenance stuff. What's occurring?'

'Nothing,' I said sullenly. Cass sighed and we both looked around the hairdresser's. I watched people laughing and preening themselves, listened to the buzz of the hairdryers and smelt the stink of spray and dye and felt like Chekhov in *Baywatch*-land.

What Cassie didn't understand was that I hadn't stopped eating when I was younger just to be thin. We'd both been at ballet school together, although Cass had never been really into dance. She'd only gone there because her father, the porn magnate, had reckoned it would give her class (I'd only managed to persuade my father to let me attend a dancing school because I'd won a half-scholarship and thus he saved money). I'd never exactly liked the place that much. The other pupils were the sort of girls who wore blue eyeshadow and had collections of teddy bears. But at least at ballet school my inhibition and lack of personality didn't seem so important. Then in my fifth year it had all started to go wrong. As I had only entered when I was thirteen, I had had to work tremendously hard to catch up. My body used to feel like it had been run over by a truck and my feet were so blistered and suppurated I used to worry about getting gangrene. But I had been so driven it didn't matter. Then when I was fifteen the nightmare occurred: ballet became boring. I sighed through pliés, yawned through *tendus*, practically cried with tedium as I had to pretend to be yet another happy peasant in *Giselle*. Maybe I was also scared that I wasn't good enough. Daddy had always said, 'If you can't succeed, don't bother.' So I stopped eating. In the end they'd thrown me out as they were worried about me dying. It had taken me years to understand why I'd done it; chucked everything away. I think it was the only way I could leave without actually failing.

The following week, I went back to the hospital. I touched my newly highlighted hair and walked in to see the plastic surgeon actually shaking with nerves. It had taken me years to get this far and it was the one hope I'd always clung to, that my past could be eradicated. The surgeon looked up and smiled understandingly as I sat down. I knew this was a bad sign. He gave me a lot of crap about going through my case and discussing it with his colleagues and how he was only doing what was best for me and that he wouldn't go ahead with the surgery.

'I'm afraid to say that I don't think the skin-grafts would give you the results you would expect.' He took off his specs and attempted to look like a kindly grandfather.

'The grafts would take up to a year and you would endure prolonged discomfort.'

'I don't care!' I said desperately.

'But I think you would. You would be unable to dance for long periods. The grafts themselves would cause some further scarring. Your skin is very sensitive. Even if we went ahead with the grafts, the scars, although we might be able to reduce them, would still be visible.'

I thought of the hours I'd spent waiting for appointments, the horrors of medical photography, the humiliation of young students looking at me in my underwear. I burst into tears.

'I really am very sorry.'

I gave up the High Maintenance plan. No point in flogging a dead horse and all that. I even tried to start eating again, but it was harder than I'd expected. The food seemed somehow to stick in my throat. I knew it was no real crisis, that if I sat back it would quietly fade away. I eventually told Cassie about my plastic surgery failure as she knew about my scars from us sharing a room at school. Instead of going down the gym with Lilly, I would head over to Cass's house after college. We'd sit in her room puffing joints and making lampshades. Then Cass would cook some dinner and I'd try to eat a little more every day. Cass herself wasn't doing so well either. She was attempting one of those Access to University courses and was behind on all her work.

Her eczema was terrible. She would sit scratching the insides of her palms until they bled, saying that she really had to cut down on the puff.

'A weird thing happened today,' she said one night as we were struggling with a particularly difficult lampshade. Like all hippies, Cassie had a fantasy of setting up a stall in Camden Market. 'Dave Hardcore asked me out.'

'Oh God.' Dave was a notorious lunatic who, since giving up his novel, *Casual Sex* (about being a casual and having sex), was now making a rave tune against racism called 'Tribal Babe' ('It's ancient native Zulu chants combined with a progressive Hardcore disco beat'). He'd recently been chucked by his girlfriend but claimed to have got over it since she'd put a restraining order on him.

'Actually, I might have a drink with him,' Cassie admitted. 'Hardcore's such a pervert, maybe my skin would turn him on.'

'Jesus, Cassie.' Hardcore also claimed to understand the lyrics of Phil Collins's songs. 'He's not normal.'

'I'm not normal. I don't even know how to give a blow-job.'

'Oh, not the old Weird and Different syndrome again.' It was something both Lunchie and I suffered from. Only I really was weird and different. I was ugly enough anyway, but the scars gave me the added benefit of being completely abnormal. Recently, the only physical contact I had had with men was medical examinations.

'I wish I was Lilly,' I said finally, unwrapping yet another piece of chewing gum. Lilly was so confident and so free of convention. She was the sort of person who, if you gave her a job as a merchant banker, would have nicked the computer and shagged the boss by lunch. 'She told me the other day that she's decided she's a renegade and if she could go back in time she'd be a highway woman.'

'She got Nico back,' said Cass.

'Really?'

'And chucked him about two days later. She said she'd just remembered why she'd chucked him in the first place. You know, that he was a wanker. She was going out in some mad outfit and asked me what I thought of it and I said I thought it was a bit much and she just laughed and said, "Sod you, I think I look great." '

I was just getting back to grips with eating again when I received notice of Sarah's latest exploits. Jinty told me via Ben via Jonny that Sarah had finally achieved her wish and been locked up in the Priory, a smart loony bin. Fulham was crazed with rumours regarding Sarah's admittance to the clinic. Some said that Sarah had finally lost her nose; that she'd blown it one morning and part of her brains had fallen out. Others countered that it was Sarah's shopping addiction that had finally sealed her fate. Tales of Sarah's supposed extravagance abounded. That her account at Harvey Nick's alone was enough to keep an African family in Calvin Klein for a year. That, pissed one night, she'd given her Rolex watch to a tramp. That Chanel cosmetics had actually invited her to Paris as customer of the year. The other goss was that Sarah had owed so much money she'd been forced back to escorting and, after a three-day coke n sex sesh, had suffered a heart attack.

'Sarah called me the other day,' I told Lilly as we sat in some Fulham pub that had gone all horribly wrong since it had put up fishnets.

'Sloaney cunt,' said Lilly automatically. Lil's hair was now fashionably cropped and she wore a top so ludicrously tight that her nipples danced when she laughed.

'Oh, Sarah's not as bad as you think,' I said. Really, Lilly was pissed off after an incident with a nubile Australian washer-up in her kitchen. Apparently, she'd taken him out, got him absolutely hanging and had then proposed sex. He'd put his head in his hands and gone, 'Oh God mate.' Having experienced sexual rejection for the first time in her life, Lilly was now certain that she was becoming a man and it was only a short step to picking up inebriated sixteen-year-olds.

'Sarah wouldn't tell me why she'd gone in,' I continued, 'but she seemed to like it there. They've got a gym and everything.'

'I've got to get fit,' said Lilly, not listening and swigging a pint of cider.

'I just want to be beautiful and unobtainable,' I countered. Like Sarah. She said, however much they paid her, that she never kissed them.

'I just want a man to put his arms around me.'

'The last time someone put their arms around me,' I mused, 'it was a policeman and he arrested me.'

Lilly laughed, despite the vague truth behind my statement.

Lil and I then got totally cunted. She picked someone up and took them back to her place for sex. I staggered home, having lost it completely due to not eating for so long, vomited for an hour and then re-arranged my wardrobe.

4. The Mystery of the Packet

'D'you like me new T-shirt?' asked Chingford Susie, getting into my car. 'Me and Tracey had them printed especially.' Susie opened her jacket to reveal an undersized pink number with *Slappers Go For It* emblazoned in silver across her breasts.

'Subtle.' I started up my rust-mobile, almost stalling as I caught sight of my thighs splayed grotesquely on the car seat. They were like something out of a horror movie.

'Trace got it as a sympathy present for me having sex with an Albanian at a party in Dalston.'

'I thought you were going out with that Bellbottoms with the braces.'

'I am but . . . I mean, he's seventeen, I'm twenty-six. It's gettin embarrassin. I'm sure I only went out with him cos of grannie-bashin.' Susie had worked for several months with old dears whose bums she had wiped and whose beards she had plucked. This had led her to start making eyes at nine-year-olds. 'Sides, he can't get it up.'

'Oh not again.'

'I know.' Susie did up her seatbelt. 'I'm thinkin about gettin a splint to take around. I mean, what is it about me? A gel can get para, you know.'

'Not you,' I said, driving off. This was exactly why I rated Susie. Like Lilly, she had a kind of unshakable self-confidence. Her mid-twenties life crisis had lasted just one day during which she had booked herself a flight to Australia where she'd decided to train as a reflexologist ('I've always ad this thing about feet').

'Funny, this sex business,' I mused as we passed two fat people kissing each other at a bus stop.

'What would you know about it, cobweb fanny?' Susie opened the window and started throwing out some of the rubbish I'd accumulated under her seat. Empty fag packs, cans of Diet Coke and, mysteriously, a dirty pair of knickers flew into the night. 'Jesus, this car smells worse than Satan's arse.'

'Actually,' I admitted, 'I've given up trying to have sex this decade. I even went out and bought this book called *Sex For One: The Art of Self-Loving*.'

'Any good?'

'No. I was hoping for a thirty-second guide to instant finger-highs but it's all about sixties encounter groups and consciousness raising.'

Susie pulled a scrappy piece of paper out of her bra and gave me some directions. 'Why don't you just fuck someone?'

'That's too obvious. Anyway, I can't bear sex if it involves me. Normally I wouldn't mind, but Love is in the Air at the moment. Even Cassie's got a boyfriend and before him she hadn't even got off with someone for four years.'

'No wonder she's such a bleedin zoid.'

I was actually quite disturbed by Cassie's new amour, even if she was seeing Dave Hardcore, a bloke so perverse he'd wanted to film his ex having an abortion.

'I just don't understand how you manage to have a boy-friend,' I'd said to her the previous evening. For once Cassie had not been stoned and was drinking a glass of whisky. She said she was admitting her contradictions but actually her dealers were dry.

'I know, it's bizarre, it's like, I'm abnormal, fucked-up, useless – just like you – but here I am, being normal, in a relationship.'

'Amazing.' I felt more isolated than ever.

'But I still make a point of walking naked in front of Dave in broad daylight cos I'm so convinced he can't of realized what a mutant I am.' Cass looked down at the scabs on her hand.

'Really? That's so courageous. I used to think I was brave but actually I was just reckless.'

'You need a man to protect you.'

'No, men need to be protected from me.'

Susie and I were travelling to some dodgy rave where Tricky Dicky, a DJ we knew, was playing. We'd both been obsessed with Tricky since meeting him a while ago at Chan's. He'd been fairly non-descript but had sported one hell of a bulge.

'I bet he's got a stoker,' Susie had said and instantly swapped phone numbers. However, Susie's would-be romance had been interrupted by her sudden nervous breakdown and subsequent cherry-picking runner to Israel. And since she'd been back in London her rampant promiscuity and grannie-bashing had left little time for blokes that were non-certs. Now, before she left for Australia, she was determined to solve at last The Mystery of the Packet.

'I need some meaning in my life,' she claimed, adjusting her bra as we arrived at the venue (some rat-infested disused warehouse). 'Besides, sex is my hobby, like you and dance. Tricky will be like an audition for me.'

I nodded, thinking this was a pretty pathetic defence for Susie's nymphomania.

'And I've seen a lot of penises in my time. There are small ones out there, you know. Ones that look like Walnut Whips. If Tricky's got a big one I wanna know about it.'

Tricky was on the decks when we arrived, smoking a spliff and chatting about football. I remarked to Susie that he'd put on a lot of weight since I'd last seen him.

'I know, rank, isn't it? I'm thinking of chaining him to a radiator for a week to slim him down.' Susie hated having sex with fat blokes as she said she could feel their stomachs slapping against hers. 'I know I shouldn't say nothing. I've decided not to have kids in case they develop my fat arse. I wish there was some sort of test they could do to check.' Susie turned to Tricky. 'All right?'

'Yeah, you?'

'Fucked off. You stood me up last night.'

'Sorry, I got pissed with me mates and ended up down a bowling alley in Streatham.'

'Sort us out then.'

We dropped some E and then danced around and had a few spliffs. It was the average casualty city night out featuring retina-destroying lights, stomach-churning drum n base and a crowd that looked like an NA bash gone horribly wrong. I remembered Lilly once saying that she thought that the widespread use of ecstasy was some government plot to turn the young into imbeciles. However, as I started coming up half an hour later, I began noticing how friendly everyone was and how good the tunes were and all the boys with nice haircuts.

'I love you, Susie,' I shouted close to her ear.

'Oh no, not again.'

'No, I mean it this time,' I screamed, passing her a spliff. 'It's not just the drugs talking. You see, we've all got to love one another. It's like the tune says, "It's time to get up and get along."'

Two blokes danced in front of us like apes receiving electroshock treatment, only pausing from their dementions to scream, 'Oy! Oy!'

'Yeah, right.' Susie took a drag on the joint and stared at me strangely. 'You look like Keith Chegwin. Christ, everyone looks like Keith Chegwin. I'd better snog Tricks before it's too late.'

I was left on my own on the dancefloor and whiled away a couple of hours muff-chucking at any bloke who went past. Others called me a prick teaser but it was just my way of saying hello. At a particularly bizarre moment of pelvic grinding, a bloke came up and asked if I wanted a drink. I was thirsty and he didn't look obviously deformed so I agreed. We chatted at the bar for a while and he told me that his name was Dwayne and he was the fifteenth child of an alcoholic country and western singer now dead of cirrhosis. He seemed to be my kind of bloke. It all goes blurry here and I vaguely remember snogging and tooting and refusing to go home with him and then agreeing to meet for lunch the next day. Susie and I drove back in the car feeling fairly satisfied with ourselves: we'd both touched tonsils and Tricky had asked her to a party.

Alone the next day, I decided that I would meet Dwayne for lunch. I sat in the Dôme drinking a beer and worrying that I couldn't remember what he looked like, that I had chafing on my chin and please God let him not have a beard. Dwayne arrived a few minutes later looking equally nervous. Luckily, facial hair was not an issue. We drank and talked and he told me that he'd been a roofer until he'd fallen off a roof and broken his leg and that he now worked as a photocopying assistant. I admitted to being an alcoholic barmaid who masqueraded as an arthritic dancer on her days off. It also turned out that I'd once shared a flat with his half-sister, Joleen, a notoriously unsuccessful nymphomaniac. We ended up snogging in a gay bar in Camden Town and I agreed to meet him the next evening.

Our second date was a whirl of horrendous parties stretching across the bathrooms of London. I saw it through a coke-induced air of calmness, being one of the few people that toot made quieter and more sensitive. We went back to my place for some drunken sex. Then we lay in bed looking at one another.

'I can't believe we get on this well,' said Dwayne.

'I know. I mean, I always think strangers are enemies you haven't yet met.'

There was a lot of hand-holding, eye-gazing and general soppiness. We agreed to meet the next evening.

Before I went out, I telephoned Susie to see how she was doing in her search for a solution to The Mystery of the Packet.

'Oh, don't ask. The other night I went to a party with Tricky but it was lame. So then we all went back to Tricks' and smoked smack and played Sega.'

'Oh, not Sega.' Both Susie and I hated computer games.

'Never again. I still feel severely shit. Anyway, he just got the nods and blanked out and I couldn't even ave a look as there was other people in the room.'

'What about last night?'

'Even worse. I ended up with some nurse and went round his place and played games with ice boxes.'

'Oh dear.'

'And I've got to meet Bellbottoms tonight and how'm I gonna explain the ice-burns?' Susie sighed. 'Anyway, how's it going with Ronelle?'

'Dwayne. OK, I guess. Actually, he's all right.'

'Don't do another runner, whatever you do.'

'I won't,' I lied.

Dwayne and I spent the evening with some dope-head friends of his who all claimed to be musicians because they'd once picked up a guitar. Afterwards, we went back to my place and he commented that I was the most undomesticated girl he'd ever met.

'Have you looked in your fridge recently?' he called from the kitchen.

'I try not to.'

'Well, it contains precisely one eye mask, two carrots, a tub of lard and a packet of Rizla.'

'Oh, I was wondering where the Rizla went.'

Dwayne got into bed and we played around for a while before I took some sleeping pills.

'Why d'you need them, honey?'

'I don't sleep, really. Haven't since I was twelve.'

He looked perplexed. 'I always sleep well.'

He curled up around me whilst I stroked his hand. I had a feeling I was doing something I shouldn't. It was nice being warm and held but . . . someone who slept well? That meant he couldn't be like me. Fuck-ups never slept well, probably because our consciences were never easy. I had made a mistake. Dwayne wasn't one of us.

I nervously broached the subject with one of the other barmaids at the Escape, Gerry. Gerry was an ex-dancer who acted as my guide and general mentor.

'You're pretty fucked up Gerry, aren't you?' I said hopefully.

'Totally.'

Gerry turned to one of our two customers and handed him a Budweiser. 'Three quid.'

'Three quid?!'

'Got a problem with that, mate?' asked Gerry with unmistakable menace in her voice.

'Christ, no.' The guy threw down a fiver on the counter and scuttled off.

'Now your boyfriend, Paul,' I said. 'He's a bit of a state.'

'Tell me about it. He's just started that therapy and comes out with fucking "revelations" most nights. The other evening we were in this cab and the radio was playing Elvis. The cab driver goes that he hates Elvis and changes stations. Then Paul tries to jump over the back seat and starts screaming, "My Dad loved Elvis." '

'Yeah . . .' Paul really was mad. He worked as a scaffolder and used to do Tai Chi on site. 'Now, d'you think we should only go out with fuck-ups, or would it be better for us to see normal people?'

'I dunno.' Gerry walked to the side of the bar, lit a spliff, and started spraying air freshener everywhere. 'I mean, my first boyfriend's now a woman called Rebecca. And then there was Darren; well, we once agreed to share sexual fantasies and mine was having two men at once so he punched me.'

'What d'you reckon, Tim?' I asked the barman who was leafing through a copy of *Tropical Fish Monthly* underneath the counter.

'God knows. I once read Chekhov and he said that what women wanted was originality in a man, like a bloke who wears felt shoes all year round. That's why I'm still doing my fish mobiles.'

'Right.' I downed another vodka. I was drinking too much, again. 'Oh screw it, I refuse to care.'

Gerry looked at me seriously. 'One day, Tara, you're going to have to find a way of dealing with your problems other than by knocking back the vodders and saying, "I refuse to care."'

I drove up to Chingford the next day to say goodbye to Susie. She was leaving for Australia that evening.

'How's it been going?'

Susie looked down at her stuff on the floor, which she was trying to cram into a tiny rucksack. 'It's been a fucking nightmare. Bellbottoms made me have Sunday lunch with his family yesterday. Sod it, I'll never fit this load in.' Susie picked up half her clothes and threw them in the bin. 'I should've done it years ago,' she said, looking at the mound of Oxfam rejects.

'What about Tricky?'

'Aven't seen im since the party. He stood me up the other day, OD'd or something, so I ad to shag that nurse. When I woke up, the nurse ad buggered off and his mum made me watch a video of her ballroom dancing in Torremolinos. I can't wait to get on that plane.'

'So you never solved The Mystery of the Packet?'

'Nah. I'm not that bothered, really. One of Tricky's mates told me he was impotent.' Susie grinned. 'Sod it. Men, they all do a runner in the end.'

'Tim says that all his girlfriends emigrate.'

'I'm not surprised.' Susie was bitter as she'd once tried it on with Tim at the Escape but instead of getting off with her he'd chatted about his fish mobiles.

'But hang on . . .' I could feel my face contorting in a rare act of thought. 'How can you accuse other people of doing runners when you're leaving at least three blokes who think they're going out with you to fly to Australia?'

'Oh no. See, there are two types of people: bolters and stickers. I just stick with a lot of people.'

'What about me?'

Susie raised her eyebrows.

'I know. Sometimes I think I was born with no facility for intimacy.'

I took Dwayne to a staff party at the Escape. He was happy and drunk and I was happy and trying not to get too drunk.

'He's really nice,' said Gerry after meeting Dwayne. I was relieved she didn't mention Dwayne's clothes. He was wearing cowboy boots and a Lurex shirt.

'Yup,' agreed Tim. 'Not one of your normal sleazebags. He can speak English and everything. Don't blow it, Tara.'

'What makes you think I would?'

'That shifty look in your eyes.'

I watched Dwayne knocking back Tequila slammers and

dancing in a peculiar manner.

'You need to fling,' said Tim, staggering slightly. I always liked Tim when he'd had a few as he was a very charming drunk. If he'd become an alcoholic, I'd have married him.

'What?'

'When you meet someone, you have to be brave. You have to fling yourself into their arms and sometimes they'll catch you and sometimes they'll step aside and you'll hit the floor. If they step aside, you may get bruised but you'll get up again. But if you're caught . . . You've got to fling, Tara, or you'll never know whether they'd have caught you or not.'

Afterwards, Dwayne and I left the Escape for a late-night drinking bar where we smooched for a while.

'Listen,' he slurred, 'let's get this straight. I'll always be honest with you.' Cool, I thought, because I'll always be dishonest with you. 'I want you to be my girlfriend.'

'Good,' I said.

'I haven't got a lot of money, though. I know that bothers you.'

'You talk as if I was some gold-digging leech.'

He coughed.

'Maybe I was, but I've changed.'

'So?'

'Of course I'll go out with you. Hey, I love you!'

'I love you too,' he said.

'Good.'

We then went back to his place where, tired and pissed, we both collapsed asleep on one another.

When I awoke the next morning, it all felt different. We lay hungover and dreamy and then I called a cab and got dressed. Something felt weird. He knew I was abnormal.

'I'll call you later,' I said, and kissed him and left.

I never called him. He never called me. I never flung.

5. Dangerous Freedoms

'My dance is called *Empty Skies*,' I said, standing nervously in front of my choreography class. 'When I was improvising I realized that I had nothing to express but my own shallowness so *Skies* is all about being empty and vacant.'

'You're doing a dance about nothing, then,' said my tutor, Sam. Several students yawned. It was Friday morning and no-one could be bothered to pretend to care any more. They lay on top of one another or sprawled against the studio mirror, sighing and picking spots, their dancebags spilling out stinking leotards.

'I . . .'

'Yes, yes, get on with it.'

I duly did my piece, noticing out of the corner of my eye that three people had fallen asleep and the rest were examining their toenails, the floor, indeed anything except me. I ended on a leg-lift, wobbling and almost falling over, turned off the tape and waited for the abuse to start.

'There's certainly a lot of emptiness there,' declared Sam. 'Actually, though, the movement's not too bad. It's more your face.'

'It's not my fault,' I protested desperately. 'I couldn't sleep last night and all the dust here is giving me spots.'

'I'm not talking about the condition of your skin.'

'It's more that your face is so blank,' said one of the girls helpfully. 'I mean, the piece would be all right without your face.'

'Thanks.'

'You're sort of blank from the neck up,' mused Sam. 'You race around the studio leaping and rolling and indulging in your various movement clichés and yet your face is totally impassive. You express nothing.'

'I was internalizing,' I said, sinking into a pit of inadequacy.

'Your piece does have a certain creativity, though. Maybe you could get someone else to perform it,' said Sam.

'Yes,' agreed the 'helpful' girl. 'Someone with a bit of life and energy in them.'

'So I'm too fucking crap to be in my own bloody choreography,' I said, grabbing my tape from the cassette-player.

'Don't be so hostile, Tara. All we're doing is suggesting that you examine all your options here, leave no avenues unexplored . . .'

'Yeah, I get the point.' I was useless. My head was fucking me up again. My body was quite willing to do anything I wanted, but my head . . . it was always there; destroying my life, adding unwelcome 'blankness' to my dancing.

'Maybe you should wear a mask,' said the girl.

'Maybe you could do something about your body odour

problem.' There was a Class Gasp. 'Sorry.' I could feel the tears beginning. 'Excuse me.' I pretended I had something in my eye.

'Tara,' said Wiesna, a mad Polish girl who did Dance History with me, 'there is much to be proud of in your *Empty Skies*. I suffered, I really suffered when I was watching it.'

'You did?' I choked hopefully in between sobs.

'Choreography is most difficult. It is because we are so free to do what we want here. We show, even without realizing, some deep hurt. It is a dangerous freedom we have.'

I nodded, clutching my knee which had begun to ache.

'Maybe I do your dance for you.'

I sat down and gave up.

After choreography, I rested on the stairs icing my knee. The paranoia about my knees was getting worse. The right one didn't seem to feel right and so I worried about it and then I worried that worrying was praying for something you didn't want. I knew my knee ligaments were shot. They'd been stretched too far, they'd never heal. It was funny, really: giving up uni to dance, to discover that dancing was no longer an option. Two operations later, I'd got back on my feet. Swimming, weight-training, body conditioning, back to class, winning a place at the Laban Centre for Movement and Dance. But the fear of crippledom still haunted me: I now had no illusions that I was brave. I was a coward, terrified of pain and injury. I could never go back to those months in bed after the operations. The quiet, ice-cold terror: it's all too late. The obsessive self-pity, with my first waking thought being, Why me? The deranged bitterness (I used to hope for a nuclear bomb as it was obvious I was on the way out and didn't see why everyone else shouldn't go as well). Now all

I could do was ice my knees and pray. Yes, the final insult, I had Gone Religious.

'Could you spare some ice?' asked a girl standing beside me on the stairs.

'Sure.' I cracked the ice-block in two and handed her a piece. I vaguely remembered her from jazz classes. She wasn't technically that hot but she had a nice kind of loose flow. She sat down next to me and put the ice on her shoulder.

'Torn ligaments?'

She winced with pain and nodded. 'I'm Caro,' she said.

'Tara.' We exchanged half-hearted smiles. She looked down at my knee, which was now a red-raw colour from the ice.

'What's wrong with your knee?'

'To be honest, I don't know whether it's my knee or my head that's going wrong.'

'I know what you mean.'

'You do?' I had assumed she would think I was mad.

'Yeah, I've got so many old injuries that I'm basically just held together by strapping tape. Every time I get a twinge I think, This is the one that's finally going to end it all.'

Staring at Caro, I had to admit that she didn't look so hot: sporting the traditional dancer's anaemic paleness, spots and dark shadows under the eyes.

'Do you ever think about giving up dance?' I asked.

Caro started laughing in a hysterical, desperate sort of way. 'I think of nothing else. I don't know what I'm doing here.' Caro and I leant to the side of the stairs to let some girls go past. 'Actually,' she said bitterly, 'despite the broken health and final bank demands I think it's the other dancers that piss me off most. All the fucking anti-leotard faction with their nose-rings and shaved heads and radical bisexuality.'

'That's really scaring me,' I admitted, wiping my wet knee

with a sweatshirt. 'I always hated fringe dance but recently Lloyd Newson's become like a god to me.'

'That one who did the piece on men having sex with other men in lavatories?'

'That's him. I always thought that he needed psychiatric help and that my friend Lucinda was a fool for dancing with DV8 but now it's my life's dream to lick the sweat off his arse.'

'Lucinda,' mused Caro, rolling her neck around. 'Not Lucinda Miles, the loony bulimic smack-head?'

'Oh dear, she thought no-one knew.'

'She once tried to make me eat a rat with her.'

'Oh, not you too.'

'I didn't mind. We'd just done this nightmare audition where a choreographer asked us to re-enact the worst time in our lives. Lucinda just threw up on the floor and started skidding around in her own vomit. When she's bad it's kinder not to look but when she's good . . . she got the job. At least she's not average.'

'That's my nightmare.'

'I know. Becoming a workaday dancer. Shit, I've gotta go, I've got notation.' Caro stretched her arms over her head and flexed her back. She had quite big tits. 'See you around.'

After our talk, Caro and I often sat with each other on the smoking wall outside college, where she would bore me with all the details of her recent relationship breakdown. I was sadly grateful for any company. I didn't really have any other friends at dance college. In fact, I'd never even tried to make any as on my first day at Laban I'd bumped into someone I'd known at ballet school and just hung out with him until he was expelled. Now friendless, I only occasionally chatted with other dancers about blisters or laxatives. Thank God for Caro, despite her whining.

'What I can't stand is that I'm becoming really wet,' she'd tell me though tears and smoke. 'I sat on a bench for six hours yesterday just hoping he'd go past. I didn't even want to talk to him, I just wanted to look at him. I even call his answerphone so I can hear his voice on the message. I've just lost *all* dignity. Pathetic, eh?'

'No,' I lied.

'And I get these awful stabs of pain when I think of when we were together, as if someone was knifing me in the chest. I've started listening to songs that remind me of him.' Caro tried to smile. 'We met at a nightclub in Luton. Our Tune was, "I Like to Move It".'

'Nice,' I said.

'I think about suicide all the time. I imagine him standing over my grave looking gaunt in black and going, "I'm gutted. Caro was fantastic and I always loved her but I've realized it too late." Then he spends the rest of his life mourning my loss and weeping over old photos of me.'

I nodded understandingly at Caro. The worst thing was that I did understand. I had a similar dream: me topping myself and then all these articles in glossy Sunday supplements saying: *Tara: Young, Talented, Beautiful – Why Did She Have To Die?* And then loads of quotes from people saying how amazing I was and how guilty they felt. But I realized that I couldn't kill myself until I got some decent photos to go with the article.

'I get so miserable I can barely move,' Caro continued. 'I burst into tears in class yesterday.' She suddenly thumped the wall. 'And you know what makes me most bitter? I loved him even when he had acne.'

Thinking of acne reminded me of Dwayne, the photocopying assistant I had failed to fling with. His ambition had been to become a flamenco guitarist.

'But I know I can never be great,' he'd once informed me, guzzling a pint of Guinness. 'I like my social life and football on Sunday afternoons too much. I don't even bother growing my fingernails.' But for people like Dwayne, whose favourite wine was Jacobs Creek and who liked Mike Leigh films, it didn't matter, whereas I *had* to be successful. For one it was obvious that I was an artist and needed to express myself and all that (even if all I could express was emptiness and paranoia). Also, I had nothing else – the emotional capacity of a baboon and a sex life less active than that of an amoeba. But I did wonder if I had the dedication. We were always being told that dance was about loving pain ('You feel the pain? It's a good pain, no?') and enjoying suffering. I rarely bothered warming up for class and lessons were so dull I'd even spot my pirouettes to the clock. I thought bitterly of Lucinda. Lucinda and I had grown up together and she was now a dancer. A much more successful dancer than me. She starred in things like gothic horror lesbian ballets. What irritated me was that it was a well-known fact that Cindy was a heroin addict and hadn't done class for two years and yet she *still* got work (although admittedly Cindy worked mostly in physical theatre and her roles were the type where she'd run on stage, scream, 'No!' and tear all her clothes off). And I couldn't even do a crappy little bit of choreography.

When I showed my next re-working of *Skies* to Sam, he sighed and said, 'There are two rules in dance, Tara. One: don't piss on the audience. Two: there's a divide between dance and masturbation. Today, you crossed that divide.'

Most of the class tittered and giggled. As I didn't even masturbate, I was less than amused.

A couple of days later, I twisted my ankle in ballet. It had been a bad class anyway. Tonty, my ballet teacher, had watched my *port de bras* and said it was lucky for me that he had a sense of humour. Then, in *petit allegro* he decided on a 'use them or lose them' method of teaching and had threatened to cut off my arms. By *grand allegro* I was hysterical, certain that my knee was about to give way. I went across the diagonal and the next thing I knew I was sprawled on the floor. Tonty accused me of faking the injury to get out of the difficult *ménage* we were about to do, but I ignored him and went and fetched some ice. I was sitting in the atrium icing my throbbing ankle when the door flung open and Caro came through on a stretcher, screaming in between using her gas mask. I watched with horror as she was rushed past me. One of the other girls told me later that Caro had fallen during class and injured her back. I immediately had images of Caro in a wheelchair for the rest of her life, miserable and incontinent, only kept alive by monthly fixes of the *Dancing Times*. I honestly worried about Caro but obviously made no attempt to call her as I was far too wrapped up in my own suffering.

A week later, my ankle was actually worse. It swelled and throbbed and was painful to touch. The following week I had my choreography and contemporary assessments. I was fucked. After a particularly torturous ballet class I collapsed in the corridor, gasping with pain. One of my more sympathetic contemporary tutors was heading in my direction. I called out to her and explained about my ankle.

'Go home, eat loads of cake, rest and see a physio.'

Admitting defeat, I drove home. I then lay in bed all evening reading a book about concentration camps and thinking pathetically about Primo Levi's quote that his depression had been, 'Worse than Auschwitz.' The only person who I thought could cheer me up was Susie, and she was in Australia. Bitch. Then the phone rang.

'Tara? It's Lucinda.'

'Lucinda!'

'We must meet, it's imperative. I've found How to Live.'

I agreed to meet Lucinda the following evening after physio.

Lucinda had been my childhood friend. We'd met at kiddie school in Fulham, united by our wild unpopularity. Ecstatic at finally finding someone who liked me, I'd skipped my silent morgue of a house to hang out at her place. There her father would play classical music, her mother would sing arias and Cindy and I would eat (there was so much nosh around that my resounding memory of that time is opening the fridge and reeling with the stink of rotting food). After my family left London, Cindy and I saw each other less regularly but I always stayed at hers in the hols when I attended the Royal Ballet summer school. Together we had smoked our first cigarette, puffed our first joint and swallowed a bottle of dog worming pills to see if they gave us a buzz. Cindy even got interested in dance herself, assuming that if I could do it there was no reason why she couldn't.

The last time I'd seen Lucinda had been a couple of years before when I'd bumped into her on Fulham Broadway. She'd just come back from America and told me her parents were away. I'd foolishly re-entered her house. The mess was unbelievable — worse than my flat — and there were two people smoking heroin in the sitting-room. Lucinda chased contentedly and asked me if I was willing. I left. I couldn't believe it. Lucinda had become a scag user. What was worse was that all of Fulham seemed to know about Lucinda's Addiction.

'Lucinda's been fucked for years,' said Ben, who knew Cindy through Hardcore (who turned out to be one of her dealers). 'The last time I saw her she was trying to catch a rat for Hardcore to eat.'

'What?'

'The brown stuff's only used by total losers. Even her own sister Nina doesn't speak to her no more.'

'I remember seeing Lucinda's father in Safeway,' Jinty added. 'He was wheeling this huge trolley of food around and I asked him if he was having a party or something and he said, "No, Lucinda's back from America. She's bulimic, you know." Nina says her puking's stripped all the enamel off the bath.'

So I had avoided Lucinda. Not out of any moral stuff, but because I knew I was way out of my depth with heroin.

Debbie, my old physio, greeted me at the Remedial Dance Clinic, scene of my many scenes when my knees had been bad. She checked my ankle and tutted.

'Acute sprain.' She stared in disgust at the swollen monstrosity before her. 'Complete rest from weight-bearing activity for two weeks.' I thought of my exams, an important audition I had coming up. Shit happens.

'I'm surprised you're at Laban,' Debbie said whilst lasering my ankle. 'You've such a little ballet body.' It was true in a way. The other students there were the sort of girls who had big calves and who could do press-ups for breakfast. Funnily enough, though, the teachers were always going on about my 'natural physical facility' and wondering why I didn't progress faster. I found this bitterly amusing as I thought I had the body of a middle-aged woman after two Caesarean sections and that, injury-wise, I was basically in trouble from the waist down. I was glad that Laban wasn't like ballet school – where we were all anorexic bunhead soldiers doing regimented *tendus* at the *barre* – but I still felt like I didn't fit in. One of the contemporary tutors used to bitchily refer to me as, 'Our own little swanette,' and I never understood what the 'thinking' dancers were going on about (existentialist ballet, my arse).

'But if I don't dance what am I going to do for two weeks?' I asked Debbie.

'There are other things in life than dance,' she laughed. 'Either watch class or take a few weeks off and put your feet up.'

I left the clinic utterly terrified.

Lucinda and I were meeting in a small café in Parsons Green. I stirred my coffee and wondered if Cindy would have changed. Thing was, we'd always found normal life so difficult; Lucinda permanently in trouble with the teachers, and me having no friends. We reckoned that at birth everyone else had been given a copy of a book called *How to Live*, but we'd been forgotten. I still wanted my copy. I supposed that was why I'd turned up.

'Tara.'

'Cindy.'

I stood up and hugged her, towering over her tiny frame. I could feel her jutting bones and smelt stale cigarette smoke on her hair. 'How are you?' I asked, sitting down and staring at Cindy's smooth face. She hadn't changed at all.

'All right, you know. I've given up the smack and booze.'

'How's the eating?' This question cost me. Until I'd lived with Lucinda she'd never had any problems with food.

'Bad. But I'm going to AA. Groups are where it's at.' I

ordered another coffee. Lucinda had the cheek to ask for a skimmed cappuccino.

'You've got to come,' she said.

'But I'm not an alcoholic.' I wondered if Cindy had heard rumours.

'AA's not about drinking. I hadn't drunk for a year before I went. It's about who we are. You had an eating disorder by the age of ten and I used to vandalize my own parents' house. Our heads have always been one hundred per cent out to get us. If anyone else treated us the way we treated ourselves they'd be arrested.' Lucinda paused for breath and I stared intently down at my coffee, totally floored by her honesty. 'Don't try to fucking avoid me,' she said, pointing her finger at me. 'Tara, I've had money, I've travelled the world, I've done great jobs, I've looked good *and it's never been enough*. I'd always end up sitting alone with my head going off and then having to chase or binge or whatever to shut it up. I didn't stop using heroin cos of some moral shit. It just wasn't working any more.' She handed me an Alcoholics Anonymous pamphlet, *Where to Find*.

'Why'd you call me?' I asked finally. Lucinda looked very small and sad and raised her chin.

'I . . . I wasn't good to you.' She shook her head. 'That's why I want you to come to one of the meetings. I know you must still feel the same. There's a meeting on Sunday morning that's absolutely brilliant.'

'I'll come,' I agreed with absolutely no intention of going. Cindy stirred her cappuccino.

'Tara, just give it a try. I thought it was just me but it isn't.'

It was only later that I realized that Lucinda was on Step Nine: trying to make amends.

* * *

I spent the next couple of days in bed with an ice-pack on my ankle, watching TV and eating Jammee Dodgers. I tried not to think about what Lucinda had said, convincing myself that she was just mad. But I didn't have much else to think about and I was also feeling very alone, like a sulky teenager whom no-one understood. In fact, Lucinda seemed to understand me better than I did. There'd been the farcical 'relationship' with Dwayne, after which I'd finally been forced to admit that I was incapable of going out with someone for longer than three weeks; and that I wasn't sure I was capable of any emotion for anyone other than Poor Little Me. There was also the fact that when I wasn't lying in bed I'd be standing naked in front of the mirror, gobbing on my reflection, wishing I could be someone else, even for just a day. Then, of course, there was the worry about my ankle and getting behind at college. And then just Paranoia. It was funny, as I'd always taken the piss out of my sister Jinty and her supposed 'panic attacks'. But I was beginning to wonder if I was actually suffering paranoia attacks. Memories seemed to be doing a runner with my sanity. I saw Lilly, cars, packets, police stations. And I thought of Lucinda, my dopplegänger, saying that even heroin couldn't shut her head up.

'I've started playing my answerphone in the shower,' I told Gerry at work (although this didn't stop me demanding why no-one ever returned the calls I never made).

'Silly cow,' said Gerry, passing me a sea breeze she'd just mixed. I was serving from a stool as I claimed to be unable to stand up for longer than five minutes. 'When you're injured you should lie in bed and be nice to yourself. You know, eat chocolate and have sexual fantasies.'

'I think I'm becoming obese.'

Gerry sighed at me and lit another joint.

'I've always longed to be happy-go-lucky,' I said eventually.

'It's not fair. I'm behind on my rent, you know. I'll probably become a vagrant.'

'Jesus!' Gerry threw some air freshener at me. 'I talk to you and somehow death loses its sting.'

'Sorry.'

Gerry and I turned to watch a group of lesbians rampaging down the stairs. Tim, who was sitting quietly at the other end of the bar, looked up from the mobile he was making. He was sporting a psychedelic Hawaiian shirt, as he'd recently decided to wear amusing clothes to disguise his lack of personality.

'Listen,' Gerry hissed, stubbing out her joint. 'Shut up and let's get pissed. I'll tick us a couple of Es off the bouncer and then we'll go out.'

By eight-thirty the next morning, I was in my first AA meeting.

It wasn't that my night out with Gerry was so bad; I'd had worse. Our first stop was Pushka, a sort of fashion victim club where people went dressed as Barbie dolls and car seats. I looked completely out of place in black combat trousers and a *Slappers Posse* T-shirt Susie had given me. Within minutes, Gerry was up on a podium getting sexy with several black men. Meanwhile, I shuffled around, waiting for the E to start working, and eventually ended up snogging a Venezuelan called Freedom. At six in the morning, we followed a crowd to some seedy illegal dive off the Charing Cross Road. Entering, we were asked if we had any drugs on us and, when we protested we didn't, were advised to buy some as we were going to need them in there. It was a horrible 'club' – freebasing in the loos, blow-jobs on the stairs, some girl breakdancing wearing no knickers – and everyone was un-friendly and had bizarre facial piercings. Gerry and I took some more E but then decided to leave. She dropped me off in a cab and, alone in my flat, I started to freak. All I wanted to do was sleep but my body was twitching and jolting and my head was like a thousand nails being dragged along a blackboard. I showered and changed but it got worse. I think the Es must have been trippy as the next thing I knew I was convinced there was a ghost in the room trying to kill me. Panicking, I grabbed my *Where to Find* and got the hell out.

Still Eing my tits off, I tubed it to Camden Town and then walked around looking for the Sunday Gratitude meeting. Peering out from behind my sun-specs, I was sure people were staring at me. It's all right, I told myself, no-one can tell, I've been home, showered, changed.

'You looking for the meeting, love?' asked an alcoholic tramp over the road. 'It's up there.'

'Thanks.' So I did look like a freak. Entering a dimly lit doorway, I climbed a tatty staircase. I couldn't believe I was doing this and yet it seemed so depressingly inevitable. I stood outside a smoky room full of seemingly normal chattering people, took a deep breath, and entered.

'Tara!' said Lucinda, seeing me. 'I knew you'd come.'

'I'm finished, Cindy,' I said and burst into tears. I was, as so many members would tell me later, sick and tired of being sick and tired.

The meeting began with a bloke giving a 'chair' where he spoke about his drinking and recovery: 'I entered AA on me knees. Well, I was that pissed I fell down the stairs and landed on me knees. By then I was drinking me pints through a straw cos the shakes were that bad I couldn't hold the glass. Then I started looking for wakes in the paper, to get free booze. I'd turn up round some stranger's funeral, neck all the alcohol and roll around going, "We go back fuckin years, us." In the end, I'd sold all me furniture, was living off me mum's pension and was waking up after blackouts seeing policemen with guns and realizing I was being nicked in another country. I fought I was one of the incurables. But I was saved, freed from the insanity. My life now is beyond me wildest dreams.'

Afterwards, I went to a café with Lucinda and we were joined by John, another AA member. He had long greasy hair but good cheekbones. It was from John that I learnt about the Programme and the Twelve Steps (John called himself one of the Programme Patrol and Step Police). We had to admit powerlessness over our lives, hand our wills over to a higher power, stay sober and then things would just fall into place.

'We're not condemned to be the walking dead,' said John, pointing at me with nicotine-stained fingers. 'Now, I've got a job and a flat and my self-respect back.'

It was funny, as that's how I'd always kind of felt, like a ghost.

'You live in a world of fantasy, don't you?' he accused. 'You've always felt alone and abused and yet somehow destined for greatness.'

'Have you been telling everyone about me?' I asked Lucinda, feeling betrayed. Both she and John laughed.

'Tara,' said Lucinda, 'we *all* feel like that.'

I spent the next two weeks at AA. My ankle still injured, it was really just a case of doing meetings instead of class, the Programme rather than pliés. I rather enjoyed the secrecy of the Fellowship and all the little slogans like, 'We're Only as Sick as Our Secrets' and, 'What is Denial? Don't Even Know I am Lying'.

I never actually spoke at meetings, but I felt an inward sense of relief as people admitted to things that could get them sent down for ten years. John actually revealed that he had murdered someone in a blackout, and he now ran meditation workshops. Lucinda once blurted out that when she'd been on smack and living with some bloke, she used to open all his post and once found a letter saying he'd won a computer. Now it had been the dream of this bloke's life to own a computer. So Lucinda contacted the company and sold it for heroin. I wished I was capable of such honesty. Maybe my guiltiest secret was that I actually didn't regret anything I'd done, I was just worried about being caught. That I didn't care about anything or anyone, really. And how could I face up to the past if I couldn't bear to live with the guilt?

In the end, I told everyone about my AA membership, curious to see what the general opinion was on my latest fad.

'I'm pleased for you if you think it's helping, Tara. But they haven't made you sign anything or taken any of your money, have they?' (Hippie Cassie)

'About time.' (Jinty)

'Any hot men?' (Lilly)

'Watch your mouth. I'm sure they've got police spies there.' (Ben)

'You're not an alcoholic. You should be worried about your chain-smoking. Is there a Nicotine Anonymous?' (Merchant banker Seb, who was always trying to give up puffing)

'How can you be an alcoholic? You throw up after three vodkas. In fact your problem is you don't drink enough. I used to worry about me drinkin but since I came to Australia and started drinkin more I don't worry, me.' (Susie)

'Cool, you could be doin some business there. After me last trial they sent me to NA. Loved it. Went on a mission to liberate me comrades, didn't I. They're all clients now.' (Dave)

'Jinty told me, darling. I . . . I went once. Rather dull,

really; as if they were trying to bore one into sobriety. I actually thought of setting up my own support group called STOP. It would be for people who weren't actually alcoholics but couldn't stop drinking.' (My mother)

Obviously, I ignored everything everyone said. I wasn't terribly sure why I was at AA, not being an alcoholic or anything, but all the other members kept telling me how much better their lives were since they started attending meetings. I was sure it was only a matter of time before I was presented with my copy of *How to Live*.

Amazingly enough, my fatally sprained ankle began to improve and my physio Debbie agreed I could start *barre* work again. I returned to Laban, which was now in the examination period, to find it looking like Charing Cross casualty on a Saturday night: people limping about on crutches or lying groaning in corridors. Those that weren't injured generally had flu or were in intensive psychiatric treatment. I felt a deep sense of belonging as I strapped my ankle in the atrium.

'Tara!'

I looked up to see Sam, my abusive choreography tutor, standing over me.

'Where have you been? You look terrible.'

'I've been injured.'

'Why didn't you come in and watch class?'

I stood up and tried to think of an excuse. 'I just couldn't,' I finally admitted. 'I couldn't bear watching when I should have been up there doing it.'

To my amazement, Sam put his arm around my shoulder. 'Sometimes you remind me of myself, Tara.' He smiled sadly at me. 'You know, it is possible to try too hard.'

*   *   *

In my delirium of self-obsession, I had forgotten all about Caro. It was thus something of a surprise to meet her outside the administration office later that day, looking tanned and happy.

'Caro! Are you OK?'

'Fantastic. I'm just making my arrangements to leave.'

'Oh my God, your back,' I said, thinking she was in some huge paranoid form of denial.

'No, it's fine, I was only winded. But the folks were worried about me so they sent me to Greece for a couple of weeks. I sunned and swam and stared at the stars and decided to take a year off.'

'But what will you do?'

'Enjoy myself.' Caro looked down shyly at the floor. 'You know, since I stopped dancing I've finally found my voice.'

I realized then that Caro and I weren't nearly as similar as I had thought. Her crisis in dance had been brought about by the failure of an important relationship; mine was simply that dance was my only relationship. It was the greatest love affair of my life. There were tears, there was heartache, it stole all my money and physically abused me, but I'd have done almost anything for us to stay together. I considered setting up a helpline called Dancers Anonymous.

I went to a meeting that night, at which Lucinda gave a heartbreaking account of her struggle with eating: 'The strangest thing is that people think that it's because I'm a dancer that I have eating problems when in fact I think it's the reverse: I'm a dancer *because* I have eating problems. The dance world is practically the only place where I feel almost normal because *everyone's* obsessed with food.'

I remembered a quotation I'd once read from the choreographer Merce Cunningham, who'd said, 'Dance is not for restless souls.' I was a restless soul but I still wanted to dance.

Then John, Cindy's and my AA guru, started to speak, explaining that he was going through a bad patch. 'I know I should be grateful,' he said, thoughtfully sipping his tea. 'I came from hell to a steady job, decent flat, OK girlfriend but . . . I thought I'd be this great fucking star lighting up the world and people'd just look in wonder as I sped past them. It's not what I imagined.' He shrugged and lit a rollie. 'High class problems, I guess.'

I knew what John meant. I sometimes felt schizophrenic: so afraid of failure that I didn't even bother trying, or trying too hard and messing up as I put all the effort in the wrong direction. I'd once loved to dance, a silent child with no voice, and yet I had this disgusting body. I wanted to be anyone else but me.

After John, some old man told of his eighteen-year slip and lying covered in his own excrement in gutters. I noticed that he now wore a fur coat and was smoking a Havana. So I *wasn't* too far gone.

I somehow heard my mouth opening and me shouting, 'My name's Tara, I'm fucked, I've told so many lies.' In a vague, general, roundabout sort of way (i.e. without actually saying what had happened) I admitted stitching up Lilly, my own best friend. Desperate to confess, I even thought about telling the full story of my time as a cocaine courier for CJ, but I kept remembering what Ben had said about police spies.

Afterwards, everyone patted me on the back and John hugged me and said how proud of me he was and I stood in the shabby, smoke-filled room and felt like a total fraud.

6. Hardcore's Funeral

There was a horrible sense of inevitability when Rupert and I were reunited at an AA meeting. We'd gone out years before, united by our self-pity, arrogance and love of cocaine. Our 'relationship' had lasted about three weeks, after which a bit of my nose had fallen out and he had entered the first of his many treatment centres. I stopped mixing with our old crowd, finding them dull and Sloaney. Also, they had grown to hate me. But I always had fond memories of Rupert: the two of us at parties lying on sofas stuffing cocaine up each other's noses or sitting under tables playing with water pistols. He'd attempted to contact me a couple of times over the years but I'd never returned his calls, ashamed of my physical degeneration. What a joy it was, then, to see that Rupert also looked terrible: puffy of face and flabby of body.

'Tara!' he exclaimed, coming over to sit next to me when

the meeting had finished. 'I can't believe it! What are you doing here instead of NA?'

'Family tradition, I spose. What about you?'

'Oh, I've kicked the coke. I only do heroin occasionally now. When I came out of my last centre, I decided to let myself drink and gave myself three months to decide whether I was an alcoholic or not. After ten days, I was sitting in a police station with my head broken open. So here I am.'

There was an awkward silence. We both got up and stacked our chairs at the side of the room.

'What do you do now?' asked Rupert as we straggled our way outside.

'Nothing really,' I sighed. I was feeling particularly disillusioned with dance, having just failed a jazz audition at Danceworks. I'd been told my technique was fine but my personality needed 'adjustment'. I wasn't going to let it get to me, though. I had better things to do with my life than performing high kicks on the *Les Dennis Laughter Show*. Probably. 'What're you up to?'

'Same as. I work in a book shop in Putney and stay in a hostel nearby.'

'But?' Rupert was from an extremely smart Anglo-Irish family who'd once owned half of County Monaghan.

'Dad died six months ago. Drank himself to death. Everything's mortgaged to fuck. No more coke, no more treatment centres.' Rupert laughed. 'Not that they ever did any good. They were more like drug education centres.'

'But you're off it all now?'

'Basically.'

I thought this was like saying you were sort of pregnant.

'I live a pretty normal life. Work, meetings, community service. I had to help with occupational therapy for twenty schizophrenics this morning. We were trying to teach them to make breakfast but most of them just stood screaming at the cooker or attempted to stab themselves.' He sighed and fingered some scratches on his face. 'I know it's all my fault but it's not really what I'd expected.'

After our first encounter, Rupert and I started bumping into each other quite regularly at meetings. We were both still in the AA tourist stage and would sit at the back wearing sun-specs and pretending to be journalistic observers. Lucinda had gone on tour so it was nice to be with someone who didn't spend all their time shaking my hand and telling me to keep coming back.

'It's so strange seeing you again,' Rupe said to me as we waited for the Joys of Sobriety meeting to begin. 'I always wonder what happened to my ex-girlfriends.'

'They probably regained their senses and went on to live normal lives.'

'You were always such a bitch.' Rupert shook his head and looked down at the floor. I could see he was starting to go bald. He'd always had a dangerous hairline. 'I can't believe I ever loved you.'

'You didn't.'

'Maybe not.' He shrugged. 'Did you ever love me?'

'No, not really. When I was younger I never loved anyone. I thought love was some sort of consolation prize for poor people. Now I tell entire clubs I love them. I guess it means about the same thing.'

I took a sip of tea out of my now very bitten polystyrene cup. It was all so weird. Rupert had been my male Lucinda. I'd met him at a party and, despite his good looks and confidence, had somehow been convinced that he was like me. I'd later learnt that his entire family were alcoholics.

Even his grandma used to dry-retch in the morning. He told me that his mother was the sort of woman who rode bicycles half naked whilst smoking a cigar. My mother was the sort of woman who wore ill-fitting dresses to drab dances. But I'd always had a strange sense of déjà vu when Rupe and I were together; as if identical ghosts were haunting us.

'Do you miss your father?' I asked him, watching the meeting fill with unlikely suspects.

'I try to.' Rupert folded his arms around himself. 'He was such a fat, disgusting bastard. He used to sit in his chair in front of the television, neck a bottle of Black Bush, pass out and then wet himself. I always used to give him a good bunny punch when I passed as I knew he wouldn't remember it in the morning.'

'I'm tormented with guilt,' I blurted out suddenly.

'I know.' Rupert reached for my hand and I instantly recoiled. 'I wasn't much help, was I?' he said finally.

'Rupe,' I sighed. 'You're looking at the wrong person for comfort. I sometimes think I'm suffering from that Compassion Fatigue.'

Death was in the air, it seemed. A few days later I discovered that Dave Hardcore had been killed. He and some mates had been car chasing and he'd gone out of a back window and broken his neck. Dave had always been a sick boy but he'd still functioned under the crazed illusion that he was some kind of Renaissance figure. In the past he'd claimed to be an actor; even if the only acting he ever did was in court. Then, on the basis of, 'That Marquis de Sadism got published so why shouldn't I?' Dave had attempted to be an anarchist writer. Claiming dyslexia, Hardcore proceeded to record an offensively poor Zulu rave tune, and his most recent sexploit had been trying to make a porn vid, *Donkey Sex* (his mother ran a donkey sanctuary in Dorset). Even the drugs he'd dealt had been shit.

'Things won't be the same without Hardcore,' said Ben, who'd run around with Dave for years. 'No more letting off cans of CS gas in pubs, no more nights down Mad Frankie Fraser's gaff, no more death threats.'

Cassie, who'd still been going out with Hardcore, was devastated. 'I can't believe it,' she sobbed.

'At least you've got lots to remember him by,' I said, looking round her room which was stuffed full of hot goods Dave had been storing there.

'It's so confusing.' Cass applied some more E45 cream to her eczema. 'To be honest, I'd really been wanting to finish with him. If it wasn't bad enough with Dave making me watch *Genital Hospital* every night, then he seemed to think that just cos Dad runs glamour mags we should form some sort of porn empire together. He actually wanted to film us having sex and then sell the recordings.'

'Oh God.'

'He couldn't understand why I wasn't flattered.' Cassie handed me a joint. It was all sticky with the E45 cream. 'I keep remembering our last row and can't seem to feel anything genuine. I'd refused to be videoed again and he stormed out going, "Women, I'll never understand them," and I just stood there thinking that that was the single most predictable thing he could have said at that moment.'

Indeed, in Dave Hardcore's rare sober moments, his notorious perversity had been replaced by an unbelievable talent for stupidity, as in, 'I could've been in *EastEnders* if I'd got the part,' or, when watching the footie, 'Big pitch, innit? Amazing how big pitches are, really.' Dave had basically been a grotesque living caricature of a lad, never happy unless boozing, tooting or telling lies about his sexual prowess. No wonder all the other boys were grief-stricken. But girls too said they would miss Hardcore. His death seemed like the end of an era; the doors finally closing on our teenage years. In times of boredom, Dave had always been there, handing out microdots and leering at any girl present, going, 'I'm here to be used and abused. Take liberties!' There'd always been the comfort that however sad, however drug riddled we became, Dave could always be counted on to be more degenerate than us. I wished Susie had been there to comfort me but she was still in Australia, working as a gynaecological model for medical students taking their exams. Susie got all the best jobs.

Since Cassie was now dining out on two eighths a day and Hardcore had been estranged from his parents due to the donkey video, it was left to Ben and the Bolivian Posse to organize the funeral. Nothing was too grandiose or too vulgar for them: gospel choirs and wreaths the size of elephants for the funeral, a nightclub and top London DJ for the wake (Hardcore techno, of course, it was what Dave would have wanted). My sister Jinty, who'd described Dave as a wart on the hand of humanity, found the histrionics 'repugnant'. But his death did my head in. Watching the boys writing lists, stressing out and drinking possibly lethal amounts of Jack Daniels, started to remind me of other funerals. It was the kind of thing I knew I should discuss at AA but I still had problems opening my mouth there. Also, I was getting tired of the meetings with all their stewed tea and emotional vomiting. If the meetings were happy and positive, I'd moan about how I always went to the advanced groups and where were all the fuck-ups. If they were down, I'd whine that what was the point of going to AA when all you did was get depressed. And it wasn't as if I was an alcoholic, anyway.

'I don't think I can take another "sharing",' I said to Rupert one day as we waited for a meeting to begin.

'Me neither,' he sighed. 'Let's go to the pub – only joking!'

I laughed, despite the fact I'd been ready to agree.

'You don't look good,' he said as we walked to a café. 'Is it that friend of yours' death?'

'Dunno.'

'You still haven't spoken about her with me.'

'Her?'

'Jesus, Tara, you make an art form out of repression.' Rupert looked at me kindly. I'd forgotten how unusual his eyes were; almost a dark orange colour. 'Amaranda. You never talked to me afterwards, you know.'

'You dumped me.'

'I dumped you! You bloody chucked me by answerphone.'

It was a bizarre coincidence, I suppose, meeting Rupert and another death occurring. The last time Rupe and I had been seeing one another, my sister Amaranda died. She'd killed herself, to be honest, downing several bottles of top pharmaceutical grade tranquillizers. The inquest called it misadventure. I remembered after her funeral, emptying her bank account, thinking, Cool, I can pay off my overdraft. Ama had been slight and skinny and used to read those dreadful self-help books like *Daddy – Please Don't Hurt Me* by Ruth M. Abrahams PhD. I once found a questionnaire in one of the books asking, 'Have you ever attempted self-mutilation?' and Ama had ticked the yes box. I had been totally unable to understand. I, who at the time was suffering with a collapsing nose and the desire to acquire the body of a six-year-old Ethiopian. For some reason I thought of Hard-core sitting in Ben's garden, leafing through *The Big Anal* and fantasizing about his non-existent talents, and what he could have been if he'd been straight enough to do it ('I could've been dyslexic, me, if I'd been middle class').

Cassie had said the funniest thing about Dave. That despite his faults, his many, many faults, she'd always be grateful to him. He was the first person to make her feel normal. She'd never felt normal before. 'Even him wanting to make the porno vids was kind of sweet in a way,' she'd said. 'My eczema honestly didn't seem to have crossed his mind. I think he genuinely thought there was nothing wrong with me.'

I'd used to call Ama a freak.

I went to Hardcore's funeral. The service itself was sickeningly amusing and giggles were heard in the church when the vicar referred to Dave as 'sensitive' and 'articulate'. But by the time we were standing by the grave the atmosphere had deadened somewhat. Dave's mother was there, looking shabby and fat, staring at the rest of us with something like horror. Cassie became hysterical and had to be led away. After we arrived at the nightclub for the wake, everyone dispensed with their façades of self-control and the bogs reverberated with the sounds of emergency supplies of cocaine being snorted. Then the girls stood in one corner smoking with stiff upper lips whilst the boys sobbed into their lagers.

There were some of the old crowd from the Brixton sixth form, which Dave, Lucinda and I had attended. Pathetically I started looking out for Mark, our old pal. It had been a joke of Dave's to torment me with false 'news' about Mark. That Mark'd become a crack-head and was living in a Bronx ghetto. That he'd seen Mark the previous day and he'd become a second-hand car salesman in Dagenham. Once, even, that he'd spotted Mark in Soho dressed as a nun and wearing roller-skates. I had a silly thought that Dave was practically the only other person I'd still known who'd remembered that time in my life.

'God, that Hardcore,' I heard Ben saying, his voice slurred with drink. 'Was he mad or what? We were round his flat one night, clean out of money and bored shitless. So what does Hardcore do? Gives himself a Tennents enema with a spare syringe.'

'Mad!' said Touchy-Feely. 'I remember him boring those holes in the bathroom wall so he could watch the girls pissing. Said he loved water sports.'

'Mad!' said Ben. 'Nothing that boy didn't know about the Arsenal.'

'Or arse,' said Peanuts. 'He once told me he'd picked up a girl and turns out she was a fucking transvestite. So he thought sod it and gave it up the shitter.'

'The best was the 0898 Bestiality Hotline,' said Ben.

' "Speak to dogs you'd like to get to know better!" ' they all screamed in unison.

Over in the girls' corner, conversation was somewhat different. They talked of snogging Hardcore (all of them), fucking Hardcore (most of them), going to raves with Hardcore (all of them, many, many times). Hardcore had viewed himself as the Forrest Gump of the rave scene: at every pivotal moment in House History, Dave had supposedly been there. He was there when no-one else was; when nothing was happening. He claimed to have DJ'd the first ever rave, to have personally road-tested E in England, even, in his more fucked moments, to have given 'Nightcrawlers' the idea of playing Michael Jackson backwards (this after I told him that Chingford Gary had called Kiss and discovered why the lyrics never made sense. Hardcore asserted that he often played records backwards and musical spies must have been listening).

'I remember going to this rave off the M25 with Hardcore,' said Lilly, looking particularly ridiculous in a spotted ra-ra skirt. 'He stuck a trip in his eye and then did a shit in the middle of a field.'

'I once had sex with Dave on a dancefloor,' mused Sarah, now back from her treatment centre. 'Then he took me to Smithfield to look at severed pigs' heads. Anyone got any more toot on them?'

I wandered back through the sweaty crowd, thinking of the icon of outrageousness that had been Hardcore. He really had had no shame. Unlike the rest of us, he never worried about his drugs intake, never gave a minute's thought to his future. Which was lucky, I supposed. I felt a hand on my shoulder.

'Are you OK?' asked Jinty, who was sipping Perrier through a straw. 'I don't think I've ever seen such a bunch of addicts gathered together before. It's absolutely disgusting.' She looked closer at me. 'You're crying.'

'I am?' I felt my face and found it wet with tears.

'It must be tough for you at the moment,' said Jinty. 'What with these idiots and you meeting up with your old boyfriend again.'

'Rupert wasn't my boyfriend,' I protested. 'More just a guy I snogged.'

'Let your feelings out,' Jinty patronized. 'Be with your grief.'

I decided that the only solution was to leave and exited the smoky club. It was still daylight so I went to visit Rupert.

Arriving at Rupert's hostel down in Putney, I found he wasn't in. I remembered that he actually had a job and went to a bar to wait for him. It was one of those dingy pubs full of old men killing themselves and I sat huddled in the corner downing vodkas. I thought of John at AA saying that the reason he'd drunk had been in order to anaesthetize his feelings. But I didn't see what was so wrong with that. People took painkillers for headaches, why not booze for mental misery? But then I remembered Ama once saying to me, 'You know, Tara, I can see you in ten years' time. Wearing lovely clothes and living in a lovely flat and yet drinking yourself to death.'

And here I was. In a revolting old boozer with some gimmer on a stool having a tuberculosic coughing fit next to me. I decided to get out and made my way back to Rupert's. As I entered his road, I saw him on the other side, his back bent and a small plastic carrier bag under his arm. I called out to him but he didn't seem to hear me.

'Rupert!' I said, running across the road.

'Tara!' He clumsily gave me a kiss and we entered the hostel and walked up to his room. It was absolutely minuscule and, on first sight, looked immaculately tidy. It was only when you looked closer that you realized the room wasn't tidy but was empty, totally devoid of any personal goods. Rupe made us some tea and we sat on his bed chain-smoking Marlboro Lights.

'You know,' he said, smiling sadly, 'I reckon I've worked out why I used to fancy you so much. I think I'm attracted to emptiness.'

'Oh, thanks.'

'And of course you always looked like the sort of girl who knew how to give a boy a good spanking.'

'Probably an inherited talent,' I mused.

I thought of Dave and his favourite game, feel-who-it-is-in-the-dark. I thought of Ama confessing to me, 'I don't know what to do,' and me telling her she could pay back the fucking money she owed me for a start.

'I was only such a bitch cos I liked you, Rupe,' I said finally.

'I know.' Rupert looked down at his tea. 'We were powerless, you know. We couldn't have saved them.'

'Maybe.'

He sighed and stood up. 'I've got to pack. Luckily I've fuck all to pack.'

'Where are you going?'

'Home. Mum's had a nervous breakdown so I've got to go back and sort out the estate.'

'You're crazy!' I couldn't believe what I was hearing. 'To go back now's fucking suicidal.'

'I have to or I'll never be able to live with the guilt.'

Rupert returned to Ireland two days later. He never contacted me and I knew what had happened.

7. Looking at the Ceiling

Lilly and I were sitting in Housing Benefit waiting for her claim to be messed around with. I was there as a kind of reverse bouncer, designed to prevent Lilly from attacking the staff. We'd been hanging around for three hours and were suffocating with boredom and the forty fags we'd smoked.

'Social Security's ruining my health,' snarled Lilly, sparking up again. 'Sometimes I think going legit would be easier. Six months and I haven't seen a fucking penny of rent. If I hadn't been cheating I'd have been fucked. What about the people who don't cheat, eh? What happens to them?'

'Whatever,' I murmured, having heard this rant about five times already that afternoon.

'It's a fucking disgrace!' Lilly screamed whilst throwing around random threatening looks. 'They treat us like pigs.'

'Yeah,' I agreed, watching an alcoholic tramp roll off his chair. Lilly sighed and I realized gratefully that she was moving from anger to despondency.

'Sometimes I feel like I've spent my entire life in benefit offices,' she said morosely whilst playing with a hideous charm bracelet she was wearing. 'I used to sit with my mum when she did dodgy emergency claims. She was a fucking genius with the social. But by fuck did she earn her money. We used to queue outside before the offices opened.'

'How is she?' Lilly's mother had cancer.

'Terminal. What with that and the fucking Restart interviews I've got enough on my plate without eviction notices.'

'It's your number,' I said thankfully, looking at the machine. Lilly and I wandered through to an interview room (no wonder the DSS always reminded me of police stations) and Lily meekly greeted some old hag. I always thought it bizarre how big, hard, revolutionary Lilly was floored by authority. She was ashamed, I think, that because of her gypsy childhood she was unable to read and, in particular, write properly. This was the other unspoken reason for my presence. I'd do all the forms for Lilly so that she didn't have to admit to any of the official bastards that she didn't understand them.

After half an hour of excuses and promises that Lilly's money would be sent to her 'within the week', we went off to sit in some greasy spoon. Neither of us was feeling too chirpy. A day at the social was bad enough, but we'd also both been sacked again. Me from the Escape for calling the manager a cunt and Lilly from her vegetarian-anarchist café for attempting to glass a customer.

'It looks like we've hit rock bottom,' I said after we'd paid for our teas and realized that we had twenty-four pence left to our names. 'We're going to have to become hostesses and give hand-jobs in seedy Soho bars.'

'But we've already done that.'

'That's the worst of it. We've hit rock bottom AGAIN.'

'True.' Lilly scratched some spots on her chin. 'It's amazing to think that we've been sacked from the worst jobs in the world.'

'At least we hated them.' I lit my last cigarette. 'Maybe we should become hookers. Sarah said it wasn't so bad. She just used to look at the ceiling and work out what she was going to buy the next day.'

'You know, I think you're right.' Lilly poured a huge load of sugar into her hand and lapped it up in one. 'I haven't been shopping in ages.'

'Lilly, I was joking.'

'Listen, if that girl who lived in that skip outside my old squat could be a successful prostitute, I don't see why we shouldn't.'

'Don't be stupid.' The idea of anyone actually paying to have sex with me was patently ludicrous. 'No, it's just more piss-shit bar work for me. Sometimes I think I'll never escape the Confines of the Counter. I'll be like ninety and still pouring pints and waiting for the next audition.'

'What do you think I'm gonna fucking do? Brain surgery?' Lilly ran her fingers through her cropped, greasy hair and sighed a sigh so long it could have travelled to the moon and back. 'I can't face kitchen portering any more and bar work's the only other job that still pays in the hand. But I fucking hate doing pubs. I could only cope with the Parrot by nicking. I used to price insults. You know, if the manager called me lazy I'd nick a fiver. If he called me stupid, I'd nick a tenner. It was my only enjoyment, you know, ripping the tills. But now that's all over.'

I cowered in my chair. Since Lilly's caution, her nicking had had to cease and I was scared she still blamed me for her criminal demise. 'Lil—'

Lilly put her hand up. 'Please, no more of your lame excuses; I'm too tired to have a go at you. Besides, I've lost my nerve. I go into shops now and even pay for Tampax. I never realized how much life cost . . .' Lilly paused to pick out some grit from underneath her fingernails. 'But the nerve's gone. It's weird. When I got picked up and the rozzers were going on at me, it was like I'd been there before; like I'd been paranoid all those years without even realizing it, if you know what I mean.'

'I know,' I admitted.

At first, Lilly and I attempted to ignore our precarious financial situations. Lilly decided we were to go 'on the jib'. She'd picked up the phrase from Dave Hardcore. Being on the jib basically meant never spending any money and, if possible, making a profit out of doing nothing. Lilly had, of course, been jibbing it for years with her many scams and dodges but her new challenge was to jib without breaking the law or giving blow-jobs to men who used inflatable condoms. So, on the pretext of looking for bar jobs, Lil and I jibbed round the West End. I'd get back from dance college and we'd change and warrior-paint ourselves and then stand beside smart bars looking moronic. We never paid for a drink. We never paid for cigarettes. If Lilly particularly disliked the blokes she'd lift their wallets. We took Smollenskys; we took the Atlantic; we took Browns – but we never did anything. Even the hangovers weren't so bad as we hadn't paid for them.

Despite our jibbing triumph, I began to tire of fat men trying to molest me and of attempting to look fascinated as they bored on about the difficulties of dog ownership in the city.

'I don't know why I bother talking to you,' said a bloke who was trying to make a date with me for the following evening. 'You're so pissed you won't remember a word of this tomorrow.'

'Wrong!' I slurred. 'Actually, I act much more drunk than I actually am.'

Besides, I knew that I was only delaying the inevitable. I would find myself woozily eyeing the bar staff as Lilly encouraged our prey to order champagne. It was only a matter of time till I changed counter sides, joining the staff in their obvious naked desolation. Or maybe I was just projecting. I was dreading going back to bar work so much that I knew I'd have to do it soon or I'd never be able to face it. I began to think that the biggest of the big lies we're asked is, 'What do you want to be when you grow up?', when in fact everyone knows there's no choice.

It seemed to me almost inconceivable to remember that when I'd first started club work I'd quite liked it. I'd just dropped out of uni and was living in London. Totally insecure, I'd gone to the worst nightclub I'd known, assuming that only somewhere that sad would take on someone like me: Fifi's. What a lucky break. I'd arrived during the most corrupt management reign I ever witnessed in a club. The entire place was on the take; the staff parties were so obscene that the cleaners had threatened to resign if they had to straighten up another. Fifi's operated on the principle that not only was the customer always in the wrong, but also they knew what they were risking when they entered the club in the first place. The poor punters had their drinks gobbed in by the bar staff, their money stolen by the glass collectors, their bodies brutalized by the bouncers. When one punter complained to the management (Terry) that all the staff were drunk, Terry'd cried, 'Buy them black coffee!'

'Listen, mate, they told me to fuck off.'

'Well, why don't you, then?'

The customer was then shown the unofficial back exit down an extremely long flight of stairs. Fifi's – what a place! It was so relaxed we used to sleep behind the bar. But then new management took over and the entire staff were sacked. We were all 'security risks'. No-one much minded being given the shove, though. Pissed all night, no hassle, money there for the taking – we'd all known it was too good to last.

My next stop was The Line, so named after the manager's infamous cocaine habit. Rumour was the guv had even accosted a cappuccino machine mender because he'd had a Colombian accent (the workman had been obese and about sixty) and told him he was being held hostage until emergency supplies were shipped over. Drugs were everywhere. The chef dealt trips over the kitchen counter, the bouncers would sell a different brand of E in each lavatory cubicle and we were allocated free coke as a job perk. Unfortunately, the manager's alcoholism and toot addiction started turning him into a loony-tune. He began wearing lipstick and reading gay 1970s San Franciscan porn beside the bar, only rising occasionally to scream, 'What we need is Goth music!', before passing out. He sacked me most nights but his drinking was such that he'd always forgotten by the following evening. Sadly, one night he actually wrote himself a note saying, 'Remember to sack Tara,' so I finally got the shove.

Next came DOA (Dead On Arrival), a club so rough even the bouncers wouldn't go into the loos. On my first night I was given Instructions: 'Listen, if there's trouble Shaz will start putting up the boards behind the bar and I'll go outside and grab the chairs. Your job is to throw the slop-trays over the punters. If it gets bad, just start throwing glasses.'

'OK . . . but why will you get the chairs?'

The barman looked at me like I was a village idiot. 'So as I can smash them up, stupid, and start throwing them at the crowd.'

DOA specialized in showing 'new' bands; the sort of bands who would never last long enough to be old. Our favourite was The Cunts, who came on stage completely naked apart from barbed wire wrapped around their heads and demonically attacked their guitars whilst screaming, 'We're The Cunts! Here to Offend!'

At DOA there were threats, fights, gratuitous violence (and that was just amongst the bouncers), guns, stabbings and fun with CS gas. When a bouncer threw out a crack dealer one night, the dealer said that he was going to get a bunch of his mates down to machete the lot of us. We prepared for a siege and martial arts weapons were handed out. A car pulled up and three guys leapt out carrying machetes.

Suddenly one of the would-be attackers looked at one of the bouncers and said, 'Fuck me, it's Leroy. When d'you get out mate?' It turned out they'd been cell-mates inside so we were safe. But there were times when DOA did go off. People walking out of lavatories with no teeth. Me finding a bloke lying in a corridor, covered in blood and begging for me to get him an ambulance. I could see blood was spurting out of his neck and knew it could be an artery and that I should try to stem the flow. But I just thought AIDS, and screamed for one of the bouncers. A girl staggering back into the club and going, 'Oh God, oh God, I can't believe it, oh God I've been raped . . .'

There were the bad times, too. The clubs I'd worked

before the Escape and after DOA. So many, so similar, they had merged into nothingness. Calling ambulances to collect punters who'd OD'd one too many times. Staff becoming so terminally alcoholic that they had to be thrown out of the club. Managers trying to molest you in the cellar. Staff-transmitted diseases. Comical wages that barely covered the cab fare home. Vomiting in the slop-trays. Police taking away the barman who'd been on the take. The clinical boredom of doing the same thing every night, listening to the same crap every night and thinking, Oh God, this is it. I've gone and fucked it. No social life. Just the same old faces grey with smoke, booze and lack of sun. Twentieth century vampires. The Escape hadn't been any better. Totally boring. So boring that I used to go inside, sniff the air and think, Christ, I've only just walked in and I'm already sick of the smell of this place. At least, though, during the eighteen long months I'd been there, I'd always been able to drink myself into oblivion. I was never really sure whether Kevin, the manager, knew that I drank, or didn't care that I drank as long as I didn't show it. Whatever, I drank. Of course, since being in AA I'd cursed myself for my liquid diet but I was also well aware that I'd never be able to stick bar work sober. If you're doing something every night that you hate but there's no other option (and what else can you do – nights, no experience, at college – but bar work?) then you have to escape from it somehow. And then I'd been sacked. To be honest, it wasn't just because I'd called Kevin a cunt. Actually, he'd found me paralytic on the bar floor going, 'Don't mind me, I'm a Buddhist.' He'd told me to get up and I'd called him a cunt and thus were my services terminated. Kevin had told me not to take it personally but it's hard not to take getting sacked personally.

Anyway, I didn't care as I'd decided to become a waitress.

There was no way I'd be able to stop drinking if I continued as a barmaid and besides waitressing money was better. So I gave up jibbing and trooped round several restaurants claiming extensive experience but no references due to a pending sexual molestation case. To my amazement, I couldn't get a job. I did a couple of trial shifts but my lies – experience, skills, any aptitude for waitressing whatsoever – were quickly uncovered. I was beginning to feel like someone from the north, when I was offered a job at a small Italian café in Battersea. Decked out in black-and-white, I did the bar for the first couple of shifts and was then allowed on the floor. I discovered that I was an even worse waitress than I had suspected: simply hanging around being vague, dropping plates and going, 'Sorry.'

The manager kept looking at me, punching his forehead and shouting, 'Oh my life!' At the end of the shift he gave me thirty quid and said to me, 'To be somewhere you do not belong, that is disgusting.'

I had agreed and walked out feeling slightly hopeless. It was obvious I was good for nothing but bar tending. Two days later, I procured a job at a fashionable easy listening club in Soho. It was full of people with goatees doing poetry readings and drinking expressos. I was asked to leave after a week due to my getting blind drunk one night and passing out in the Blokes'.

My finances became so desperate that I started going to AA again (I'd recently given up as it wasn't the same without Rupert and his dangerous hairline) just so I could have tea and biscuits for dinner. Lucinda, now back from touring, would watch me wolfing down Custard Creams and give me maniacally understanding looks whilst telling me I had to stop lying to myself. She was off the smack and claimed to have sorted out her eating, though I was suspicious it couldn't be that sorted if she still had the body of a concentration camp victim.

'You don't need money,' she'd say as I started on the Party Rings, 'you need mindfulness. Instead of doing the washing up to get it done, you need to start enjoying doing the washing up. I spend a lot of time practising breathing.'

I thought this was easy to say for Lucinda, who had a cushy contract with a Belgian minimalist dance company (their latest piece was called *Chair* and explored the act of sitting down).

'You need to forget about bar work and concentrate on your sobriety.'

Instead, I decided to forget about Lucinda and AA. Lucinda said that it was a mark of my illness that I was continuing doing something which I knew was destroying me.

Fair enough.

I had a lucky break. I was doing one of my traditional wanders down the King's Road when I bumped into Sarah. She was on one of her traditional shopping expeditions and was carrying half of Harvey Nicks. She immediately dragged me into the Dôme for a drink. Apart from Dave's funeral, I hadn't seen her since she'd gone into rehab to save her nose. The clinic had obviously done her good and she looked particularly stunning.

'Moshino?' I queried, feeling her skirt. She nodded smugly.

'What're you up to then?' I asked.

'Nothing much. Remember, it's not what you do, it's who—'

'—you screw.'

'No romance—'

'—without finance.'

Sarah looked me over. 'Well, you obviously need reminding. You look appalling.' I felt my low self-confidence plummeting even further. Sarah tended to have this effect on me.

'It's not my fault,' I pleaded. 'I'm unemployed.'

'Sacked again? Any police involvement?'

'No.'

'Good, then I should be able to help you.'

'I'm not becoming a prostitute.'

'That's lucky. You wouldn't get many takers with that haircut.' Sarah grinned. 'Sorry, only joking. No, you know that I'm running Jonny's nightclub at the moment?'

'Serious?'

'Serious.'

'What an idiot.'

'I know, he's fucked up, trusting me. I live there as well.'

'YOU LIVE IN A NIGHTCLUB!'

Sarah's, or rather Jonny's, or rather Jonny's father's, club was in Chiswick. It was called Bimbo's. When Sarah opened the door (complete with peephole) I just gasped and cried, 'It's like the club that time forgot!'

Those three lights in front of the DJ stand, a poster on the wall advertising Ladies Nite, mirrors everywhere. Sarah giggled and started playing with switches. The dancefloor lit up.

'It's like being in a Michael Jackson video!' I laughed as I jumped between flashing squares.

'Just wait,' said Sarah. 'It gets worse than you can possibly imagine. Dwarf Albanians saying, "Pst pst, babee," when you go past, girls with biker tattoos. A chap actually did come up to me one night and say, "Are you a model, love?" Really rather squalid, but I imagine you're used to that.'

'Yeah.'

Sarah turned off the lights and I followed her up to her 'flat', which was really just a couple of decrepit rooms covered in piles of clothes and make-up. Sarah had obviously made no attempt to improve her surroundings and the only 'decoration' she'd added was hundreds of empty champagne bottles with candles in them (she always said that candlelight did more for the complexion than a dozen facials). Sarah opened a bottle of Moët and we drank champagne from chipped mugs.

'So how did you end up in rehab?' I asked as we sat down on her bed (the only surface without discarded outfits on it). 'I heard so many rumours.'

'Well, no-one must ever know.' (It was amazing how all of Sarah's conversations were peppered with, 'No-one must ever know.') 'I had a heart attack.' She grinned and lit a cigarette. 'Funny, eh? Things had been getting a bit out of hand. I owed money. A lot of money.'

'Coke?'

'Not so much the coke although that reminds me . . .' She reached under the mattress and pulled out a wrap. 'No, it was more the shopping that destroyed me financially. I just couldn't stop. It was an obsessive, compulsive thing apparently . . . anyway, I went back to escorting. I was doing it all summer.'

'You're joking.' I'd had no idea. All that summer when Sarah and I had lazed on Parsons Green she'd been hooking by night.

'Well, I hardly wanted to advertise the fact. Anyway, one night I was with this American government chap. I'd been working all week; I must have been doing coke solid for about five days. Well, we did the business and then I got up to get dressed and the next thing I knew I was in an ambulance and then lying in a smart London hospital. They said I'd die if I didn't stop. So Jonny paid for me to go into rehab.'

'But?'

Sarah was presently engaged in rolling a note for a toot. 'No, this isn't really using. It was the escorting that made me use so much. I couldn't do it without the coke. I kept thinking of . . . well, you know.'

'Jonny?'

'Don't be stupid. You know, my uncle.' Sarah had once revealed to me that as a child she had been repeatedly raped by an uncle. Unfortunately, he'd already died which was a pity as Sarah's only aim in life had been to torture him to death. If the abuse wasn't bad enough, when it had all come out her mother had had a breakdown and become convinced she was a re-incarnated Red Indian. Sarah said her mother was still totally barmy.

'Does Jonny know?'

'About my uncle or the escorting?'

'Either.'

'No.' Sarah finished snorting and handed me the note. 'The court stuff's bad enough.'

'Court stuff?'

'I'm presently charged with intent to supply and possession of a fire-arm. When I got out of the clinic I went to stay with one of the girls from the agency. They raided her flat cos of some car deal scam and found three thousand pounds' worth of cocaine and a gun.' Sarah shrugged. 'Bit of a pisser. That's really why Jonny said I could run the place and live here. I'm trying to look like a respectable citizen.'

'Jesus.' I had to hand it to Sarah; she was the hardest person I knew. She made Lilly look like a TV AM presenter.

'It's not so bad. I'll probably get off; my prints weren't on anything. And if I do a stretch, I do a stretch. I can't be bothered with paranoia any more. It was all the paranoia over the bills that got me in this mess in the first place. Shopping, freaking, snorting, escorting . . .'

'I still can't believe that Jonny hasn't realized about your escorting.'

'I know. The fool. That's the funniest thing of all. I met his father and—'

'No!'

'I know.' Sarah let out a snort of laughter. 'It's like something out of a book.'

'And he didn't tell?'

'How could he?' Sarah stood up and smoothed down her micro-skirt. 'Come on, let's go downstairs and laugh at the peasants.'

Sarah sacked some square bitch and I started working at Bimbo's the next night. Initially, I loved it. Sarah couldn't have given a shit what I did and the other barman was some Irish retard who took pride in his job and did all the graft for the pair of us. We'd hang around tooting and smoking and boozing and getting chatted up by dwarf Albanians and watch tattooed girls removing bottletops with their teeth. Unbelievably, the punters at Bimbo's were even worse than those at the Escape; a particularly unsavoury mixture of fuck-ups, wide boys and sexual deviants. But being with Sarah somehow made the clientele seem amusing rather than horrifying. Her bitchiness was famed in Fulham for good reason. She would say that people smelt of council houses, that they looked like the elephant man after a car crash, that she'd rather suck on a pavement than snog them. Such was her power that the offended would actually laugh nervously with her.

On Sunday afternoons, we would both take Es in her

bedroom before going downstairs to the club to switch on all the lights and music. Then we would cavort round the empty dancefloor, Sarah screaming, 'If you don't want to fuck me, fuck off!' Sarah would always dance to her reflections in the mirrors, perfecting pouts and poses. I would watch and copy.

After a couple of weeks, though, the old manager of Bimbo's returned. He'd been on holiday for two months and was now living with Jonny. The agreement was that he and Sarah would split nights. He was called Savage and he hated Sarah because she'd stolen his shifts and he hated me because I was her friend. On her nights off, I would catch Sarah getting ready to visit Jonny at another of his clubs and I would groan inside. Working with Savage was a nightmare. There was no hanging around the bar with him. It was all clean this, clean that, smarten yer fuckin act up. He only laid off when he was pissed and reminiscing about his days as a Millwall thug and how he used to hang up banners at New Cross station saying 'Prepare To Die' and saw all the other fans off in an ambulance. When I asked Sarah why she didn't get Jonny to sack him (Savage openly referred to Sarah as 'Pissflaps') she said sadly that she couldn't as he was Jonny's best friend.

'They're fucking inseparable, those two. Spookily so. They'll sit for hours in that flat watching old Millwall videos and boasting who they decked at what match. At least I know Jonny's not fucking around, I spose.'

Lilly claimed to be madly jealous of my new job. She was working at a pub in Clapham. Since she had got the sack from her vegetarian-anarchist café it had taken her ages to get a job too. Everywhere had been on the books, but how the fuck was she supposed to survive on three quid an hour? She'd eventually been offered in the hand by the Clapham place and was grimly sticking it out there, even though most nights she wanted to attack the manager.

I went to visit her one evening after college. I'd been totally knackered and couldn't face seeing Savage so I'd pulled a sickie. Trust me to end up in a boozer on my night off. Lilly was violently washing glases, apparently smashing as many as she cleaned. The other two barmaids were stocking a fridge and giggling inanely.

'I'm beginning to think,' said Lilly, staring thunderously at another broken glass, 'that it really is them and not us. I mean, we fuck around and take the piss but that's normal. It's people who don't fuck around that are weird.' Obviously, I agreed. But then Lilly decided to disagree with herself. 'No, it's us and not them. I mean, my behaviour isn't normal.'

'Yes it is.'

'What would you know about normality?'

'Oh, thanks.'

'Sorry. Oh sod it.' Lilly threw down her cloth. 'I mean, I really do think I'm becoming a man. It's not just the facial hairs this time. I have oral sex with punters on the back stairs.'

'What a result!' I suspected that if I was ever lucky enough to have sex again, the man would have to draw diagrams to remind me what to do.

'I mean, I'm fucking a different stranger each night.'

'Fantastic!'

'And I feel like shit. Everyone thinks I'm a slag. The blokes all call me Loose Lilly.'

'That's just sexist rubbish.' I wanted to grab Lilly and shake her. She'd always been so free of convention and now here she was worrying about what people thought.

'Ignore them. You just like sex.'

'You don't understand.' There were tears in Lilly's eyes and her face had gone bright red. 'I don't *want* to fuck around. I don't know why I do it. It feels good at the time but then I wake up in some stranger's bed and I don't know where I am and I walk the streets looking for a way home and . . .' She shook her head. I drank some vodka.

'Lil,' I said slowly, 'I drink too much behind the bar.'

Lilly looked up. 'So what's new?'

'No, I don't mean pissed on a fun Saturday night sort of stuff. I mean comatose on a dead Thursday stuff. I sometimes do think I'm an alcoholic. I just get so fucking bored. You're bored so you fuck some guy and I'm bored so I empty the bar. Like you say, it's natural.'

'Do you really think so?' asked Lilly, looking strangely vulnerable.

'I . . .' I lit another cigarette, pausing to wonder if it was my constant chain-smoking that was giving me chest acne. 'I don't know, really. I don't seem to care what happens to me . . . But Sarah drinks as much as me. She says her drink and drug use isn't a habit now, just habitual, and that she's clean apart from when she's at clubs.'

'But she runs a nightclub.'

'I know.'

When I next saw Sarah, I told her I was going to cut back on the alcohol. Sarah agreed that our drinking had to stop. She admitted that she often thought of placing herself back in treatment just so she could cease boozing for a day. But Sarah went out that night and I got pissed behind the bar anyway. I wondered if the AA bores were right and I really was a hopeless dipso. Around Sarah, my alcohol use didn't really matter, but I knew that if Savage ever realized how much booze I was nicking, Sarah could never protect me from getting the sack. That I desperately needed the job and the money didn't stop me. I just hated the job so much I had to block it out somehow.

'I wouldn't worry,' said Seb, my merchant banker friend, whom I phoned after work on a drink n dial. 'All jobs drive one to drink. I'm doing Qualitative Research at the moment. We call it Quality Restaurants. I'm practically comatose every afternoon.'

I called Jinty afterwards. 'Bloody hell, Tara, you know you should avoid people like Sarah and working in disgusting nightclubs. You only end up getting drunk, trying to escape your life rather than sorting it out. And don't telephone me this late again.'

Whatever. I didn't see that I had a choice. My dance college was private, and it was with great difficulty that I even paid my fees, let alone supported myself during attendance. I didn't want to feel like the other students' ageing grandma, grabbing desperate snatches of sleep outside the studios whilst they frolicked around me. I didn't want my exhaustion to turn class into a nightmare. During *pirouettes* one morning, Tonty had positioned himself at the end of the diagonal, saying, 'I am standing here not for my health and beauty, which are legion, but so I can see your eye focus. I am prepared to excuse Tara from this exercise as due to her inability even to keep her eyes open, she has developed a dangerous kamikaze style to her turns.'

Bitter and self-pitying, I chain drank and smoked like a fish, and still wondered why I looked so shit.

It didn't help that whilst I longed for someone to put their arms around me and tell me it was going to be all right, Lilly had actually found such a person: Peanuts. Peanuts was a friend of Ben's who'd just been inside after being found with ten thousand Es in his car door. Lilly didn't seem to be as embarrassed about going out with him as she should have been. I supposed that it was because, as Peanuts had been down for five years, he was probably one of those rare souls who had a sex drive temporarily grotesque enough to equal even that of Lilly's. Lil constantly crowed to me about her new-found normality.

'No-one at the Pie and Eel thinks I'm a slag any more,' she boasted. 'I told them my promiscuity was just a phase cos of the tragic discovery of my mum's cancer.'

Even Sarah had cut back on her coke habit as she was having a fling with one of the Bimbo's bouncers who was a fitness fanatic. She now spent all her time having secret assignations in the gym.

'You're crazy,' I'd told her. 'You've broken your cardinal rule: don't poke the payroll.'

'But he's *so* fit.'

'Jonny's bound to find out.'

'I don't care.' Sarah's face hardened. 'He's up to something, anyway.'

'What?'

'I found this flyer and it all became obvious.'

'What?'

'Forget it.'

Exhausted in ballet one morning, I pulled a thigh muscle. I drove home from college feeling like the Gazza of the dance world: the foul temper, the tears, the injuries, the weight problem, the tacky nightclub scenes. But it was one of those bright, crisp days and I wanted to be outside. For some reason I found myself heading towards Brompton Park Cemetery. I went to look for Dave's grave, toying with the idea of committing some random act of hooliganism (he would have wanted it that way). I managed to identify the grave – there was no headstone yet – by a huge rotting wreath saying, *Hardcore Never Dies*. I tooted a line in remembrance of Dave and considered what he'd do if he were me.

'I'D STOP BEING SUCH A WHINGEING CUNT,' I could hear his devil's-child voice tell me, 'AND FUCKING GET OUT AND SCORE SOME DRUGS AND SEX.' I knew that in a way Dave was right. I wondered if the Betty Ford Clinic club was on that evening. Suddenly, I saw a familiar pint-sized figure walking towards me. It couldn't be . . ., it was.

'Cindy!' I screamed. 'What're you doing here?'

'Step Nine: making amends.'

'You didn't . . . ?' I remembered: Dave had been one of Cindy's old dealers.

'He was the fuck of the century, wasn't he?'

I smiled and shuffled some earth round with my shoe. Lucinda hadn't contacted me since I'd left AA. I think she thought I was a bad influence. 'You OK?' I asked.

'Yes. Still struggling with the eating but it's improving. The company's doing well.' She smiled and moved her weight from one foot to another. 'And I'm sort of seeing someone.'

'Oh, not you too.' I looked at her enviously. Not content with being thinner, more successful and richer than me, Lucinda now had to have a boyfriend as well. 'Do I know him?'

'Definitely not,' she said, a wry grin spreading over her face. 'I met him on tour. He's over here doing an aerobics course.'

'Oh.'

'We went to IKEA the other day.'

'IKEA?' With the mention of that one word I knew we could no longer stay friends.

'How're you, anyway?' she asked, ignoring my bafflement.

'Oh all right. Bored.'

'Remember the mindfulness. You have to actually enjoy things so that you don't have to block out what you're doing.'

'Yeah.' I thought Lucinda should try working at Bimbo's on a dead Thursday night with Savage ranting on about how many people he'd stabbed. 'Well, gotta go.' I left her reading poetry to a wreath.

It all came on top. I went into work one evening and Savage greeted me with a grin. 'Great to see yer,' he said, slapping my back. I had a feeling something was up. 'Go up and see Flaps.' I went up the stairs and found Sarah packing. Jonny had found out about the fit bouncer. Sarah had to leave. I'd obviously been sacked into the bargain.

'I can't believe he's chucking you out like this,' I said as Sarah tooted a line off a suitcase.

'Fuck it. This place stinks anyway.'

'Where will you go?'

'I'm going to crash at this girl's place in Notting Hill Gate. Would you help me over there, darling?'

I agreed and we got down to packing Sarah's stuff. She had so many clothes that we just ended up throwing them in bin-bags. Then we called a cab and loaded the stuff inside. Savage didn't help and just sat at the bar cackling with laughter.

'Cunt!' said Sarah as we finally drove off. 'I'll fucking do that Savage one day.'

'I'll help.'

Sarah burst into tears. 'You know that flyer I found round Jonny's flat? It was for the fucking Black Cap, that fucking turd-thief place.'

'What?'

'Jonny's queer.'

'Sarah, you can't tell that from a flyer.'

'He and Savage are lovers.'

'How do you know?'

'I know. I suspected it for ages and then I confronted him and he said, "What on earth makes you think that?" '

'So?'

'Liars always answer a question with another question. Stalling for time.' She lit a cigarette and I could see the cab driver about to ask her to put it out and then decide he valued his life. 'Want to know the funniest thing? I loved him, I really did. I thought he was my other half.'

I remembered when I'd first met Jonny. I'd looked at his haunted, coke-blurred eyes and thought, He's like me. Obviously, I'd warned Sarah against him, but as usual she dismissed my advice.

'Oh, you'll be OK,' I said vaguely.

'You bet I will. I'm still HIV negative and you know that case you carried down that was really heavy? There are ten bottles of Moët in there, darling. And I've been ripping the tills all along.' Sarah wiped her eyes and looked out of the window. 'You know,' she said quietly, 'no-one, no-one's ever loved me best.'

We arrived at Sarah's friend's flat in Notting Hill Gate and unloaded her baggage. Her friend turned out to be an idiot Sloane who had a picture of Bob Marley on her bathroom wall. I stayed to quaff some of Sarah's illicit champagne and then decided to leave due to the fact that I could never stand any of Sarah's friends. They were all appalling trustafarians to whom everything was a 'total mare' and were much trendier and prettier than me. I took the tube back to Fulham and wondered what to do. It was eight o'clock, I'd been sacked, I had no money, my flat was like Calcutta. My destination was brutally inevitable: The Escape Club. I arrived as Gerry was opening the door, a fag hanging out of her mouth and flab protruding from beneath a small top. She greeted me and I followed her down to the dingy cellar that masqueraded as a nightclub.

'How's everything?' I asked.

'The same,' she said, turning on the lights. I thought how quickly I'd forgotten the place: the grotty smoke-marked walls, the hideous 'decorations' (some drunken art student's ludicrous daubings) the sick-stained floor, the broken disco-ball.

'Where is everyone?' I asked, running my finger over the scummed-up bar counter.

'Kevin's got a night off. He's stalking his girlfriend, I think. Tim's coming in late. He's depressed cos another of his girlfriend's emigrated.'

Poor Tim. He always met girls when he was pissed and being charming. But the girls soon scarpered when he was sober and going on about his fish mobiles. Gerry wearily started unlocking the fridge padlocks.

'So who's replaced me?'

'No-one, really. Kev tried a few people but they just did one shift and never came back. Can't blame them really.' Gerry stubbed out her fag and lit a spliff. 'Have you blagged a job then?'

'Just been sacked again.'

'I'm still aiming for the big elbow but Kevin just won't budge. Drink?' I nodded and we started to work our way through the bar.

Gerry called me two days later. She and Tim had spoken to Kevin and had asked him to take me back. Kevin had been dumped by his girlfriend the night before and said he didn't care what they did any more as his life was over. So that Friday I started back at the Escape.

'Thanks guys,' I said to Gerry and Tim, happily re-entering the place I'd sworn never to go near again unless I was torching it.

'It's all right,' said Tim, putting an arm around me. His hair was longer and had started curling into ringlets. His Hawaiian shirt was so loud you had to shout over it. 'We quite missed you, a bit.'

'You did?'

'There was no-one to take the piss out of when you left. And you made us look good by being so crap.'

'The punters asked after you as well,' said Gerry. 'They all claimed to be on a promise with the skinny bimbo lush.'

The things I'd say for a drink. 'Where's Kevin?'

'He's off getting emergency psychiatric treatment. He'll be in later.'

'I'd better get myself a drink now, then.' I went behind the bar and poured myself a large vodka. 'Have you ever seen that film *Groundhog Day*?' I mused. 'You know, the one where the bloke keeps waking up and living the same day over and over again? Sometimes I think my life's like that.'

'God, you're so ungrateful,' said Gerry, looking like she was going to throw her rolling mat at me.

'Oh no,' I protested. 'I really am grateful. I'm just tired and poor and confused and feel like I might chuck in my dancing career for some decent clothes.'

'You haven't got a dancing career,' said Gerry.

'True.' I looked at the ceiling and shrugged. 'My bar career isn't exactly meteoric either, but at least I'm back where I belong with you two no-hopers.' They didn't contradict me and I started setting up the bar. Then Gerry went into the loos to spliff herself stupid and Tim started reading *Carp Talk* magazine. I leant on the bar and sipped my triple vodka. I thought of Sarah, who'd gone to sign on that morning, and Rupert, coming out of a dreary AA meeting saying, 'It's not really what I'd expected.' And Hardcore, lying in his coffin sprinkled with cocaine to help him on his way. What a bunch of losers.

8. Sharking

Seb's new merchant banking career had obviously driven him insane. He'd rushed up to me on Fulham Broadway one afternoon, screaming that he was having a party.

'A party? What, now?' I stammered.

'Don't be ridiculous. Friday.'

'But . . . or is it a bet?'

'I'm asserting my individuality.'

'Oh.' I hadn't seen Seb, my old uni pal, for ages. He'd always had a liking for military gear but dressing as a Nazi stormtrooper was something new.

'You don't understand the pressures I'm under to conform. Wearing suits all day. Liaising. Brainstorming. Going to think tanks.' Seb wiped his nose on the cape he was wearing.

'But at least you get well paid.'

'That's the trouble with you poor people,' he ranted. 'Obsessed with money.'

'Is banking that bad?'

'Worse. I've started practising Office Sabotage. I pour coffee into the computers and steal files. Several secretaries have been sacked over my antics.' He giggled with glee and pulled me into the nearest pub.

After Seb had ordered most of the bar ('Gin. Doubles, sir. Gin's fantastic, gin's *British*') we sat down and he told me of his party plans. 'You know the sort of party you go to and lock yourself in the lavatory and cry for five minutes solid?'

I nodded.

'That's exactly the sort of party experience I want to give people.'

It turned out that Seb had heard of some club in Glasgow called Misery where apparently the whole idea was that you went there to have a miserable time. The beer was awful, the music depressing and the bouncers came up and hassled you if you looked like you were enjoying yourself.

'I want to throw a party so bad,' he continued, knocking back his gin, 'so horrendous, that it will actually drive people insane.'

'But why?'

Seb looked around the pub with feverish eyes. 'I don't have a lot of friends, you know that.'

I nodded.

'I know people think I'm square, dull even.'

'Not at all,' I lied.

'But I can be fun, I can be a laugh.'

I thought that all the evidence pointed against this.

'Only I don't want to be. I work all day as a banker. No-one understands me. Why should I suffer alone?'

This was surprising. I wouldn't have thought Seb was

suffering. He had been given a job in Qualitive Research (or Quality Restaurants) by an embarrassed uncle. He was caked but did sod all. It seemed amazing that someone so rich could be so bitter.

'So exactly how are you going to produce this worst-ever party?'

'I don't actually know,' he admitted. 'Got any ideas?'

I hadn't, really. I'd been to so many bad parties, generally involving getting drunk, throwing up and having a long walk home. 'It's difficult,' I said. 'I mean, you're new to Fulham. You don't really know the history of shame and degradation that's been parties round here. It'll be hard to do anything worse.'

No-one even held house-parties any more, due to the overwhelming inevitability that they would end in tragedy or court appearances.

'I suppose I'll just have to torture people with mediocrity,' Seb sighed. Then he grinned. 'Actually, "a party of mediocrity and drivel". That's rather British, isn't it?'

I arrived late on Friday evening after work. I was drunk and had chest acne. It had been a bad day. In ballet we did the Spanish Dance from *Swan Lake* and I was told I was supposed to look lethal, not ludicrous. I was also accused of Lacking Commitment at college when I failed to be excited about the repertory role I was offered (dancing as an aboriginal poet). Then it was off to work where Kevin was still in the process of having several nervous breakdowns. I vaguely asked him how he was and he said, 'Oh, depressed, suicidal, paranoid-schizophrenic,' and asked if I had any tranquillizers on me. I wondered if I should tell him about the club Seb had mentioned called Misery. It seemed like the Escape would be the perfect place to put on a Misery night. Even Tim had been depressed, worrying that his fish mobiles would never amount to anything.

At first when I entered Seb's flat, it seemed to be like the average Fulham suicide gathering. There was already a girl crying in the hall while her best friend comforted, 'He's not worth it, really'. A bunch of Sloanes called Sethra shared half a joint ('It's amazing because *everyone* I know's been at Eton!') and some suspicious-looking, six-foot-four black guys with gold teeth talked into mobile phones. Two girls wearing mini-skirts nodded and whined, 'God, I *hate* media parties.' Someone was going on about how depressed they were. Most of my 'crowd' stomped around demanding narcotic assistance (none of them really knew Seb but they were always grateful for a party to crash). Yet there was something amiss. This was not a party that had gone wrong, it was a party *designed* to go wrong.

'Wine?' asked Seb, spotting me thorough the clouds of smoke.

'OK.' He gave me a polystyrene cup. I took a swig and spat out the liquid contents.

'Liebfraumilch!' Seb laughed. 'South Africa, Land of the Free!' He walked away, swishing his cape.

'All right?' said Lilly, peering up at me from underneath a table. She was half undressed and smeared with lipstick. She grabbed my arm and pulled me under the table. I always forgot how strong she was. 'Mum's dead,' she told me.

I said I was sorry. Seb overheard and shot me a look of triumph. He seemed delighted by my discomfort. Lilly's mother had been dying of cancer for a few months. Recently Lil had been spending all her time down the hospice, torturing her mother with some of the dreadful poetry she had been writing. I'd thought a lot about going to see Lilly there, but obviously I'd never made it. I didn't like hospital-type places and besides I'd always loathed Lilly's skanky mother, who I'd only ever seen when she was mouthing off about her latest OD or begging money off Lil. It actually amazed me that Lilly cared about her at all. Lil said I didn't understand. Her mother had been a gypsy, unable to cope with normal life. She used to sleep on the balcony because she couldn't stand being indoors. I didn't see how this explained the burn-marks on Lilly's arms from where her ma used to stub out fags on them.

'How's your dad? Jinty told me he had a heart attack.'

'Oh.' I watched Seb putting on a CD of Samantha Fox's greatest hits. 'He's OK.' It had been my father's second heart attack. This was amazing in itself as my father had no heart. I'd asked my mother if he was in a great deal of pain. She'd said no, which I thought was a pity.

Lilly lit us both cigarettes and showed me some marks on her knuckles. 'I was talking to Seb about my mum and he said I needed to express my rage.' Lilly threw back her head. 'I just beat up Peanuts.'

Lilly, after a brief fling, had just been chucked by Peanuts. He claimed she was fucking him into an early grave and that he needed more time to re-establish his drugs business.

'How is he?'

'Oh, nothing that modern dentistry can't solve. I can't believe I ever went out with Peanuts. You know, when I first met him I actually did a double-take at how rough he looked. Then I end up going out with him.' Lilly took my wine and downed it in one.

'It's amazing. You think it could never happen to you.'

'Your mother dying?'

'No, going out with someone like Peanuts. He used to piss in my toothmug.' Lilly burped. 'I look a fucking state, don't I?'

'No, no,' I lied. Lilly's face, due to the amount of make-up smeared all over it, actually looked rather like a faded watercolour painting.

'And my breath smells.' She blew several bottles of Liebfraumilch at me.

'Not at all,' I said, trying not to cough.

'I hate everyone here. They're all cunts.'

I looked up from under the table. Two girls were dancing and shrieking, 'We're not sisters. We're lesbians!' A semi-naked bloke sat in the corner playing the bongos. A film projector was showing a backwards-running copy of *The World at War* on the wall. Someone had fallen asleep and had 'Suck My Cock' written on their forehead.

'They're fucked,' I said.

'They're cunts. Roll me a spliff. I want to go to the bathroom for a wank. Oh God, that's what men do. I'm a bloke, aren't I?'

Lilly staggered up and tottered off, leaving me staring at a sea of bottoms. I saw Seb's platform-loafers passing me and heard his voice saying, '. . . you see, what people don't understand about Baroness Thatcher is that she has the most *tremendous* sense of humour . . .'

I needed cocaine.

Ben was in the kitchen talking to Peanuts. Peanuts had an ice-pack on his face and looked strangely pleased to see me.

'Right, Ta!' he interrupted Ben.

'Yeah.' I looked at the other figures in the bright room. One bloke was being sick in the sink and another was hot-knifing over a broken milk bottle. Two Sethras were discussing what fucking a black bloke would be like.

'Heard from the whore?' asked Ben. I shook my head. Jinty had gone to Africa. It wasn't enough for her to leave Ben or to leave Fulham or even to leave England. She needed another continent. She said she was finished with Ben for good this time. They'd never been a happy couple (Jinty regularly attempted to strangle Ben's parrot and Ben often threw wardrobes at Jinty) and such was their incompatibility that it was one of the great Fulham debates as to Why Do Ben and Jinty Go Out Together? Jinty was a New Age teetotaller who went to Life Dance workshops and read Environmental Studies at ULU. Ben was a cocaine dealer who read the *Sun*. Their only shared experience was sibling suicide.

'Ben, have you—'

'She ruined my life. She took it all.' Ben took a drag on his whale-sized spliff. 'She said I acted like a rapist.'

'It was probably all the Andrea Dworkin she was reading,' I comforted. Actually, it was more like Jinty had always viewed sex as yucky, especially with Ben. She said he used to tweak her breasts and call them Devil's Dumplings and that his idea of foreplay was rolling on top and going, 'You know you want it.'

'I asked her if she found me, like, erotic,' Ben continued, 'and she said I reminded her of a pet Labrador she once had.'

'Piglet was a nice dog,' I mused, snatching the spliff from Ben.

'I try to have sex with her, I'm a rapist. I pick her up from college, I'm stalking her. I give her flowers, I'm treating her like an idiot. I never want to see the bitch again . . . d'you think she'll come back to me then?'

I remembered driving Jinty to the airport. She'd kept wheezing and faking asthma attacks everytime I lit up. She was sick of people smoking around her. She was sick of watching snowboarding videos. She was sick of Ben going on about what he was going to do with his life and why didn't she give up college and look after him. And she was sick of me being such a self-pitying alcoholic tramp and the whole bloody lot of us, bloody addicts. OK, maybe she was avoiding Life Issues by going to Africa, but at least she had somewhere to escape to. We could all rot in our own filth for all she cared.

'She'll be back,' I said, and then asked Ben for some toot. He threw two wraps at me, telling me to go on and fuck off. I picked up the wraps and left the kitchen.

I went out into the hall, which was packed full of sweaty bodies shouting at one another. By the time I reached the bathroom I could have petitioned for at least three counts of sexual battery. The bathroom door was locked and there was a large queue outside, most of which had obviously decided the situation was hopeless. Blokes pissed out of the window, girls puked in the corner and hand mirrors were pulled out for chopping. I got one of my wraps out and stuffed half of it up my nose.

'Tara!'

'Oh, Touchy,' I said, turning round to see the grotesque figure of Touchy-Feely leering over me. Touchy was one of Ben's Bolivian Posse. He was a notorious shark and his promiscuity rivalled even that of Dave Hardcore's. He'd once come back to my place and when I'd asked him if he wanted anything had said, 'Yeah, you, spread-eagled on yer bed.'

'Missed you,' he leched, putting a hand on my shoulder. 'Still . . . ?'

'Dancing.'

'Dancing, yeah. I used to be a ballet dancer, me.' As Touchy was six-foot three with a serious weight problem, I found this difficult to believe. 'Could ave gone pro but I ad other interests, know what I mean?'

'Not really.'

Touchy moved closer and transferred his hand to my face. His touch felt disturbingly pleasant.

'I've always liked you, Tara. We always have a little flirt when we meet, don't we? I think it's cos you're so relaxed, so at ease with yourself.' I wondered how someone could get someone else's personality so wrong. 'So, are you coming home with me then?'

'Got any Es?' At the sniff of a deal, Touchy's sharking snapped to business mode.

'Sorry,' he said, swapping doves for dosh, 'forgot, you know. You're one of the lads really.'

I guess Touchy meant it as a compliment.

I squeezed my way back towards the sitting-room, my head wired with coke and the hardcore experimental industrial techno Seb was now playing. It was the kind of music that gives you a headache and a stomach ache at the same time, the kind of music that ruins lives. The projector was now showing reels of people dying in the Ethiopian famine whilst a naked performance artist did genital puppetry against the backdrop. Quite a lot of people were leaving. I should have guessed Seb's next move.

Wildly flicking his cape around, he moved towards the stereo and put a tape on. At first we were confused. A tune was playing that was so bad, so appalling, that we assumed it was some sort of joke. I slowly began to realize that it was a looped tape of Dave's old recording of 'Tribal Babe'.

'Apparently, it's become some sort of theme tune for the BNP,' said Seb, laughing hysterically. About half the party then exited when the performance artist invited people to shit in his mouth. I walked back out of the room to see Lilly being cornered by Touchy in the hall.

'Seb told me,' he said gently, 'about your mum. My mum's dead, too, you know.'

'Really?' said Lilly.

I knew for a fact that Touchy's mother was alive and well and living in Tottenham.

'I need some comfort,' said Lilly.

'What?' Touchy looked confused.

'A man's comfort,' said Lilly.

The shark was being sharked. It was too much for someone with the brain of a stoat. Touchy said he was feeling depressed about Dave. He had a headache.

'Do I have to be so obvious?' hissed Lilly. 'I'm offering you a fuck.'

Touchy said that he had to take a piss.

I passed the kitchen. I could hear Ben.

'. . . she ruined my life. Without her my life is meaningless.'

'Oh, cheer up, mate,' sighed Peanuts.

'One's dead and the other's buried. There'll be no more laughter.'

Seb ran up beside me. 'Having a good time?'

'Oh, yeah,' I said, putting a falsely bright look on my face.

'It's not just me,' he chortled, rubbing his hands with glee. 'A few drinks, a couple of lines, the right environment . . . it's not just me. The whole of Fulham is insane!'

I sighed and lit a cigarette.

'You look very attractive when you smoke, Tara,' Seb said finally, raising his eyebrows.

'What?' I looked like a pig in a wig.

Peanuts rushed passed us, drinking a bottle of tomato ketchup. Someone was graffiti-ing on the wall. A bloke was pissing in a pot plant.

'There's something I like about you, Tara. Something I can't quite put my finger on.'

'And it will always be that way,' I confirmed.

'I can't understand it.' Seb shook his head and slurped some more Liebfraumilch. 'I've never been rejected before.'

'I find that difficult to believe.'

'You're frigid, aren't you?' said Seb.

'Fucking hell.' Seb had always made jovial attempts to rape me at university but it had been a game. I used to joke to him that I was a lesbian, I was frigid . . .

'You need to go home and confront yourself,' he gibbered, looking around for another bottle.

'You need fucking psychiatric help.'

'I could never work you out at college,' he said. 'But now I've realized there never was anything to work out. There's nothing there, is there?'

I remembered Jinty and myself at the airport. She'd hugged me and I'd been unable to restrain myself from flinching. She'd sighed and said I'd become impossible. Not just because of my 'constant substance abuse', it was as if I'd 'gone blank'.

I went and locked myself in the lavatory and cried for five minutes solid.

It was Cassie who got me out, knocking on the door and screaming, 'Don't be scared!' She'd just arrived at the party after going down the Ministry. But Cassie never went to nightclubs.

'But Cass, you never go to nightclubs.'

She grinned and winked at me. She was obviously on E. But Cass never took E.

'But Cass, you never take E.'

'I've given up puff, remember?'

I remembered. Three weeks previously Cass had decided to chuck in the old weed. By that stage she'd been stoned for eight years. She'd never had a job, lived on the dole and her father's allowance and used to hot-knife for breakfast. But her skin was bad (she'd even got eczema on her pubes, was nothing sacred?) she was failing her Access to University course (she'd actually twisted her tonsils from yawning so much during lectures) and her father had stopped her allowance (nothing personal, he'd gone bankrupt). But I'd never dreamt that Cass would actually manage to get off the green.

'How've you been?' I asked, watching in amazement as Cassie jumped up and down the hall with me.

'Drunk, mostly. I've been going through half a bottle of JD a day. I guess that's normal. And angry and violent and full of eight years of emotions I was too stoned to feel. I'm not sure if that's normal.'

Cassie led me into the sitting-room where she began leaping around to Italian marching music, deftly avoiding various bodies prostrated on the floor. I couldn't believe it. Cassie was the sort of girl who always sat at the side of parties and acted as some sort of automatic spliff-making machine.

I saw Seb marching someone to the door. 'You urinated in my plant. Leave.'

'I thought it was a bed. I mean, toilet.'

I saw that the urinater was Touchy-Feely.

'What about my girlfriend's tits?' said another bloke, walking up behind him.

'What? Oh, I was reading her future. You know how some people read hands? Well, I read breasts.'

'Outside.'

'I do Kung Fu!'

'So what?' said the bloke and decked him.

I turned back to Cassie who was dancing happily in the pale, early-morning light. The deranged mind that was Seb came up behind me.

'Missed one,' I said. 'Cass's actually enjoyed this evening.'

'Vale of Tears,' he predicted, as Cass walked up and hugged him and thanked him for a wonderful, wonderful party.

Lilly, who must have been under some table or other, swayed up to us. 'I need to speak to you, Cass.'

At this moment Lilly decided to confess to Cassie that she had been fucking Dave whilst Cass had been going out with him. Cassie, always good-tempered, had said, 'At least it was just you.' Lilly had said, 'No, there were others.'

Then Seb had collapsed into the debris of his party. 'I feel like Janis Joplin,' he moaned, attempting to eat a lit cigarette. 'It's like I make love to a thousand people and then go home alone.'

'The party wasn't that bad,' I said.

'I know. I must be the only person in the world who actually wanted to hold a bad party and even failed at that.'

'You can't lose 'em all,' I comforted. 'Anyway, I didn't have a good time.'

'But you're frigid,' he whined.

'OK, that's enough.'

I decided I needed some sea air. I wasn't drunk any more, just wired, and as it was obvious I wasn't going to sleep for three days I might as well go on an adventure. I enticed Cass and Lil into my car on the pretext of getting more drugs and left Seb with his face in his hands going, 'I'm an invisible museum that no-one wants to visit . . .'

When I told the girls I was driving us to Brighton they took it pretty well after the initial protests of, 'Kidnap,' and, 'But you're completely fucked.' Besides, Cass and Lil were in so much torment they could barely see the motorway.

'I'm a mutant,' said Cassie, crying in the back. From the happy dancing queen of the party she had been reduced to a scabby, raw-skinned wreck.

'It's just the old weird and different syndrome,' I said.

'No-one, no-one, will ever love me.'

'But Cass, you're *pretty*.'

'Why am I in this car?'

'We've been kidnapped,' Lilly reminded her.

'Why do I bother? I'm a walking scab.'

'Why do *you* bother?' snarled Lilly. 'I got dumped by *Peanuts*, rejected by *Touchy*.'

'I was so jealous when you got dumped by Peanuts,' said Cass, wiping snot off her face.

'What?' Lil and I shouted.

'It's like I'm always on the outside; watching everyone else getting together and falling in love and splitting up and being bitter and shopping each other to the DSS and all the normal stuff. I just know it will never happen to me.'

'But you went out with Dave,' I said. I knew I was coming up on the E as I was beginning to find driving a sensual experience.

'Hardcore. The first boy I'd been out with for four years and he wants to take me on a Pilgrimage of Pain and start a magazine called *New Cunts*. And he's having sex with most of Fulham while he's seeing me.'

I looked in the rear-view mirror and saw Lilly squirming in her seat.

'I'm a mutant,' sighed Cass. 'A hopeless case.'

I wanted to tell Cass that she wasn't weird or a mutant; that she was cool and normal. But I knew what she meant.

I remembered Cassie at school, never once raising a sweat in class, sitting in academic lessons chewing her pen and staring out of the window. Her only ambition was to lie in bed all day eating sweets. She'd been much the same when she left school, only then puffing had entered the equation and if anything she became even lazier. I don't think either I or Lunchie ever realized the reason for her constant apathy.

Cass said she'd never actually been unhappy as a child. Her father, Reg, did run sub-standard porno mags and wear too much gold jewellery, but he loved Cass. He used to come to school performances with his latest bimbo and watch Cassie stumble through her always minuscule parts and then start cheering and crying at the end. And her mother used to write to Cas every week, sending her pictures of her half-brothers and inviting her to visit. Both her parents had been distant in a way (her father working so much and her mother not the huggy type) but there'd been no tragedies, no abuse. I wondered if something Cass had once said was true, that it was almost as if a part of her had been left out. Maybe it was the eczema (and poor Cass was so *ashamed* of it) but I had a feeling that Cass would be pretty similar even if her skin was normal. Sitting on the edge of things, not watching contentedly but almost obsessively, as if she was trying to work out how other people managed to communciate with one another.

We arrived in Brighton and I parked the car, scrabbling for change to put in the meter. It was a beautiful day. Not English lukey warm sort of rubbish but really hot with a clear, bright blue sky.

'Fresh air!' said Lilly, breathing in deeply. 'The last time I breathed fresh air I was having sex in the garden.'

'Nice, isn't it?' said Cass, leaning on some railings. 'Look at those birds, they're dancing.' We watched the flock of birds circling over a derelict pier. I thought of all the spontaneity my movement had lost. I'd gone into dance because it was only when I was moving that I felt free. Now all I did was worry about pirouettes and placement. We walked down onto a pebbled beach. There were already quite a few people around putting up windbreakers and deckchairs.

'My mum would have loved this,' said Lilly, staring at the sea. 'Come on, let's go for a swim.' Cass and I began to mumble a stream of excuses: 'Too cold,' 'No bathers,' 'Pollution,' 'Just got over flu.'

'Oh come on,' Lilly implored, already tugging at her trousers. 'We'll just go in our bras and knicks.'

'But we've got no towels,' said Cassie.

'That's right,' I said.

Lilly looked quizzically at us. 'Am I missing something?'

Cass and I looked down at the beach and started scuffing the pebbles with our shoes.

'My skin's really bad,' Cass admitted finally.

'What? Oh fuck that. The sea's good for eczema anyway.'

'It is?'

'The salt, you know.'

Cassie looked at me hesitantly.

'Well, what's your problem?' said Lilly.

'Nothing,' I replied.

The other two began to undress, Lilly ripping off her clothes and scattering them anywhere, not giving a toss about her forest-like bikini-line, Cassie carefully removing her garments and folding them neatly. I took a long time undoing my shoes.

'I'll be down in a sec,' I said. I watched Cassie following Lilly down to the sea, her arms pathetically trying to disguise the red-raw patches of eczema covering her body. I took a deep breath and began to remove my sweaty rags.

For I had scars. Not the cool, white silvery line-type scars, but huge great revolting monstrosities. My father used to beat me. I'm not talking the odd slap, I'm talking belts, cricket bats, hands over gas rings. I took off my top and looked at the familiar ugly sight on my right arm and felt this awful pain go through me. I'd lived in Sussex as a child and my parents would take us to Brighton occasionally. Me, Ama and Jinty. And Ama should have been with me. I remembered her saying, 'I was scared, my entire childhood I was scared.' I'd told her there were things we could do to stop Pa beating us – stand up straight, stay away when he was drunk – but I'd lied. There'd been no rules. I couldn't protect her.

I look off my jeans and headed down to the sea. I noticed a young boy stop and stare at my leg. There was a particularly bad scar on my right thigh from where my father had got me with a hot iron. I refused to care.

'Looking at my leg?' I suddenly asked the boy.

'No,' he muttered, staring down at the pebbles.

'It's OK,' I said, 'I don't mind. Want to know how I got the scar?' He shrugged his shoulders. 'Bondi Beach, Australia, two years ago. A shark got me.'

'Serious!' he cried, looking up at me.

'Yup. Only a baby shark, luckily, so I fought it off, but I still had to have skin-grafts and stuff cos of the scars.'

'Wow.' He stared at my scars with something like admiration. 'And you're still going back in the sea?'

'Yes, I'm still going back in the sea,' I said, smiling at him. And as I waded into the froth I thought, I believed we were losers but actually we're winners. Seb worked in a job he hated, to support a life he loathed. Lilly had cared for a mother who had thrown her on the streets when she was eleven. Cass was trying to give up spliff even though she had nothing to give up for. I continued drinking despite AA membership. As I waved at Cass and Lilly, who were laughing and splashing water at one another, I thought, Let's face it, we're fucking heroes.

9. The Summer of Porn

'I think I may die of excitement,' said Sarah, who was sprawled on her sofa idly sniffing a firelighter.

'Tell me about it.' All my summers seemed exactly the same: no-one to see, nowhere to go, no money to pay for it anyway. The Eskimos may have a hundred words for snow but Sarah and I had dozens for doing nothing: idling, malingering, chilling, lurking, lounging, loitering . . .

'At least you're not pregnant.' Sarah threw her firelighter across the room. 'You know, baby-farming isn't quite the lark I thought it would be. No coke, no smoking, no bulimia and an addiction to sniffing firelighters. I really am a state.'

She was, actually. Normally immaculate, Sarah had now put on two stone and started wearing caftans. And she smelt a bit.

'My doctor's no fucking help,' Sarah continued. 'I went to

see her yesterday and told her I was depressed and she just said, "Oh God, so am I," and started crying.'

'Maybe we should, like, go out.' Sarah's sitting-room was boiling and I could feel trickles of sweat running down my sides. 'We could go for a walk or something.'

'I've never seen the point of going for a walk. You just arrive somewhere and then go back. Besides, I panic if there isn't concrete around.'

'Well, let's get down to some writing.'

'Oh, why don't you just piss off and go child-snatching.' Sarah was referring to my new 'man', Chunks, who was nineteen.

'Why don't you go back to whoring? I hear some perverts like pregnant women.'

Sarah gave me a look of utter evilness. 'You really are a foul-mouthed little tramp, Tara.'

We both sighed and looked out of the window, too hot to be bothered to row.

'Fancy watching another skin-flick?' said Sarah finally.

'No, not really,' I said. I felt like I'd spent the entire summer viewing girls being raped by hideous bikers or sticking double-dildos up themselves. Sarah got up and switched on the video. Her stomach was so huge that she could barely bend down.

Sarah had never intended to have the baby. In fact, I'd taken her to hospital for the termination.

'God, I'm tired of abortions,' she'd sighed when we walked into the hospital (this was her fourth conception). We'd trailed around antiseptic-smelling corridors and eventually ended up in the loos, where we did a few toots. Sarah had a nosebleed.

'Fucking nose,' she'd said, sticking lavatory paper up

her nostrils. 'I should have had it replaced when Jonny offered.'

'Are you OK?' I'd asked. Sarah wasn't even wearing make-up.

'What do you fucking think?' she'd snapped.

There had seemed to be a weariness about Sarah, as if she'd lost the heart for abortions. When I'd taken her for the second termination it had been more like a day out. She'd turned up at my place completely coked out of her head after persuading four male acquaintances to pay for the operation. Then she'd attempted to punch one of the 'walking-abortion' pro-lifers on the clinic steps. Whilst we sat in the waiting room beside crying women, Sarah had giggled and discussed anal sex. Afterwards, we'd gone back to my flat and when I tried to be solicitous, asking how she felt and if she needed anything, she'd put on a suffering face and said, 'Darling, I'm far too tired to eat anything. I'm in pain, so much pain . . . what's good for pain?' I'd shrugged. 'Actually, I've heard champagne is. The bubbles, you know. And some coke, too; it's an anaesthetic, really. And a good video to take my mind off things . . . and maybe a pizza.' That particular abortion had cost me ninety quid.

'Funny the way things work out,' Sarah had mused, sitting on one of the sinks and lighting us both cigarettes. 'At least this time I know who the father was. Jonny was the only person I fucked in the treatment centre.'

A nurse entered the lavatories and was obviously about to say something about our smoking.

'My entire family's just been killed in a car crash,' said Sarah.

The nurse walked out.

'Peasants!' Sarah pulled a wrap out of her jeans. 'Sod it, I'll eat the rest.' She tried to dab half a gram in her mouth, but ended up dropping the wrap on the floor. 'Oh Christ, I've had enough! I feel like the nun in *The Nun's Story*.'

'Have you no shame?' I asked in genuine amazement.

'No, idiot, it's this book about a nun who can't deal with being a nun and is racked with inner turmoil. I read it when I wanted to become a missionary.'

'You wanted to become a missionary?'

'I'd just started my periods. Anyway, the nun eventually had to leave her Order. She realized that although all her struggles seemed different, they were all about the same thing.'

'Which was?'

'Obedience. She couldn't be obedient.'

'And you?'

I thought Sarah was going to say that all her problems were the result of her shopping and cocaine addictions, but she sighed and just said, 'My uncle.' She threw her cigarette into the sink and lit another one. 'It's pathetic, I can't get over it. Other people get over it. Other people say it makes them stronger and helps them write bestselling self-help books. But I just hear his footsteps. I smell his breath. It's like he haunts me.' Sarah removed her nostril tissue and looked at the bloodied papers for a second. 'I'm going to have the baby.'

'What?'

'The doc said stimulants weren't that harmful to the foetus.'

'What about the drinking?'

'I'm always drunk, so what could that matter?' Sarah slid off the sink. 'Do you remember I told you about that flat I was staying in where they found some Class As and a gun?'

'Oh, yeah.' That was why Sarah had started running Bimbo's; so she could pretend she was normal.

'The police dropped the charges. No prints and shit. The coke was mine, you know.'

'What about the other girl?'

'Not my problem.' Sarah bent down and painstakingly swept up the cocaine she'd spilt on the floor. 'It's as if I've been given a second chance.' She started stuffing toot up her raw nostrils. 'I need to make a fresh start.'

Of course, I thought that pregnancy was just another of Sarah's larks. That she'd read some article in *Tatler* about fashionable baby-breeding and had thought it would amuse one. I waited for the call asking me to re-accompany Sarah to the hospital. But the weeks ticked by, her stomach grew larger and she started smoking menthol cigarettes. There was no mistaking that Sarah was actually going to have a baby. Of course, she still wasn't exactly the maternal type. Once, when Lilly met us in the street, she'd said excitedly, 'Sarah, wow, you're so lucky,' and had put one of her spade-like hands on Sarah's bulge. 'It must be amazing, like, having something growing inside you.'

'Yah,' Sarah had yawned, reaching for a menthol. 'I imagine it's rather how having cancer feels.'

Both Sarah and I developed a kind of sleeping sickness that summer. Even the smallest movements seemed impossibly hard and exhausting. I became so soporific that my only method of cleaning my flat was vaguely throwing TCP over the floor every couple of days. It soon became infested with cockroaches so I gradually moved more and more of my stuff over to Sarah's place. She didn't mind. Her trustafarian flatmate had gone away Sloaning for the summer and Sarah was lonely because she was too idle to see anyone. At least Sarah had an excuse for her indolence, what with being preggers and having given up the Class As; I was just sick of struggling. I didn't have enough money to return to dance college that September and it seemed easier just to give up. I was still terrified, though, that I was turning my back on one set of options to discover that there weren't any others. I asked Lucinda for help but she was helpless herself.

'Don't ask me what to do. The company's collapsed after Fredrique slit his wrists in an unfashionable nightclub. I was thinking of doing a six-month circus course in France but John from AA's got me into a treatment centre.'

'But I thought—' AA, a straight boyfriend, IKEA . . . I'd thought Lucinda had become normal.

'I tried to throw myself under a bus yesterday. I really thought I'd cracked it but the puking's worse than ever now. I just can't stop. I've even had a rectal prolapse.'

Of course, I felt sorry for Cindy, but I was also sneakily relieved that she was one of my kind again. I even felt slightly jealous. Why couldn't I go to a treatment centre?

The only fun I'd had that summer was Chunks. Chunks was a new barman at the Escape who was taking on Gerry's shifts whilst she was travelling in Thailand. The first night I worked with Chunks, I'd watched him strutt down the stairs and felt my body collapse.

'You're gorgeous,' I'd blurted out.

Chunks told me that he worshipped Kenny Rogers and often thought of growing a beard. He walked me to the tube after work and said, 'Don't kiss me yet, I've got to spit'. The next evening, I asked Tim what he'd thought of Chunks.

'He's an idiot,' said Tim firmly. This was strange as Tim wasn't usually bitchy. 'Chunks showed me a tattoo on his shoulder. It was a bottle of Pils with *Holsten* engraved beneath it. "I used to be a bit of drinker, me," he said. Then he started talking about his glory days when he used to go down Ritzy's in Tottenham.' I decided Tim was jealous of Chunks.

A few days later Chunks and I both got hopelessly drunk behind the bar, skidding a funny kind of dance-on-beer-slops around each other, and then he swayed all the way back to Sarah's with me. We snogged on the wall outside her house and I went inside. I felt my hair as I ran a shower and found a huge slug tangled inside it.

Sarah worried about money. She was claiming whale-sized benefits off the social but her old credit card bills kept on rolling in. She thought of writing a bestselling book called *Hetties, Dykes, Trannies and Junkies*. I thought about writing a trilogy called *Fat*, *Fucked* and *Finished*. But we never actually did any writing and just lay sweating in Sarah's sitting-room, me smoking and Sarah greedily inhaling the fumes. Then Inspiration struck me. I was leafing through one of Sarah's copies of *Tatler* one afternoon when I saw a photo of someone I recognized. It could only have been Jem, who was pictured in Old Compton Street wearing a ridiculous monocle and carrying a video of *Women With Beards*. The article beside the photo was entitled 'From Eton to Soho: My Journey of Shame' and told of Jem's travels from gorgeous, pouting Eton schoolboy to world-famous contemporary dancer to pornographic master. It was obviously lies (Jem had sported horrendous acne as a teenager and had been a shockingly bad dancer) but I was intrigued.

I always longed to be an artist, he withered, *but I liked cocaine too much. When I danced, I thought about suicide more often than sex. There was something about the way I moved that just enraged people. Dance lost me all my friends. Total strangers would come and attack me after shows. I often received death threats. Dance betrayed me; pornography saved me.*

I knew then that I would become a pornographer.

*   *   *

Jem had arrived at my ballet school in the middle of the fourth year after being sacked from Eton for what he coyly described as matters of a carnal nature. Even then his dancing was noticeably terrible (he used to bound around like an over-excited puppy and sometimes drooled in class) but ballet schools basically took any boys who could put one foot in front of the other. Cassie Lunchtime and I had become Jem's acolytes, delighting in his madness and degenerate nature. Jem hadn't lasted long, though. In the third term there had been a school choreography competition. Whilst the other pupils did pretty little dances about butterflies, Jem had composed a horrific piece about neo-Nazism and rape which ended up with Cassie being strung on a cross whilst I waved a Swastika flag at her. It didn't go down well. Jem was taken into sick bay where he was asked if he was mentally trauma-tized. He tried to get out but they'd locked the door. He left four days later. The next time we met was on our first day at Laban. Jem had been as appalling as ever – both in terms of dancing and personality – and the two of us had decided we hated everyone else and just hung around bitching about how bored we were. Unfortunately, Jem had been asked to leave at the end of the first year as he'd 'forgotten' to turn up to most of his classes. So I was left with no friends and a reputation for being a snob. I still thought he owed me one.

Sarah had managed to obtain Jem's phone number from a friend of hers at *Tatler* to whom she sold over-priced and over-cut cocaine. I'd then called Jem and demanded to see him. I couldn't believe it when he opened the door of his Soho flat. I'd been expecting some bed-sit dive infested with rent-boys, but instead I was greeted with a stunning penthouse love-pad.

'How the hell do you afford this?' I'd asked immediately.

'Oh, it only costs me a fiver a week.' Jem was wearing a red velvet smoking jacket and carrying a magnum of champagne from which he poured me a glass. 'I've been taken up by a millionaire philanthropist.'

'You're going through a gay stage, then?' Jem had been permanently tormented by the uncertainty of whether he was gay or straight. The only thing he knew was that he wasn't bisexual.

'No, I've just come out. I've been a closet hetro for all these years. I know people will find it difficult to accept, but I can't sacrifice my sexuality for the sake of fashion. Anyway, I'm celibate at the moment. Gerald just likes to look at me. He's taking me to Tuscany next week so he can watch me sunbathing.'

I had to hand it to Jem: I still didn't know anyone who could talk as much crap as him. Exaggerations, half-truths and blatant lies flowed effortlessly from his lip-glossed mouth. Annoyingly, he'd also somehow become very pretty since I'd last seen him.

'I have to be celibate,' he continued, 'because of the pornography.' Jem popped a fag into an absurdly long cigarette-holder. 'I don't make love or masturbate in order to allow myself to reach a frenzied sexual peak when I write.' He paused expectantly.

'Do you make money from this . . . filth?'

'Tons. I'm a member of the Guild of Erotic Writers now, and I record a telephone series about a gay massage parlour.' Jem puffed frantically on his cigarette-holder.

'But I'm behind on my stories now. Tara, you must simply lock me in the cupboard so I can write more pornography!'

I sipped my champagne and looked steadily at him. 'Jem, listen, I'm interested in writing porn, too.'

'You!' He guffawed with laughter. 'Dearie, I hate to point it out, but you're not exactly over-qualified for the job.'

'I've had sex.'

'Yes, but . . .' Jem grimaced. 'You perhaps don't tend to exude a lustful, blatant type of unashamed sexuality.'

'No.' I sighed. 'But that doesn't matter. I have this friend, you see, who used to be a hooker. She can give me all the material I need. Please, Jem, I'm broke.'

With much bad grace, Jem eventually scribbled me out a few addresses and phone numbers in between jibes regarding my poor dress sense. Then he flopped down on his white leather sofa and began drinking champagne from the bottle.

'Do you miss dancing?' I asked him finally when he'd stopped going on about his *Tatler* triumph.

'I wish I did more, really, but life's too fun. I can't think why you still bother.'

'Oh, I've never really had a life. Anyway, unless I raise some dosh I'll have to give it up.'

Jem stroked his chin and put on a thoughtful look. 'Thing is, Tara, you always had "something". Something unpleasant and disturbing, but "something" nevertheless. Is there anything else you'd like to do?'

'I'd quite like to go to a treatment centre.'

'Dance and write porn, dearie.'

I went back to Sarah's that evening bursting with enthusiasm. We would take up pornography to fund our hopeless life-styles! We tried to think of a few story titles but then Sarah said her stomach hurt and she wanted to lie down and I was a bit sozzled from the champagne, so I went to bed too. Then I saw Lilly the next day and got stoned. Sitting fog-eyed on the bus I realized that unless I got it together very rapidly the porn would never take off. That evening, I decided to shock myself out of my apathy. Chunks was off and when as usual some vile stranger invited me to go out after work, I accepted. We went to some tacky bar and boozed for a while. Then we headed back to his place, walking hand-in-hand through the rain. We drank almond tea, I gave him a blow-job and then wanked him off in the kitchen as I waited for my cab.

'This is amazing!' he said. 'I go for a late-night drink and the barmaid leaves with me and . . . wow! I must be the luckiest man alive.' I shrugged my shoulders, washed my hands and left. What was I like?

When I told Sarah what I'd done, she tutted in disgust.

'That's appalling. You could have picked up a hundred for that. I remember when—'

'Hold on.' I grabbed a pen and a phone-pad. 'Go on.'

It was simple as that. I'd throw a few random words at Sarah – lesbian, double-penetration, mutual – and she would listlessly recount a torrid tale from her escorting days. If she couldn't think of anything, we'd put on a video to inspire us. Mostly we just watched a faded copy of Dave's old fave *Genital Hospital*, but sometimes I'd go down to Soho and rent us one (the worst vid we saw was one about disabled people having sex with pigs). At first I tried to write the stories in a sexually exciting way, but I soon gave this up and decided to take the more factual approach. Then I'd type them up and send them off to one of Jem's addresses. Sarah had a go at writing too, but, if my stories were dull, hers were genuinely disturbing, always ending with the men dying in a brutal and distressing manner. To my amazement, *Erotic Stories Monthly* and *Fiesta* accepted two of our more lurid attempts and other magazines were showing interest. I also started record-ing a telephone series called *The Torture Goddess*, about a convent-educated dominant prostitute. The 'recording studio' was a foul flat off the Edgware Road and was run by a sweaty Greek man. I hated going there and was terrified he was going to molest me, but it was by far the best paid bit of my porn crusade. I'd sit by a microphone mumbling through a couple of stories whilst I watched out for the Greek making advances and then run out clutching a one-er. With half the porn-takings and my wages from the Escape, I was slowly able to start paying off the mountains of debt I had accumulated over the year.

I was still seeing Chunks. Well, it was perhaps more a case of when we were both on at the club we'd get pissed, go out afterwards and then he'd come back to Sarah's with me and we'd stagger inside for a night of silliness and then he'd hold me close and I'd just sigh inside and he'd go on about how he fancied a kebab. There was perhaps one small point of awkwardness: he had a girlfriend. Seeing someone who was seeing someone else was something I'd always sworn never to do, so it was perhaps inevitable that I'd find myself doing it. We talked a lot about his girl, Maria. Chunks and Maria had been going out for two years. They no longer got on, he claimed, and fought all the time. He'd never been unfaithful before, apparently, apart from a one-night stand with some black girl in a cupboard. Funny thing was that I believed him. Chunks was honest in a way I was incapable of being. I once told him he was special and he went on about it for weeks, asking exactly what I thought was special about him as no-one had ever called him special before. He didn't understand that I was the sort of person who not only always said things I didn't mean, but also often said things without any meaning whatsoever. Whenever Chunks came back to Sarah's, I'd have to rush around the flat removing 'evidence' (stories, videos, books, magazines). I was actually having nightmares about vice police from the porn squad turning up and arresting me and then Chunks giving evidence for them in court.

Just after Sarah had gone to her doc about being depressed, she suffered internal bleeding. I took her to the hospital and she stayed the night. The doctor said it wasn't serious but that Sarah should stay indoors and not over-exert herself. Her indolence reached new bounds. She once even asked me to go to the lavatory for her. To bribe Sarah to dictate the stories, I was forced to provide her with an endless supply of cream buns, minty Viscounts and firelighters. It wasn't easy being a porn writer. I was always hungover from the Escape and Sarah was always exhausted from being pregnant; she would forget what she was saying and I would forget what I was writing. Jem was no help. I telephoned him for advice and he said he was all porned out. So it was just me and Sarah, sweating and sighing and falling asleep mid-sentence. We were so dull that everyone seemed to forget about us. Only the terminally kind Cassie ever visited. She had now been transformed into a raver and spent a lot of time telling us about her clubbing experiences.

'I took drugs and they played loud music,' was typical of her insights. She looked quite good on it, though, and had lost lots of weight. She'd even scored with Touchy-Feely, seeming to be on a life-long experiment with fucking ugly, perverted men. 'It's like that Summer of Love back in . . . was it '89 or '91? Anyway, I'm not sure but you know what I mean? You know, loving everyone, taking loads of E, feeling great, you must remember.'

'No, not really.'

'No, neither do I.' Cassie scratched her legs. 'It was around then I took some dodgy trip and altered realities for two years.'

My wages for *The Torture Goddess* telephone series were raised. Sarah said she hadn't been without sex for so long since she'd been out of nappies. Chunks and I became an 'item'. We went out for lunch twice a week. He took me bowling and to cockney nightclubs off the North Circular; I took him to Dance Happenings at the South Bank. He used to play me 'Regulate' by Warren G (he hated 'that head-banging dance crap') and I used to hum the sample in bed. We drifted along in a haze of nothingness. Chunks told me that one night he and Maria had been in bed and she'd asked him which underwear he found sexy: 'Fuck knows,' he'd said.

'Lacy? suspenders? Black?' Chunks had shrugged his shoulders, turned over and put on his Walkman.

Another evening, Chunks had stayed at mine till four and then collapsed in a cab back home. On returning, he'd found all the lights and the TV on and an empty bottle of wine beside the bed. Maria woke up when he tripped over some shoes on the floor.

'I waited till three a.m. for you,' she'd slurred, obviously half-cut, 'and it's now – ' she'd looked at the clock ' – four-fucking-thirty. Where the fuck have you been?'

Chunks had made up some story about a crisis in the club, but he didn't think Maria believed him. She threatened to cut off his balls if he was having an affair. I was haunted by the image of Maria, sitting in bed staring at the television, downing a bottle of wine and wondering where Chunks was. By fucking, Chunks and I were turning each other into wankers.

Ironically, the sex wasn't even that good. Well, it never really was with me. My idea of adventurous sex was leaving the side-light on. I realized that a lot of people our age would have had lunch-time sex rather than lunch. And I didn't even like food that much. I sometimes wondered what Chunks thought of me but I decided it was safer not to ask. I just kept my mouth closed and my legs half-open. Anyway, Chunks and I were mostly too drunk to talk properly. We were both hopeless drinkers; swaying, falling, colliding with alcohol, mutilated by hangovers. Although Chunks was the sort of guy who swaggered rather than walked and I was the sort of girl who stammered rather than talked, we were both a bit shy. We didn't really know how to communicate.

'There's something sexually wrong with us,' Chunks had said to me one night.

'What?' We'd just had sex. Of sorts. Pitch-black. Groans. Not much to write home about.

'We're not like . . . what's the problem?'

I'd shrugged.

'Were all your other boyfriends blatantly thick or something?'

'Blatantly thick's perhaps unfair. Stupid, obviously.'

'What's wrong? What are you worried about?'

The sky fell open and collapsed on my head.

'Stop looking at the ceiling. Stop giggling.'

I couldn't say anything. I worried that if I started talking I'd never be able to stop.

'Are you nervous . . . you know, physically?' Chunks took my hands. 'I've felt the scars, I know about them, I still think you're beautiful.'

'Chunks, I . . .' The room was growing light. I pulled my hands out of his. 'You'd better go.'

Sarah decided to give up her flat. She admitted that one of the reasons she'd been so tired all summer was that she'd been scared of sleeping due to all the terrible nightmares she'd been suffering.

'I thought if I didn't say anything about them, then they'd go away,' she told me as I returned from a recording session to find her swigging sherry and packing up the flat. She was horribly drunk and her face was all red and blotchy. 'I keep seeing my uncle and I have these nightmares where I'm having the baby and I'm screaming and the nurses think it's cos I'm in pain, but actually it's cos I never wanted the fucking brat and it's all too late.'

'Do you wish you'd had an abortion?'

'I knew I'd be dead in six months if I didn't stop everything.' Sarah looked down at her enormous stomach. 'And this is the only way I could stop.'

So Sarah moved back to her mother's and I moved back to my flat. I tried to continue writing the porn, but without Sarah's input I had nothing to write. So I gave up and chucked dance college a few hundred so I'd be allowed to return. I didn't really know why I was going back, but it seemed better than real life. Then Chunks threw his girl-friend out of their flat.

'I was having dinner and she was rowing at me and I just thought, "I wanna kick your fucking face in," so I told her she had to go.'

'You're finished?'

'Totally.' He was standing on my doorstep. 'Can I come in?'

'Yes, sorry, of course.' I led Chunks upstairs.

'I'm blatantly drunk,' he said and collapsed on my bed. 'I just had fifteen pints.' We watched *Three Men and a Little Lady* and he started crying. I put my arm around him but he turned over, saying his stomach hurt, and passed out. I couldn't sleep and got up and took a Temaza and wandered over to the window. I leant out, smoking a cigarette. It was one of those brown, drizzly nights and the air smelt of damp pavements. I watched some drunk weaving his way up the road and I had the weirdest thought: I can taste all the tongues I've ever had in my mouth. I tried to work out if it meant anything, but decided it probably didn't and went back to bed.

The Sunday before I started dancing, I paid a quick visit to Sarah and presented her with some booties I'd found going cheap in a Sue Ryder shop.

'You really shouldn't have,' she said, showing a trace of her old self and throwing them over her shoulder.

'Sorry,' I apologized and gave her the last share of our porn-takings.

'So how's it going with the child?'

'I don't know, really. He went home last night and Maria had broken in and was hiding behind the door. She hit him over the head with a plastic bin and then punched him.' I was unable to stifle a giggle. 'Sorry, I can't seem to take it seriously. Do you think I'm a nasty person?'

'No, indifferent and coarse, perhaps, but not nasty.'

'He took me out for lunch today.'

'What, raided his piggy-bank, did he?'

'No, got his pocket money.'

Sarah gave me a smugly amused look. 'You're so funny, Tara. I could hand you ten tabs of anything and dare you to take them all in one go and you would. But you couldn't wake up with a chap and have breakfast and think, "This could go somewhere," without leaving the country.'

'I don't see why you're in such a good mood,' I said eventually.

'Well I've just heard some good news about Jonny.'

'He's gone straight? He's coming back to you?'

'No.' She started cackling. 'He's caught herpes.'

I only saw Chunks once after I went back to college. He was sacked from the Escape one night for picking a fight with the bouncer and then came round to see me. Neither of us was drunk and we watched television for a while before going to bed.

'I can't believe it,' said Chunks, rolling off me. 'I can't get a hard-on with you when I'm sober.'

Without alcohol to lubricate our bodies, we had no idea what to do with our flailing limbs and awkward bones. There didn't seem to be a lot of point in going on. I had nothing to offer but paranoia and insecurity. Even while I was fucking I was still being screwed.

10. Not Just a Phase

'It feels like my world's getting smaller and smaller,' said Jinty. 'At first I was just scared of clubs and parties and then it was tubes and crowds and now it's just everything. I'm getting panic attacks for breakfast. I think I'm becoming agoraphobic.' Jinty burst into tears and I clumsily patted her hand. A Louise L. Hay *Overcoming Fears* tape was still playing in the background and scented candles lit her perfectly neat bedroom. This didn't seem real. I was the fucked up one, not my careers-conference sister.

'I miss Ama,' she sobbed. 'And I've run out of Rescue Remedy.'

I had no idea what to do and pretended to admire some of Jinty's African artefacts. I hadn't seen her for a couple of weeks and had only turned up that evening by accident. I was supposed to be having dinner with my merchant wanker Seb but he'd cancelled at the last minute due to having to go into detox (apparently he'd collapsed at work two days previously and the doc had done tests and discovered that Seb's liver was shot). Bored and listless, I'd been unable to find anyone else to go out with and had decided to visit Jinty as she never went anywhere. The last time I'd seen her had been just after she'd returned from Africa and I'd been helping her move into her new house. She'd sat down on her trunk and admitted that she hadn't enjoyed Africa that much.

'It was a bit scary,' she'd said, scratching her peeling tan. 'And I missed London and Ben and going to silly nightclubs in silver skirts.'

I had pointed out to Jinty that she never went to silly nightclubs in silver skirts.

'I know that now. But somehow in Africa I was convinced that I did.'

Of course, Jinty had gone back to Ben. I'd asked for details but she'd just scratched her bottom and said she needed to get a stools test done.

'Anyway, it's all different now,' she claimed, unlocking the clasps on her trunk, 'since I've become independent.' Jinty's move from Ben's to her new house in Parsons Green was paid for by Ben. I'd wished I had Jinty's kind of independence.

I hung out of her window, smoking a cigarette and rehearsing *port de bras* in my head. My ballet teacher had said to me that my arms looked like limp pieces of lettuce that had been left out of the fridge for three days.

'We never talk,' said Jinty, thankfully turning off the drone of Louise L. Hay.

'We're always talking,' I yawned.

'But never about anything.'

'What's there to talk about?' I asked. 'Neither of us have got lives.'

'You never talk about Ama to me. Our sister killed herself and we never even mention it.'

I threw my fag out of the window and got up and examined a hideous tribal skirt Jinty had brought back from Africa.

'Why can't we talk about her?' Jinty continued. 'I need to talk.'

'Yes, but I don't bloody want to listen,' I snapped. 'Can't you get another fucking counsellor or something?'

Jinty leapt up and snatched the skirt off me. 'Ben's in trouble!' she suddenly screamed.

'Oh yeah?' I'd heard rumours: that a package had been picked up by the wrong people; that Customs and Excise had paid a visit to Sarah's mum's; that the police were combing Fulham for a guy called Parrot.

'He's packing this evening and then coming to hide here.'

No wonder Jinty was upset. Would she never escape the clutches of the idiot?

'I think my phone's bugged. You know, I could be arrested for being an accomplice.'

'Don't be stupid.'

Jinty folded her arms and turned away from me. 'Just go, Tara. Go and get drunk or toot a line or write porn or whatever rubbish you're into now. I'm going home to visit Ma and Pa.'

'Jinty, I know things are bad but surely that's unwise.'

'Ma called me last night. Pa's really ill again. You should visit him too.'

'Should I?'

'I don't see why I should take all the responsibility in the family.'

'I'm not making you.'

'Yes, but if you don't go then I have to.' Jinty let out a sob. 'He could die.'

I knew that this was a moment when I should reach out to Jinty and say sisterly stuff and hug her, but I couldn't. She continued sobbing and we stood very close without actually touching.

It had turned so cold so quickly. I soon got used to scraping frost off my car windscreen every morning and sitting shivering inside until the heating warmed up.

Then I'd have beans on toast and a cup of tea at a local greasy spoon and head off to college to warm up for class. After class, I'd perch on the wall outside and have a fag whilst feeling the sweat freezing over me. Normally someone would sit beside me and we'd gossip about the latest rumours or moan about how miserable class was. Conversations were the same most days. We never talked about anyone or anything outside the dance world as dance was all we had in common. In fact, at college we were always being told that other dancers were like our family. A dysfunctional family, maybe, but a family. People we might not choose to be close to, that we might actively dislike, but to whom we were in some way related. Sometimes during spare periods a group of us would head into the music room to lie down against the radiator and try to grab a bit of sleep. All the competition and snide comments in class would be forgotten for half an hour as we huddled up to one another for warmth.

Then back to class ('Actually her tits are quite saggy,'), after which I'd change and then wearily transfer from *barre* to bar.

It was no wonder I was unable to speak to Jinty. Despite the noise, I sometimes thought that my world was so silent. Even at the Escape, I rarely spoke properly to anyone. Gerry, Tim and I would vaguely attempt to chat whilst we set up the bar (Tim was thinking of moving to Brighton, 'I could really go somewhere in Brighton,' and Gerry, back from Thailand, was doing a typing course) but then the DJ would start playing and we'd give up talking. After that, all I ever heard was snatches of the punters' conversations:

' – and that was the first time she'd had an orgasm in sixty years . . .'

' – no, I don't want another pint. I want to go home and shoot myself . . .'

' – then she asked me back to her place but she was too pissed to remember where it was . . .'

' – and that's why they call him "cunt".'

I could spend an entire night not saying anything but, 'Yes', 'No,' and, 'Sorry, I thought you said *slammer*.' Jinty, who was unable to go for five minutes without expressing herself, could never have coped. I supposed I was a great disappointment to her. She wanted the kind of sister who would sit in the kitchen drinking herbal tea and discussing Gender Issues; I was nothing more than the comedy act to complement her straight man routine. But then, as much as I annoyed Jinty, I would occasionally capture a glimpse of pleasure in her eyes when she surveyed the barren wasteland that was my life. At least she could always look at me and feel superior.

I went to visit Sebastian in the Charter Nightingale. He looked pale and bloated and frankly drugged out of his head. His room was bare apart from some revolting flowers with a card on them saying, *Best from all at Morris, Gronville and Stanley.*

'Where's your pass, boy?' said Seb weakly.

'How are you?' I asked, sitting down and pouring myself some of Seb's orange squash. I had a horrendous hangover and felt like crawling into bed with him.

'Deutschland.'

Seb played with the drip that was attached to him. I fought an urge to start whistling. When it came down to it, I didn't really know Seb. We'd only stayed in contact because he'd moved to Fulham after graduating. And even at university I'd never liked him much, finding him a bit repulsive. Seb possessed a bizarre kind of physical clumsiness, as if he was trapped in the body of someone he hated and despised. Apparently at school they'd nicknamed him 'Fingers' as his hands seemed far too big for his frame and he was always knocking things over.

'How much were you drinking a day?' I asked. I wanted to check that Seb drank more than me.

'Not much, really. A few pints, maybe a bottle of wine for lunch, some shots for breakfast. It was the nights where I was really losing it.'

'Awful, aren't they,' I agreed. At AA they'd always gone on about just getting through the days and I'd always thought, But what about the nights? All those endless hours of nothingness . . . 'But you'd think that you'd be all right, Seb. Having your job and being rich and stuff.'

'Maybe that's it. That I had everything I wanted.' Seb didn't sound very convinced by his own theory. 'Or maybe it's just some kind of existential crisis.'

'You never did know who you were,' I agreed.

Seb was always trying to transform himself. After I left college, I went up to visit the old fascist and found him metamorphosed into an aesthete, living only for the stage. But he couldn't afford the plastic surgery he thought necessary to pursue an acting career. Later Seb tried to be a renegade, wearing cowboy boots and drinking Jim Beam and riding a Harley. But he'd crashed the bike and burnt off all his chest hair from smoking pissed in bed. Then Seb seemed to give up, reverting back to getting drunk in bad pubs and punching the air and shouting, 'British by birth, English by the grace of God!' Next there had been his most recent incarnation into a merchant banker. Seb had brainstormed, lived on amino acids, kept cocaine in his filing cabinet, developed a pet ulcer and worn platform loafers. No wonder he was confused.

'I was so tired,' he said, wiping clammy sweat off his forehead, 'but sleep was impossible. I thought that if I stopped drinking I'd never sleep again.'

'I know,' I said.

Seb started sniffing in a suspiciously wet manner. ' "And there's another country/I've heard of long ago . . ." ' A few tears squeezed down Seb's florid cheeks. 'I love Margaret Thatcher, you know.'

'Oh,' I coughed. I wished I was in a film and that someone would come into the room and ask me to leave. Seb looked so horribly *vulnerable*; like a fat, ugly, alcoholic child.

'I'm so terrified of getting close to anyone, of being involved, but I'm so bloody lonely.'

Even at college, Seb hadn't exactly been a social success. It wasn't simply his extreme political views, he just didn't seem to have a talent for friendship. He always got it wrong – too keen, too sarcastic, too clumsy – and all his constant attempted transformations had done were confirm his inability to make people like him.

'And . . .' Seb gulped. 'I think I'm gay.'

I didn't sleep that night after visiting Seb. I'd like to say that it was through worry but actually I'd run out of sleeping pills.

I lay aching with relentless restlessness, the duvet over my head because my face was freezing. Then, at three a.m., Ben telephoned demanding to know when Jinty was coming home.

'I don't know, Ben. Pa's ill, so she might be a couple of days.'

'Yeah, right. I'm not fooled. I know why she's left. She's trying to avoid having sex with me.'

'And who could blame her?' I muttered.

'What? You two are both the same, you frigid whores.'

'Ben, I've got to be up at six-thirty tomorrow morning.'

'Hardcore told me you fell asleep when he shagged you.'

'I just closed my eyes.'

'You were snoring.'

'Oh fuck off and go to sleep.'

'I can't.' I heard the sound of Ben taking a huge snort of coke. 'I just don't get it. When we're together we fight all the time, but I still can't sleep without her.'

I eventually put the phone down on the idiot. Here was Ben under threat of going to prison for a very very long time and all he could do was worry about his relationship problems. Jinty was just as bad, returning home to visit our parents whom I knew she hated as much as I did. Jinty hadn't been beaten like Ama and me, but I guess she'd suffered her own shit. I remembered one day when I was in the library. I'd been up the ladder which I'd loved to play on as you could roll along the wall on it. I'd felt a hand going up my skirt and had turned round to see my father.

'Sorry,' he'd coughed. 'I thought you were Jinty.' Jinty had revealed years later that she'd been Pa's play-thing. He hadn't actually raped her but he'd always been ready for a quick feel. The worst thing was that I couldn't even bring myself to feel sorry for her. I just remembered Pa with his arm around Jinty, stroking her hair and calling her 'my slender lovely', and Ama and I sitting together late at night putting TCP on our wounds. And the fact that Jinty could walk onto a beach and look normal, whereas my body looked like something the cat had sicked up.

Seb's alcoholism invalidated his insurance so he was thrown out of the clinic after a week. He was sent home with Antabuse and beta-blockers and told to behave himself.

'What shall I do?' Seb asked me frantically over the phone. 'I told them I had a friend in AA so they assumed I'd be all right. As if you could be of any help.'

'I have feelings too, you know, Seb.'

'Really?'

I gave Seb the addresses of some meetings and explained that I couldn't go with him as I was working most nights. To my surprise, he actually went to them and seemed to see AA as an amusing alternative to the banking bar scene. Amazingly, he actually made friends there. Soon he was leaving Big Bible quotes on my answerphone and making tea for the 'City: Survivors' meeting.

'It's almost a relief to stop boozing,' he admitted to me on another of our late-night phone conversations. 'In the end, I was only drinking to get sober. What I can't understand is why you didn't like meetings. People are so friendly.'

'Oh, the meetings were OK when they weren't boring. It's just that I couldn't quite get to grips with the not using aspect of them.'

'Apparently there's a gay one in Earl's Court. I thought I might possibly go, perhaps, to have a look round.'

'Do,' I yawned, popping another sleeping pill. I was tired of Seb's constant not-drinking n dialling, his braying boasts about his new-found sobriety. Spitefully, I gave him Porno Jem's phone number, saying Jem was someone who understood gay issues.

'Thanks,' said Seb. He sighed down the phone. 'The nights have turned dark so quickly.'

'I know . . . it's that line, isn't it: "All the good times we missed having good times." '

'We did have fun, didn't we?'

'I'm tired, Seb.'

I heard on the grapevine that Jinty had returned from our parents', but she didn't call. I think she was pointedly trying to ignore me but I didn't really notice. The Escape was as grim as ever. Since Kevin had recovered from his nervous breakdown he was more of a wanker than ever. He was always strutting around warning me that he, 'Saw everything,' and that I was, 'On the edge.' More like beyond the cliff. The only person who ever visited me there was Cassie. She was now at one of those toilets-turned-unis doing Leisure Studies. She wasn't enjoying it much, though; already behind on all her essays and having to get a doctor's note saying she was too depressed to work. The truth was that she took so much E at the weekends she spent all week in bed recovering.

'I can never get it together to do anything,' she said, slumping on the bar. 'I'm a complete failure. Super-crap. I've broken up with Touchy as well. I couldn't face the pregnancy protests any more.'

'What?'

'I just got so angry cos it's so unfair that girls get pregnant, so I wasn't using any contraception.'

'So you were protesting against getting pregnant by letting yourself get pregnant?'

'I know. As a protest it had its weaknesses. Luckily I've got my period.'

I shook my head and poured us both some more Long Islands. Kevin was always trying to catch me nicking drink, but I was a fairly expert booze thief.

'I saw Sarah, you know,' said Cass, lighting a cigarette.

'How is she?'

'A bit messy. I saw her baby. She's called her Coco.'

'After Coco Chanel?'

'No, cocaine. She said she spends most of her time locked in her bathroom on the phone to Crisis. You know Peanuts got done?'

'Oh, not again.' Peanuts had only got out a few months previously. He was the sort of bloke who had Arrest Me written on his forehead.

'They'd been watching him for weeks, Sarah said. Ben's in hiding, isn't he?'

'Yeah, round Jinty's. He's become a Fulham Folk Hero.'

'Why can't I do anything? I wanted to join a sun-bed society at college but there isn't one.' Cassie started biting off the skin around her nails. For some reason her ezcema had improved (maybe because she was smoking less dope?) but she seemed unable not to fuss with her body. 'Oh, I saw Jinty last Friday. I was going to this club and she was going to a Life Dance session. She said that she had dysentery and she was worried about her career prospects.'

'At least she's got prospects,' I said bitterly. Jinty was always going to those university job fairs and coming back with carrier bags full of free goodies.

'You know,' Lunchie mused, licking her empty glass, 'I worked out my biggest paranoia last night. It's the paranoia that all my paranoias are real.'

*   *   *

Seemingly within only days of going to a gay AA meeting, Seb was trying to re-invent his personality again. He started going to underwear parties, joined a male naturalist swimming group and had one of his nipples pierced.

'I'm free, gay and happy!' he told me.

'That's a twelve-inch, Seb,' I informed him.

'But so appropriate. I feel alive! As if I could kill every Frog on this planet! And I've met someone.'

'Not from that Dirty Dick's Erotic Tea Dance you went to?'

'No, I—' Seb giggled in a hysterically knowing manner. 'You must meet him too.'

When I entered the Freedom bar in Old Compton Street, I found Seb looking like some grotesque parody of the *Boyz* lifestyle pages. He'd had his hair shaved off and dyed blond and was wearing a T-shirt announcing, *Not Just a Phase*. Sadly, Seb was as chunky as ever and was sporting a rather impressive pair of breasts beneath his child-sized top.

'I'm thinking about becoming a modern artist,' Seb said, stirring his cappuccino. 'Christ, I'm nervous. I hope he turns up.' He got out a hand mirror and started examining his face. 'Oh Christ, here he is. Do I look OK?'

'Ravishing.' I turned around. 'Jem!'

'Tara.'

'Small world.'

Jem eyed me smugly and asked if I liked his new Issay Miyake coat.

'I can never thank you enough for giving me Jem's phone number,' said Seb.

I had a hideous sinking feeling and was reminded of a saying of Cervantes' that my father used to quote: 'Don't mention rope in a hangman's house.'

We sat together drinking coffee, chain-smoking and

laughing. Seb kept saying, 'Absolutely,' and nodding at every one of Jem's fatuous statements. I even saw him attempting to hold Jem's hand under the table. The old sarcastic, verbose, bitter Seb was now a distant memory. Jem kept looking around the bar and winking at all his queenie friends.

'I can't believe it,' said Seb when Jem wandered off to gossip with a cronie of his in a kilt and roller-skates. 'When I met Jem it was as if I'd mentally imploded. I saw him and suddenly I started thinking about the two of us eloping to Amsterdam to get married and that maybe we could adopt a small child together and perhaps buy a farmhouse in Wales and grow organic vegetables.'

'Oh God, you're in love.'

'Hopelessly.'

Later, Seb went to the loo and I chatted to Jem.

'I can't believe it,' he said. 'When I first spoke to Seb I thought, Poor, poor petal, but he's been tremendously helpful with my futures portfolio.'

'Oh God, you don't even really like him, do you?'

'Well, I still haven't quite decided if I'm gay yet. Obviously all the evidence points in that direction but I think that I might actually be a gender outlaw.'

'You're a bastard, Jem.'

'Don't lecture me, dearie. You, the girl who promises ecstasy and delivers indifference.'

'I know.' I saw Seb returning from the loos with a desperately bright, vulnerable smile on his face. 'But poor Seb.'

It was only a matter of time before Seb discovered that now it was he who was just a phase.

I had some good news. I'd auditioned for a jazz company a long time ago but had been rejected because of my terrible personality. However, one of the company members there had remembered me and offered me an audition for a new contemporary piece she was choreographing. Amazingly, for me, I actually made it to the audition (admittedly with a hangover and a leotard with holes in the crutch). I got the role as a result of my mixture of 'arrogance and vulnerability'.

'Aren't you pleased for me?' I asked Jinty. 'It's a fantastic opportunity for me and I actually get paid.'

Jinty kicked around some mess on my floor. She said she'd dropped in to give me 'support' but actually I only lived a couple of doors down from her new therapist and I think she was trying to avoid going home. Since Ben had gone into hiding round her place, Jinty's agoraphobia had miraculously gone into remission. Ben was showing the strain, too. He claimed to have developed cocaine psychosis as a result of having to toot non-stop to cope with constant 'emotional sharings' and had threatened to kill Jinty if she sang 'Kumbayah' one more time.

'Why should I be pleased for you? My boyfriend's a fugitive, my dysentery still hasn't cleared up and I've got no friends.' Jinty hurled one of my ballet shoes at the wall. 'Where did it all go right for you? Your life has been . . . disgusting. Why should you be a success? I'm the success, I just don't have any talents.'

'Thanks for the support, Jinty.' I felt rather pleased: Jinty, jealous of *me*.

'Oh, sorry.' Jinty picked up my ballet shoe. 'I had a row with the Women's Group at college today. I'm doing a lot of anger work with my counsellor but I think it's all gone horribly wrong. I'm so full of hate: for you, the French, Ben. I was doing my meditation yesterday and Ben was sitting in the corner blowing up condoms and throwing them at me. Then he tried to strangle my toy seal.'

*   *   *

Seb lasted about two weeks with Jem. Then he walked in on Jem having sex. Not only was Jem having sex with two other people, but they were both girls. Jem said it wasn't his fault as he was 'commitment phobic' and he needed to do more research for his porn.

Seb gave up and went back to AA; he seemed to have commitments all over London and was tea-maker at five meetings. He still telephoned me, but we had nothing to say to one another. The only thing Seb cared about was staying sober. Not drinking lost him his few friends.

'I thought it was just a phase,' Jem said to me, 'but Seb was just *too* tedious. Always looking for the next meeting.'

Seb's dullness really did become excruciating. Speaking to him was like hearing an audio-tape of the *AA Daily Reflections* book. I realized how close I'd been: I'd gone to AA, I'd talked about the Loving Thing – Seb could have been me. Luckily matters improved when Seb was told to get in contact with his inner child. Getting it slightly wrong, he went on a three-day binge at Hamley's. His flat became stuffed with train-tracks and Scalextric and he took up trampolining.

'My childhood was grotesque,' he said. 'My mother wheeled me around in a pushchair at anti-Nazi league rallies. So I'm going to be a child again. Properly.' Now, in between meetings, Seb would race cars and shoot cowboys. He even set up a tepee in his sitting-room. We did occasionally go for strolls together and play with walkie-talkies and stunt-kites. Seb seemed strangely content and I almost envied him; but my childhood was a place I had no intention of returning to.

11. The Ghosts of Hardcore's Past

By the time New Year's Eve arrived, I'd already lost it. Having nothing else to do, Cassie and I had gone on a bender over Christmas. The two of us vomited openly, drank hopelessly and cavorted shamelessly, refusing to let the mutilating dullness of our nights out interfere with our dissipation.

'Cocaine's such a tramp's drug,' I would say, snorting a line off a lavatory seat.

'I'm going to be sick if I have any more,' Cass would groan and then order another vodka. Working overtime in the club, I was drinking so much that I became unable to get drunk. Cassie regularly passed out in the bar and sometimes leant over and chucked up in the drip-trays.

'Troub is,' she'd slur, drooling out of the side of her mouth, 'is that nobody loves me, man.'

I had become desperate. As Christmas approached, any last remnants of self-control had long been abandoned, and I would have done virtually anything to escape. I thought of shaving my head and entering a monastery; of faking my own suicide and fleeing the country; even of going home. Ridiculous, I know, but luckily Mother paid me an unexpected visit. It only took one lunch at Harvey Nicks to eliminate any crazed illusions I'd ever had of speaking to her again. It turned out that, as my father was now laid up awaiting another coronary bypass, Mother was sneaking out of Sussex to do a course at the College of Psychic Studies on Living with Sensitivity. She'd just been to a special Christmas séance. It was amazing how the more ill Pa became, the more outgoing Ma seemed to get.

'Wine, darling?' I nodded and she turned to the waiter. 'Two, please.'

'Large or small?'

'Oh, do you do large bottles?' Ma hadn't changed that much. The two bottles of Chablis arrived and we both sat looking at the table in an agonized silence. We'd barely spoken for years.

'Ballet,' said Ma finally, 'is it marvellous?'

'I'm a contemporary dancer, Ma.'

'Yes, I remember seeing *The Nutcracker* as a child. Are you terribly successful?'

'Not really.'

Ma sighed. 'Oh course, I could have been a dancer. Everyone always says I have the body for it.' Ma had the body of a human pickle. 'You're looking lovely, Tara darling.' She reached out to touch my forehead and I instantly recoiled. I saw a brief look of hurt cross her face. 'I'm so proud of you. You were always so talented.'

'Yeah.'

'Are you coming home for Christmas?' she asked eventually.

'I seem to have lost the invitation.'

'Well, your father you know . . . he heard that your friend Lucinda had become one of those crack habits and, well . . .'

'It's OK. I hate Christmas anyway.'

'Of course, it's a time that has difficult memories for all of us.'

Ama, with her usual immaculate timing, had died on Christmas Eve. I couldn't believe Ma had even obliquely mentioned my sister's death. Father had always said that suicide wasn't fit conversation for the dinner table.

'You are generally happy, though?'

'Not really.'

Ma looked at me with an insane kind of urgency. 'I hate to see you so stuck, Tara. You must move on. The college has taught me so much. I've spoken to Amaranda, you know.'

'Really.'

'And I've found a new group for you, darling. It's called SOS: Siblings of Suicide. They're looking for a new chairwoman as the last one killed herself too.'

'Cheers.' I stared transfixed at the table.

'You blame me, don't you?' said Ma finally in a small voice.

I shrugged.

'Just tell me what to do, how I can make it better between us.' Ma's eyes became suspiciously wet. Not blubbing, in public.

I did the only thing I knew how to do: 'Ma, I'm sorry, I . . .'

I walked out. I spent Christmas with Cassie, the two of us getting so coked out of our heads that we thought we were having heart attacks. Cool.

*   *   *

I didn't bother to make any plans for New Year's Eve as whatever I did it always ended in tears anyway. I thought about staying in and watching a video with a nice boy but I didn't know any nice boys. So I ended up round Cassie's with all the usual suspects: Ben, Touchy-Feely, Sarah, Seb. The room was thick with smoke and misplaced expectations.

'Where's Jinty?' I asked Ben. Since Ben had come out of hiding, he'd snorted half of Bolivia. Jinty was trying to persuade him to go to Cocaine Anonymous, but Ben was as always convinced that it was some kind of police spy ring.

'Frigid whore. We had a ruck and she won't come out. All last night she was farting in bed cos of her dysentery. So maybe I did call her a freak and a violation, fucking slag.' He began chopping out lines on Cass's copy of *You Can Heal Your Life*.

'How're you, Sarah?'

'Oh, fucking great. I couldn't decide what to wear: tent, sack-cloth, scaffolding.' Sarah reached forward for a line. She must have put on three stone and moved like an old woman. 'I need my jaw wired, my stomach stapled and my nose clamped.'

'How's the kid?' I'd visited Coco at Sarah's and, despite the rumours circulating Fulham about Coco's now legendary ugliness, had found her to be a strangely pleasing creature. Sarah hadn't been terribly interested in her baby, though. She'd just sat smoking out of the window, saying she was selling her double bed to get a single and a cot.

'Coco's all right. I've got to go home in a couple of hours as Ma won't bloody babysit. Jonny came round the other day and gave me a pot-plant.'

'Nice . . . y'all right, Lunchie?' asked Ben.

Cassie was staring out of the window with a deranged kind

of concentration. 'Yeah. I was thinking, it's funny, but somehow chickens have feelings but pigs don't.' Ben started shrieking with laughter and admitted to having already spiked Cass with a microdot. It was going to be a long evening.

Thank God for Lilly. She turned up as we opened the champagne, looking beautiful, with a shy bloke in tow. 'I'm a fucking sexual desperado!' she screamed. 'And this is Ewan.'

'Aright,' he slurred in a strong Welsh accent. 'I love this woman, see.'

Lilly shot him a look of pure sex. Obviously all the rumours were true: Lilly had gone to a rave in a Brixton squat where she'd met a Welsh fisherman. Jacking in her job, Lil had started commuting regularly to his village for sex n drugs seshes. Her trick vagina had weaved its magic spell and he'd thrown his nets to the sea and come down to London to live with her. They never went out and spent all their time fucking and taking trips. Apparently, multiple orgasms were involved.

'I love my life!' Lilly screamed. She then grabbed a bottle of champagne, poured it over Ewan's head and started licking the liquid off his face.

'You're fucking mad,' said Ben.

'Yeah. Great, isn't it?'

It turned out that, as usual, our safe-as club tickets had disappeared, so we were having to go to a party of a friend of Ben's sister's. Knowing it was bound to be horrendous, I dragged everyone down to the Escape with me first as I knew I could cadge free drinks there. It was still fairly quiet and I hung around the bar chatting to Tim whilst the others had an Obscene Olympic drinking competition. Sipping a Brain Damage, I realized that I already wanted to go home.

'God,' I sighed, staring at the bar filling up with ever-reddening faces and ever-widening eyes. 'Take me away from all this, Tim. Let's get married instead and have adorable children. Would you marry me, Tim?'

'Tara, my last girlfriend left me after three weeks because I was so boring.'

'You are quite boring, you know.' I watched Ben picking his nose and then eating the bogey. He was obviously licking his coke problem.

'I, I . . .' Tim looked down at his glass and then took a huge gulp of beer. 'I do like you, Tara, you know that.'

'I . . . well, I like you, too.'

'You know that's not what I mean.' Tim raised his hand. 'Don't say anything. I know you don't feel the same way.'

'I'm sorry,' I said lamely.

'Tara!' Gerry came up behind me, grabbed me, wished me a Happy New Year and then ran off to skin up in the loos. Tim stared at me in a strange way.

'You too,' he said finally.

'What?'

'When Gerry went to put her arm around you, you flinched as if you were going to be hit. Funny how you can see it in other people.'

Time to leave.

Sarah went home and the rest of us all dropped silly amounts of E and headed off to the dive-party in Stoke Newington. Ben bribed a doorman and we were sneaked round the back. The building was obviously derelict, virtually pitch-black and crowded with smoke and junkies. It reminded me of a school I'd been at. We managed to find a ragamuffin selling luke warm beer and stood in a corner holding our bottles.

'Happy New Year!' said some sweaty stranger, kissing me.

'Gross,' I murmured. 'Yeah like Happy New Year

everyone.' We all attempted hugs and went off to dance. It was hardcore techno. I thought how much Dave would have loved it and just how mad he'd have gone. I sat in a corner, feeling forlornly trapped in an ear-bleeding hellhole. The others – apart from Lilly and Ewan who were snogging on a speaker – merely swayed vaguely to the music and went off at odd intervals to toot in the loos. Cassie simply stood, blinking to the beat.

'You all right?' I shouted in her ear.

'Ch-rist!' she stammered in shock. 'I thought I was in bed.'

After three hours of mindlessly repetitive beats, we decided to give up and go back to Cassie's. Lilly and Ewan went off for sex and said they'd come round the next morning. The night limped on. Ashtrays overflowed, mirrors were abused, fun-sized bags of drugs were emptied; a fog of sordidness enveloped us. Cass and I lay in a stupor in the corner.

'I'm probably giving up tomorrow,' said Cass, lighting up.

'What?'

'Well, if I give up smoking, I won't be able to go down the pub and get pissed and do coke to sober up and end up dropping a couple of Es.'

'Right.' It was amazing how quickly Cass had got into the clubbing lifestyle. She had spend her entire student loan at Red or Dead and John Richmond.

'I'm still basically off the puff, though. I'm just going to do one more pill, cos if you do halves you just end up doing more.'

'Yeah.' I distributed chewing gum between the two of us and we sat munching in companionable silence. The only sounds were Cassie's stereo thumping out ambient 'ambulance' music and Ben's hushed ravings: 'Bloody monks . . . my parrot . . . Uzi the fuckin station . . . diamond trips . . . buried . . .'

'Do you remember when we took those trips?' said Cass. 'And stayed up for three days cos we thought we'd almost found the meaning of life?'

'It used to be the same down the Ministry,' I wibbled. 'Lilly and I used to call it the Ministry of Snogs. We used to sit in this lav we named the Office and think all we had to do was be less mad.'

'And then you'd be sorted.'

We both sighed.

'I'm definitely giving up,' said Cass, popping the E. I had to laugh. 'What's so funny?'

'Sorry, it's just difficult to take someone seriously when they say they're stopping while they're dropping an E. Couldn't you just be more moderate?'

Cassie shrugged and started sifting through some of the crap on the floor. 'You can't moderate drugs. God knows, I've tried for years . . .' Cass seemed to forget what she was saying and reached for a packet of Rizla. I looked at her long, thin fingers, several of which now appeared green. I shook my head.

'You were saying.'

'What we need is sex. I'm convinced I could sort out my drug problem if I had more sex.'

'I'm sure Touchy would fuck you.' Touchy was sprawled on the sofa playing with a shark-fishing game.

'I don't want to fuck Touchy any more,' Cassie snapped. 'Jesus, Tara, you've dropped four, five Es, don't you feel anything?'

I looked at the states lying round Cassie's bedsit in various stages of catatonia. 'I feel a bit nauseous,' I admitted. 'Anyhow, the more I know about men, the more I like drugs.'

I wasn't at all convinced about the having sex–being in

control of drugs connection. I'd spoken to Lucinda only a couple of days previously. She'd just come out of the Second Chance clinic and was bingeing and chasing more than ever. When I asked her what had happened to her boyfriend, she claimed not to be able to remember him. She said bitterly that she'd been clean for three months before their affair, that he'd been her downfall. The first night they were together, she'd had to get drunk to have sex. Later Cindy even pretended to be an outdoors person for him.

'I was dying to be close to someone but I just didn't have the honesty. I used to sit in bed with him and be so full of self-loathing.' I remembered how I'd hidden my porn from toy-boy Chunks and the horror of us having sex when we were sober.

'Oh, fuck it,' I said finally, watching Cass sneakily feel up her ever-diminishing breasts, 'give me another.'

It struck me that 'fuck it' was probably the most dangerous phrase in the English language. I popped the E and fell into a kind of restless sleep.

At some point I began to feel my legs kicking *grandes battements*. I realized my arms were hugging Cassie's stereo speakers. Daylight was now coming full-blast through the sides of Cass' curtains and I was more fucked than ever. Even my mind was slurring.

'Your sister breaks my fuckin heart,' said Ben, who was covered in blood from an earlier nasal accident. 'You wouldn't understand. You aven't got no heart. Frigid whores, the lot of you.'

'You really are like some fucking broken record,' I said, trying to sit up. I noticed that when I moved my head from side to side I saw little flecks of stars.

'I don't know whether to laugh or cry,' said Touchy.

'Probably electro-brainstorms,' said Cassie. 'You know, when I was nineteen, I swore that, whatever happened, I'd never have floral curtains. I have floral curtains.'

'I recently became an alcoholic this week,' said Seb.

'I used to astrotrip when I was about sixteen,' said Cass.

'YOU TALK SO MUCH SHIT, YOU GOT HALITOSIS,' said someone rapping to a Warren G tune.

'What?' I looked up and saw Dave Hardcore, my dead pervert mate, sitting on Cassie's speaker.

'THIS LOT ARE CUNTS.'

It was true. I'd never seen people take so many drugs and have so little fun.

'But maybe they've got drug problems?'

'THEY FUCKIN WISH! THEY AIN'T GOT THE MONEY OR THE BALLS FOR REAL DRUGS.'

Dave moved to a chair and started grinning inanely, sticking out a yellowish tongue with three Es on it. I wondered if he was right. That we were all searching for some tangible escape from our angst – drink, drugs, bulimia – but our basic problem was that we didn't really want to live. We weren't even directionless; instead we were circling steadily down a spiral.

'YOU ON ONE, GEL? THOUGHT SO. DON'T LIKE YER OUTFIT MUCH. YOU'VE GOTTA SMARTEN UP A BIT.'

'I know, I've been through hell, you know.'

Dave walked towards the door, whistling 'Push The Feeling On' whilst fiddling with his dick. 'YOU COMIN THEN?'

'Well, I dunno . . . you know we normally go down the pub after a sesh. D'you want to come?'

'NAH, I'M BARRED FROM MOST PUBS ROUND

ERE. MAINLY THROUGH DRINKIN, YOU KNOW.
STAY MOIST AND I'LL CHECK YERS LATER.'

Dave left and I turned back to the others. They were looking at me like I was a nutter.

'Didn't you see him?' I cried. 'I wasn't talking to myself. I was talking to the Ghost of Dave Hardcore.'

'Oh God,' said Seb.

'She just gets worse,' said Ben.

Cassie scratched her head. 'I think we should go to the pub.'

The light outside and the walk to the pub were excruciating. It was like that First World War poem: 'Bent double . . . coughing like hags'. I tried to apologize for my fit of madness but the others were too interested in recounting their own most recent hallucinations. I thought of Susie, who always saw Keith Chegwin at raves. We crawled gingerly inside the bar and ordered drinks. Cassie collapsed on a pool table and lay splayed in a micro-sequinned skirt whilst talking about karmic sex. Ben had another nosebleed, which he ineffectually tried to mop up with a beer mat. Seb started chatting with a frightened old woman in the corner. Touchy looked too ill even to attempt to score, red-faced and sweating, his eyes bulging with paranoia. The other pub-goers looked at us like we were freaks. I saw myself in the bar mirror. We were freaks.

'Christ!' I screamed. 'This is grotesque! Everyone, get out! You've no idea what you look like!'

'But I wanna play darts,' said Ben.

'I can't walk,' said Cassie.

'Fuck this.' I ran out of the pub. What should I do? Of course, I should drive home. I tried to remember where my car was. Then I saw Lilly.

'All right?' she said, smiling lazily. 'Ewan's still sleeping. I thought I'd come and find out what the rest of you were up to.'

'The others are in the pub. Don't go in there, Lil, it's worse than the time you pissed yourself on Fulham Broadway. I'm driving home.'

Lilly burst into laughter. 'Tara, the state of you, you ain't driving nowhere.'

'I've got to, Lil. Now. I've just seen Dave Hardcore's ghost and then a museum of freaks in the pub.'

Lilly touched my forehead. 'I think you're a little feverish, Tara. I'll drive you.'

'But you can't drive.'

'No worries.'

I wasn't even fit to be a passenger, rapping 'Regulate' and doing pointe-work on the windscreen. It therefore took me a few minutes to notice Lilly's lunatic driving.

'Fuck,' I said, after we narrowly missed several cars. 'Are you sure you're all right to drive?'

'Jesus-fuck,' said Lilly. 'I thought I was playing a video game. I must still be tripping.'

Somehow, we made it back to my place. Lilly went to make tea and I lay down on my bed and idly played the answerphone.

'Tara! Oh Christ, help me! I'm at Charing Cross hospital. Coco's dying and I don't know where my mother is.'

We got back into the car.

The hospital was like some mad fluorescent tripping zone. We managed to find Sarah, who was sitting on the floor sobbing. She was still wearing a dressing gown.

'Oh God, oh God,' said Sarah, stumbling to her feet.

'What happened?'

'After Mummy left, Coco stopped breathing.'

'How is she?'

'It's all too late. I loved her and I never knew. She's going to die. I'm cursed.' Sarah started screaming and we were taken away to a private room. I went outside to attempt to speak to the nurse. It was obvious she knew I was on drugs. I wondered if nurses were paid extra for shopping people.

'I take a lot of Chinese herbs.'

'Sorry, love?'

'I mean, is Coco going to die?'

A smile almost passed over the nurse's face. 'No, no, love. She's been having some breathing difficulties. Just a bad dose of flu, really. We're only keeping her here under observation.'

I then spent the next half-hour trying to get this through to Sarah. 'Sarah, it's fine. Coco'll be all right. You'll be laughing about this later.' But Lilly's comfort was strangely much more effective than mine. She just put her arms around Sarah and cried with her. It was funny as Lilly didn't even like Sarah that much, saying she was the most self-obsessed person in Fulham (and this was a strongly contested title).

'It's so difficult to love,' said Lilly to Sarah. 'When I'm with Ewan I'm always worrying that he'll go off with someone else cos of my bad skin and body hair. I sometimes wish I'd never even met him cos he makes me feel so fucking vulnerable.'

'But she's my baby and I . . . I never wanted to be fat and dressed like a Top Shop reject.'

'I know. It's not easy. But think what a trendy kid Coco'll be when she's older.'

'I never even wanted to be a mother.'

'I never wanted to lose my mum,' said Lilly. 'Coco's so lucky to have you.' The two burst into a fresh flood of hysteria and, feeling like an extra in some Hollywood B movie, I left them clinging to one another and went outside for a fag.

I leant against a wall and tried to find my cigarettes. I realized I was crying and that I wanted to be sick. I wasn't really sure what was happening any more. This was the hospital where I'd had my plastic surgery failure and the knee operations; where I'd watched my sister die. I remembered bringing Ama in. She'd taken the OD at my flat and I'd found her surrounded by empty vodka bottles and pills, most of which were mine. I don't know how, but I managed to get her in a cab. We arrived at Charing Cross hospital and the driver helped me carry her inside. *Hold on Am, just hold on.* I sat by her as she had her stomach pumped. *It's OK, they're almost finished.* I telephoned Jinty and our parents. *We'll get a flat when you leave hospital. I'll cook and clean for you and get a job in an office.* Nothing could be done. Her internal organs were shot. *Ama, I don't know what to do.* We waited. She died.

It started raining. My knee hurt. I wanted to be somewhere but I didn't know where; to be with someone but I didn't know whom. I couldn't find my fags, so I went back inside to puke.

12. My Right Knee

'I've fulfilled my mother's prophecy,' said Lucinda as she
looked vacantly at all the trendy types beginning to fill the
Dôme. 'She always said I was incapable of having friends. I
have no friends.'

'Yes, but she also told you that on the day you were
born she looked out of the hospital window and thought,
My life's over. You shouldn't take it personally.' Lucinda's
mother claimed to have been an opera singer and blamed
Cindy for the loss of her glorious career. Actually, Mrs Miller
had never sung in anything other than amateur productions.
'And according to my mother I had a "golden" childhood.'
Lucinda smiled and we both lit more cigs. It was as if we
walked with a fog of fags around us. Cindy had now
developed asthma ('Trust me to get low-grade asthma,' she
had laughed, after visiting her doctor who'd said she had the

lungs of a forty-year-old).

'Look at that girl's hideous jersey,' jeered Lucinda, eyeing one of the more tragic fashion victims. 'Living on my own I always assume everyone's perfect except me.' I nodded in agreement. 'Check her snogging that boy.' We both giggled uncomfortably.

'You haven't heard from your old shag, then?' I asked.

'Not really. I saw him in the street the other day and attempted to run him over. He wasn't amused.' Cindy attempted a casual look. 'I expect I'll never have sex again. My fanny's fucked.'

'?'

'From bulimia. It stretches your vaginal muscles to grotesque proportions.' She sighed. 'Then again, I've always been abnormal. When I was a child I used to try to reduce it by using a bull-clip.'

'Oh shut up.'

'No, the sad thing is I'm serious.'

'But your house was always packed with those sex books. What was our favourite again?'

'*Where Do I Come From?*'

'D'you remember your mother coming back and giving you a present and you going, "Oh Mummy, not *another* sex book".'

'And the diagrams.'

'And those charts you used to colour in.'

'It just proves that sex isn't simply a matter of information.' Lucinda scratched her neck, revealing a jutting collarbone. 'Intellectually I knew that I wasn't deformed but inside I was totally convinced that I was. It's like the bingeing. I know it will kill me but that doesn't make me stop.'

*   *   *

193

I'd been seeing a lot of Lucinda since my knee had forced me into (hopefully) temporary retirement. Jinty said too much, but then what did she know? Lucinda was the only person I could be with and not worry about being too morose or too loopy as she always was too. Injured again, I'd lost the jazz job. It was a hopeless battle against self-pity. If I was honest I'd been experiencing pain in my right knee for months. Terrified my old knee problem was re-asserting itself, I'd done the only thing I knew how to do: I'd ignored it. But by February I was getting shooting pains down the front of my leg just getting out of bed. Eventually, I trooped back down the Dance Clinic. The news was bad. I had a chronically inflamed patellae tendon and there was some bone degeneration. Diagnosis: total rest. To say I was completely hysterical is perhaps not putting enough emphasis on the hysterical. My ankle and now this. But unfortunately no-one was prepared to listen to my Knee Saga any more. Whenever I tried to whinge on about it people would remember urgent appointments and AIDS tests. I thought bitterly of when I'd been laid up in bed years before, sporting an incredibly itchy plastercast which I used to scratch underneath with a ruler. People would occasionally drop by if they had nothing else to do: 'How are you?' they'd ask, yawning.

'In agonizing pain.'

'Oh. I've had the best day, you know.'

'I couldn't give a shit. I'm crippled.'

'You want to think of that Christy Brown. He wrote an entire novel with his right toe.'

'His left foot, idiot.'

'It's a beautiful day, you should open the curtains.'

'I hate the world. I want to die.'

Soon even Cassie had claimed that she was too 'busy' to

visit. I'd spent an entire year wallowing in my own personal sludge of bitterness.

Now, I should have been watching class and catching up on my dance theory, but frankly I'd have found snuff movies more amusing. I lay in bed for a couple of days, the knee covered in ice-cubes that I pinched to put in my vodka. Then I realized that if I didn't get up my few good muscles would waste, so I decided to go swimming.

I walked into the changing room, put down my bags and sat on a bench. My courage deserted me. I couldn't face getting changed and walking to the pool, the feel of everyone staring at my scars and trying to work out how I got them. I went back upstairs and stood looking at the other swimmers. The smell of warm chlorine and the falling snow showing through the windows reminded me of the 'remedial period' after my second operation. It had been a long winter. After yet another plastercast had been removed, I swam every day in order to stimulate my atrophied muscles. I would trudge in riding boots through heaps of snow to reach the pool where I'd duly complete my forty laps. By this stage, I had no friends, no job, nothing. All I did was swim and take tranqs, only aware of the passing of time when I signed on. I would rather have died than gone back to that.

Getting back into the car with my unused swimming stuff, I was ready to drive straight into a tree. Instead I made my way through the dancing snow to Lucinda's. She lived in one of those nasty blocks of council flats with a kicked-in communal entrance. I'd been ringing her flat-bell and knocking on the door for ages when I finally heard a small voice.

'You can't come in.'

'Lucinda. It's me, Tara. Open up.'

'I can't. I'm in bed.'

'Cindy, you're quite patently not in bed as you're talking to me through the door.' Silence.

'Oh, please let me in. I'm cold.'

There was a shuffle and the sound of a million locks being turned. Lucinda opened the door and walked away, leaving me to follow her in.

'Sod it, I don't care what anyone thinks any more,' she said and sat down on a sofa and put her head in her hands.

Although the curtains were closed and there was a thick smog of cigarette smoke, no lack of light could disguise the mess. The sitting-room was littered with overflowing bin-bags, festering plates, half-eaten bowls of unidentifiable matter, food wrappers, laxative packets, hundreds of cigarette butts, mouldy bread, empty vodka bottles and various bits of heroin paraphernalia. But overwhelming all this was an unbelievable, almost concentration-campesque stench of vomit and shit. Even I could tell something was wrong.

'How long?'

'I haven't left the flat for four days.'

'Christ.'

Lucinda looked up at me. Her eyes were red and puffy, her jaw was badly swollen and her sweatshirt was splattered with vomit. 'I think I've reached my rock bottom. I can't go on like this. I've got to stop now.'

I suddenly thought that both Lucinda and I shared the same method of giving up: the doing-it-so-much-that-you-were-bound-to-stop method. The method's lack of success was conspicuous in both our lives.

'I can't binge again today. I've got to get cocaine to clean up the flat.'

'You Need Cocaine to Clean Up your Flat?'

'Just for today.' She looked pleadingly at me. 'To break the pattern.'

'Cinds, don't ask me. I'm trying to stay away from the stuff myself.'

'But I've never been addicted to cocaine.'

'But you were using heroin to stop you bingeing and . . .' I gestured to the room.

'I know, but this would be different.'

I cleared a bin-bag out of the way and sat down on the floor. My knee hurt. It struck me that nothing was ever different for Lucinda and me. I'd already arranged to go over to Ben's later that evening to pick up some draw to help stop me drinking.

'Do you hate me?' asked Lucinda.

'How could I hate you, Cinds? It would be like hating myself.'

It took a minute to work out why Cindy smirked so at that statement.

Since that day Lucinda and I had spent most of our time together. Our main occupations were smoking, drinking coffee in the Dôme and hanging out in pet shops. We'd both developed a craze for tropical fish after watching a programme on scuba diving. We loved the quiet, dark dampness of the fish sections (even if Sarah once caught us in a shop and gave us a lecture on how common tropical fish were). Cindy and I would crouch beside the tanks, staring in wonder at such beautiful creatures, the only sound being the hiss of the pumps. I loved the fish that looked like miniature silver sharks and Lucinda loved the bright luminous ones with floaty tails ('You never see colours like that in London, never.'). We'd chat with pet shop assistants for hours, questioning them about the merits of large tanks, discussing particular fish diseases and asking how they actually *knew* that fish only had a memory span of three seconds. It was the only time we ever seemed to relax, entering the peaceful rhythm of the aquatic section, actually forgetting about ourselves for a second. Obviously we longed for fish of our own. Obviously, we couldn't afford them. Lucinda had a sixty quid a day binge habit and I was spending everything I didn't have on physio.

Sometimes, Lucinda would come round to my flat and watch me doing my remedial knee exercises. She never did any exercise now as she was too exhausted from either starving or bingeing.

'You're so lucky to have a knee injury,' she once said, watching me struggle with my patellae pull-ups. 'It means you actually *have* to stop.'

I was about to go on one of my but-you-don't-understand trips when I realized that of course Lucinda *did* understand. The awful truth was that after the initial hysteria, my invalid status had come as rather a relief to me. To be honest, class had been becoming a nightmare: grimly gritting my teeth through exercises that just fucking hurt. And the knee had given me a marvellous excuse not to do my usual shifts at the club. It was almost as if I'd forced myself to a point where I really couldn't work. I'd been doing five shifts a week and was considering taking on more nights. But I couldn't hold down work and hold down college. I had never been able to. I remembered Sarah telling me about a nun: 'Although all her struggles seemed different, they were all about the same thing.' It was simple: the way I lived was destroying my body.

'I don't know what to do,' I said finally, giving up my exercises and putting an ice-pack on my knee.

'Me neither,' said Lucinda, drinking cough medicine in between fag drags.

'I've messed up everything.'

'Me too.'

'Are you going to continue dancing?'

Lucinda shook her head. 'No. Dancing's part of the problem. As long as I dance, I'll always be bulimic.'

'You can't give up dancing cos of that.'

Lucinda looked up and gave me a wry smile. 'You know, Tara, I never even really wanted to be a dancer. I only started to compete with you. Really, I've always wanted to be an actress.'

'But you've been so successful.'

'Because I don't care. That's what's so funny. I always got work because people thought I was crazy and wild. Actually, I just couldn't have given a shit. I never wanted to be a dancer, I just wanted to look like one.'

It was such a strange thing for Lucinda to say, that she didn't even care about dance, when it was she who had inadvertently got me back into it. One night during my swim n tranq period I'd gone to 7-11 to grab some fags. Lucinda had been outside, having just bought a pack.

'Tara!' she exclaimed.

I'd wished the pavement would swallow me up. I knew I looked like someone out of *Band of Gold*: flabby, in a filthy tracksuit, with my hair in a pineapple. I wanted to scream, 'I don't look like this! You're not seeing me!'

'Lucinda. Nice to see you.'

'God, I'm just about to go off to America again. I'm in this piece playing a child serial killer.'

'Cool.' The lights from 7-11 were so harsh I felt like I was being blinded.

'What're you up to?'

'Oh, hanging, you know,' I stammered.

'Mummy's such a liar. She told me that she'd heard for a fact you'd been crippled for life and needed help going to the lavatory.' Lucinda was fingering the extremely smart dress she was wearing. 'Oh, and that you'd become a hopeless drunk. She said she saw you on crutches waiting outside Oddbins one morning.'

'Your mother, such a joker.'

I'd had one thought: Fuck Them All. It had taken me six months. I'd given up the drink, started doing weights, cut back on the tranqs, got a job; then I went back to class. I would cry after every lesson, humiliated beyond belief at my loss of technique. That Lucinda had been the one to reform me seemed . . . ridiculous. Lucinda, who'd only got away with her behaviour for so long because she worked more in physical theatre. Who, I later learnt, had been on smack that evening. Who had saved my life time and time again despite the fact that she never thought about anyone other than herself.

The first time Lucinda had saved my life had been after I'd left (i.e. been asked to leave) ballet school. Since my GCSEs, I'd been locked in a cold war of attrition with my father. We never spoke and I spent my time at home conspicuously not eating and staring mournfully at our now empty stables. In desperation, my mother had called Lucinda's mother and it had been arranged that I'd stay with Cindy in London and attend a sixth form college there. It was assumed I'd be a Good Influence on Cindy, who had recently been picked up for shoplifting, and Cindy assumed I'd get her parents off her back. My part of the bargain was to agree to start eating again. I'd sometimes have dinner with the Miller family and watch how they stuffed platefuls without even seeming to think about it, whilst I struggled with every forkful.

Cindy and I lived in the upstairs part of the house, with our two bedrooms next to one another and our own bathroom. Nina, Cindy's sister, had the room beneath Cindy and sometimes we would tap dance at night to irritate her. Cindy also had a brother called Fran but he lived in a home and the only evidence of his existence was a photo of him on her dressing table. The rest of the house belonged to the adults. Lucinda's mother, Mrs Miller – 'Call me Caitlin, child', but I never could – wore South American ponchos and had a Buddhist shrine at the bottom of the garden. She was always going on personal development courses but Lucinda and I were suspicious that these 'courses' didn't really exist, as they so often seemed to involve her staying out all night and then returning the next afternoon with a hangover and her clothes on back-to-front. Mr Miller was fat and American and ran a classical music magazine. He was mostly in his 'den', typing, drinking and listening to music. He'd used to be a conductor until he had a nervous breakdown.

'Best thing that ever happened to me,' he said. 'I needed freedom.'

'Oh, right,' said Cindy later, 'the freedom to become an alcoholic.'

The house was always full of music. Mr Miller would play records that Mrs Miller would then take offence to ('Wagner! And he *knows* how I detest Wagner.'). She'd then try to drown them out with Italian opera, which she would badly accompany whilst pretending to do housework. The noise drove Lucinda mad ('I must be the only teenager in London who has to ask her parents to turn their music down,') but, after the deathly silence of my house, I rather liked it.

Lucinda decided that we would attend a sixth form college in Brixton. With barely a couple of GCSEs between us, the choice of colleges hadn't exactly been overwhelming and besides it had a very good arts and crafts department (I had no interest in arts and crafts but I didn't really have any interests apart from ballet, so I was quite ready to go along with Cindy). I was terrified on my first day, walking into a sea of black males with loud voices. It reminded me of my father saying to me that I'd probably end up at one of those inner city schools where they sold drugs at the gates. I'd thought, I do hope so, but the reality seemed more daunting.

'It's so cosmopolitan,' said Lucinda, who I think was probably pretty nervous too. I felt that terrible cold fear freezing me up. I was bound to be attacked or mugged.

'Daddy says they all carry knives.'

'Yes, but doesn't he also think that all blacks should be paid to leave England?'

'Will we be all right?' We walked past a crowd of blokes who wolf-whistled at Lucinda, who was wearing a very short skirt.

'Of course we will. I've got a feeling.'

That first year at college was probably the best of my life. I wouldn't go as far as to say I was happy, more that happiness seemed like a possibility rather than a sick taunt. At first I was shy and didn't speak to anyone. Lucinda was far more outgoing and soon met people through hanging out in the arts and crafts block. It was only when I was standing outside one day and did a leg stretch that I began making friends.

'Hardcore. Check this, boy.' Two blokes walked up to me, both smoking huge reefers.

'Sorry,' I said, removing my ankle from my shoulder.

'Nah, show it again.' I shyly did so. 'How'd you learn to do that, then?'

'I was a dancer.'

'A dancer. Righteous. I'm Delroy and this is Hardcore.'

'Tara. Hello.'

'A dancer, like it.'

'That's why you're so skinny, then,' said Hardcore.

'Nah, man, not skinny, like *fit*.'

'Yeah.'

So I became known as 'Dancer' and somehow my quietness and lack of street cred became acceptable. Delroy introduced me to the rest of his posse: Dave Hardcore, the dub poet, Alfa, the stylist, and Mark, the athlete. I was soon able to cuss and dis and instigate with the rest of them. Delroy would often ask me to Get Naked, with him, but didn't seem bothered when I refused.

'Dancers are like nuns, man,' he'd sigh with the rest of the posse.

In fact, I was genuinely sweet sixteen and had never been kissed. This all changed with the college Vibe Sessions. At my last school, 'dances' had been a painfully sad experience featuring luke-warm punch and boys passing a cigarette round the loos. At Brixton, they were taken deadly seriously. The week before each dance, shoplifting frenzies began and all the boys started dissing one another about mixing skills. Then on Friday afternoon, huge sound systems began to arrive (one was so enormous it was dragged in on a 'borrowed' motorized Royal Mail Pullman). We'd all go home and change and then arrive later in the evening. Everyone would spliff outside in the yard and pass around bottles of warm rum. Then we'd head into the hall for a night of dub sounds, hip-hop or sweet soul, depending on who was playing. There were never any fights – arguments were settled with dancing or rapping competitions. I learnt to move without wearing pointe-shoes and to let a bloke hold me without feeling I had to call the police. Lucinda would get pissed and stagger around the floor going, 'You know I like it,' to all the boys. The only threat was some of the black girls, who didn't like us 'messin' with their men, but we were always protected by being Delroy's Women. I knew I didn't really belong, but I could kind of fool myself that I did.

My favourite bloke in the posse was always Mark, a quiet, fairly studious black bloke who always wore a tracksuit around college as he was an athlete. He used to get me to help him with his stretching and in return would try to explain GCSE maths to me. I once went down the track to watch him run. He was obviously class, even beside the other semi-professional athletes: his body lean and taut and his running so fast and graceful. I thought he was beautiful. To my amazement, word got round to me via Delroy that Mark had said I was a 'babe'. We got together at one of the Vibes and had a bit of a snog. He invited me out on a date. I was mortified (I'd never been on a date in my life) but forced myself to meet him in a Caribbean café. He'd just come straight from the track and smelt of freshly washed skin and was still sweating slightly. I felt ridiculous in a little black dress. What was I doing there? The only white face, not very pretty, secretly abnormal. Mark looked tense too, but smiled and got up to chat with the café owner who was a friend of his mum's. I noticed that when he turned around there was blood slightly seeping through the back of his T-shirt. He sat back down and I gingerly told him about the stain.

'Shit, man,' he said, straining to look over his shoulder. 'They've been killing me recently. Coach has been making me do forty-five minutes of sit-ups a day.'

'What's been killing you?'

He went very quiet. 'I guess I gotta tell you.' He took a sip of lemonade. Neither I nor Mark drank alcohol. 'I've got keloids all over my back.'

'Keloids?'

'They're like raised scars. Black people get them.'

'From?'

'My stepdad. It's all right, when the bros found out, he left pretty sharp.' He smiled sadly. 'I gotta tell you, they don't look too hot.'

'But so have I!' In my excitement, I grabbed Mark's hand and almost knocked over his lemonade. 'Got scars. 'I . . . I . . . had a really bad riding accident when I was younger.'

Mark and I went out for about a year. I suppose he could have been the love of my life if I'd been capable of any kind of honesty, but it was pretty cool anyway. He looked after me and encouraged me to go back to class and taught me how to roll reefers and dance from my pelvis. I liked just to look at him. Actually, I liked everything about Mark, even if Lucinda said that when God had given out brains Mark hadn't been present. But Mark was a year above me. His brothers, who were all armed bank robbers, had raised enough money to send him to America where he wanted to get a college athletics scholarship. He left and we wrote a couple of times and it all kind of fizzled out. By that time, I was studying at Central and considering going there to start ballet full-time again. But it was the same old story: I wanted to dance, but I wanted to have a life. In between juggling ballet and college work and running around abysmal nightclubs on speed with Lucinda, I didn't have time to think about What Might Have Been. But sometimes I would catch my head doing a sharp turn when I walked around Brixton. Without even knowing it, I was always looking for him.

Bizarrely enough, I was reminded of Mark when I met Jem later that week. I'd just been to physio and then gone for a browse in Dance Books. Having failed to find a copy of *Miraculous Knee Injury Cures*, I limped off for a coffee in Old Compton Street. Imagine my surprise when my former dancing pal walks in wearing dark shades and a leather jacket, waving at me with an issue of *Automatic Machine Gun* magazine.

'New image?' I asked Jem.

'How clever of you to notice.' He sat down beside me and sighed. 'I'm absolutely shattered. I'm in the process of moving from Soho to East Finchley.'

'What?'

'Soho's too social. I never get anything done as I'm too busy being gorgeous.' Jem blew a kiss to the neighbouring table. 'I've had it with pornography. I want to make a movie. The most dangerous movie ever filmed. It will star me, of course, leaping across ditches, flitting to El Salvador, throwing myself out of planes.'

'The leather jacket, of course.'

'You see,' Jem gestured around the café, 'all this is shit. We don't need to go to other people, let them come to us. Believe me, within a year East Finchley will be the most fashionable address in London.' Jem took an *SAS Survival Diary* out of his jacket and made some notes. 'I was thinking I could do a dangerous dancing scene with you.'

'Oh please. Anyway, how will you get the funding?'

'I'll get it.'

And the awful thing was that I knew he would.

'PMA, Tara, Positive Mental Attitude. I'm young, I'm good-looking, I've had the best education money can buy – and I'm angry.'

'About what?'

'My lack of success. It's ridiculous. I'm obviously meant to be a star. Maybe even you are, in a twisted sort of way.'

'But I don't have any confidence.'

'Well, go out and buy some, dearie. I've been reliably informed it's Bonus Time at Clinique.'

I sat on the tube home and thought about how time

was running out. That everywhere I was beginning to see people like Jem succeed, those whose enthusiasm far outweighed their talent. I'd caught my ex, Dwayne, on telly recently, playing the guitar and singing a supposedly 'comic' country and western tune. Despite Seb's recent clinic incarceration, he was still making progress at his merchant banking firm. To those sorts, failure was just a setback and not proof that they were cosmically doomed. It startled me to realize that lack of talent was no bar to success; that in fact talent itself might be a bar to success. Look at Lucinda, probably the most talented person I knew, brilliant at whatever she tried her hand at. And what did she do now? Sat in her council flat puking up and trying to score gear. Even Mark . . . I'd never seen anyone run like Mark. Whenever athletics was on television, I'd always watch it, trying to catch a glimpse of him, always feeling a vague sense of disappointment when his name was never announced. I wondered what had happened to Mark and remembered Hardcore's old taunts about him becoming a crack-head and a waster. I wondered if Hardcore had really had any idea where Mark had ended up. I supposed I'd never know.

I'd been taught a vicious strapping technique at physio to hold my knee in place and returned to class, way behind and weak. The company I was supposed to be working with had by this time long given up on me. I felt completely lethargic and had a strong sense that things were going to get worse. We had a careers talk at college but I didn't go. I was crippled not just by my knee but by fear too. Not only did I not jump or do any fast work, I also stopped taking any risks whatsoever in class, terrified I'd re-injure myself. I realized that without even acknowledging it, I was beginning to resign myself to giving up dance. It was as if I was haunted by ghosts that I didn't even know were there.

Lucinda, meanwhile, had gone back to AA. I went with her to her first meeting and, as we waited for it to start, bored her with my theories about talent being a bar to success.

'It's amazing how much crap you talk, Tara,' she said eventually.

'I know,' I agreed, eating a biscuit whilst simultaneously thinking I should go on a diet.

'There are two reasons why people like you and me fall by the wayside: we don't show up and we use.'

'Anyone who lived my life would use.'

'Yours is a life of someone who uses.'

'I could stop drinking if I wanted to.'

'So why don't you?'

'Everyone has a drink now and then. You've got to have some fun.'

'You don't drink for fun. You drink out of desperation. Look at yourself.'

'I'd rather not.'

'You claim you can't stop drinking because of working in that appalling club. But I bet you've spent more on physio in the past few weeks than you've earnt there in months.'

I was struck dumb by the truth of this statement.

'When you first came to AA did you ever stop drinking for more than a week?'

'Drinking isn't my problem.'

Lucinda looked at the floor.

'Jesus, we don't even give ourselves a chance.'

I went to work that night and got pissed. I mused that the only thing that kept me going at the Escape was the thought that some day I could leave and do something else. But the only thing I could do (dance) was being ruined by me working there. The bar was barring success. Luckily, my problem was solved for me. Kevin said he didn't want me behind the bar any more as I was 'pathologically lazy' and besides, the club wasn't busy enough to justify the amount of staff. He did have some sympathy for my plight, though, and would let me do the door at the weekends. Coincidentally, the door was the worst job at the club and they couldn't get anyone to do it for longer than one night. Having no self-respect, I thanked Kevin for his solicitude.

I told Lucinda the next day. Sort of (it actually came out, somehow, that I really wanted to commit to dance and cut down on my drinking so I had decided to work just weekends).

'I must say I'm surprised,' she said, looking suspiciously at me. Cindy was sitting in her traditional cloud of smoke, reading slimming mags. She pulled out a packet of Lax-Ease from beneath *Weight Watchers* magazine and popped ten or so.

'Bingeing last night?' I asked.

'Yes. It took me four hours to clean up this morning. I actually fell asleep on the kitchen table with my head in a saucepan of pasta.' She sighed and threw *Slimming* across the floor. 'I don't know why I read this shit. It's like some orgy of self-torture.' She drank some cough medicine and lit another cigarette. 'Bloody Mother just fucking called. She was going on about me not visiting Fran.'

'Ignore it.'

'I can't. I haven't seen him for six months. I keep meaning to go up to Surrey but I never get round to it and then I get more guilty and can't go even more. I can't face him alone but fuck me if I'm going with them.'

'What about Nina?'

'She still won't talk to me.' Lucinda and her sister had now not spoken for over two years.

'I'll go with you.'

Lucinda grinned and shook her head. 'Tara, you're the only person I know who I can rely on to be as unreliable as me.'

'We could go today.'

'What?'

'Surrey isn't that far, and I don't have to be at work till eight.'

'But . . .'

'Come on, we're always saying that we never do anything genuinely impulsive. Let's do something different. Something that doesn't involve using.'

It was amazing that, as dancers, Lucinda and I could not tell our left from our right. We almost ended up in Brighton and by the time we eventually started nearing the clinic, Lucinda had fallen asleep, worn out from bingeing all night. I wondered why I'd offered to drive Cindy down to see her brother. Guilt? Curiosity? Boredom? Who knows. Fran had always been such a mystery, locked in an institution near Guildford for His Own Good. The whole time I'd lived at Lucinda's I'd never seen him, as Mrs Miller said that bringing Fran home only 'distressed him unnecessarily' and 'disturbed his routine'. I'd only really registered his existence in my last gruesome months at the Millers'.

By our second year at Brixton, Lucinda had started to view school as irrelevant to her lifestyle. She was seeing a rich sod called Bert who bought her great clothes and took her to rooftop clubs with ostriches. If Lucinda's new stylishness wasn't bad enough, her success with dance used to keep me up nights writhing with jealousy. She'd been attending the Young Place and, due to her tiny height (and, yes, possibly some talent) was awarded a part with a professional contemporary company dancing a child's role. I instantly stepped up classes at Central. Whilst I struggled with A levels and my Advanced ballet exam, Lucinda's life became increasingly remote as she performed and partied across London. I wasn't really enjoying Brixton any more. All the posse had left and my social life had ground to a halt again. I began cutting out meals. Lucinda was then asked to lose a couple of pounds for her role. She would look at me bitterly and demand that I wrote down everything I ate in a day. I lied to her about what I consumed and she became convinced that I had an overactive metabolism and small bones. Lucinda started fasting and taking laxatives. Within two months, she had developed full-blown bulimia. Having no shame about her condition, she used to boast about how much she'd thrown up and weigh buckets of sick on our bathroom scales.

Matters in the household were also deteriorating. Mrs Miller came back paralytic one night and admitted that she was having an affair and demanded that Cindy help cover up or we'd all be the victims of a broken home. Cindy said nothing to her father about the affair, but began to refer to her mother as a 'fat old slag' and 'cellulited nymphomaniac'. I began to realize that the house I'd thought so carefree and bohemian had its own silent set of rules. Mr Miller was made to sleep in the den because Mrs Miller claimed his alcoholic snores kept her awake at night. Sweet Nina, Cindy's invisible sister, used to have vodka-and-oranges for breakfast. Fran was not to be mentioned. It was this rule that Lucinda began to start breaking in order to irritate her mother.

'Can't Fran come back for the weekend?' she'd ask.

'I'm sure he's much happier where he is,' Mrs Miller would say, turning up her opera.

'How do you know if he never comes home?'

'A mother knows these things. Besides, I can't see you being of any help to your poor brother. Your bedroom is an absolute disgrace. I think I may have to get it fumigated.'

'You've abandoned Fran. You just don't care.'

'I've sacrificed my life for you children.' Et cetera. Et cetera.

Lucinda and I became each other's worst enemies, tormented over each other's achievements, crowing over failures. I didn't pass my Advanced. My pointe-work was 'inadequate'. The truth was that I'd begun to notice a weird sort of laxity in my right knee and was having trouble even keeping my leg straight on pointe. My ballet teacher stopped saying I should try for a scholarship. And Lucinda's boyfriend dumped her because (I was listening on the phone extension) 'If I wanted to fuck a piece of spaghetti, I'd go to the supermarket.' I knew Lucinda didn't want me living with her any more but was too cowardly to say it to my face.

One Saturday morning we both got up to go to class; me down to Central and Lucinda off to the Place. We were both surprised to find Mrs Miller in the kitchen. She looked haggard and the place stank of fag smoke. I guessed that she had been dumped by her fancy man the previous evening. For some reason, she had made us both huge cooked breakfasts and demanded that we sat down and ate them.

'Thanks so much,' I said, 'but I'm late for ballet. Shall I put it in the fridge and eat it later?'

'I never eat in the mornings,' said Lucinda. 'You know that.'

Mrs Miller then picked up the plates and threw them on the floor. 'You two freaks! Don't think I don't know what you're up to: plotting, spying. You're lesbians, aren't you?'

'You're drunk, Mother,' said Lucinda calmly.

'I may be drunk but at least I'm not a freak. I can't even bear to look at you now, Lucinda.' She turned her head away and made a choking sound. 'You repulse me.'

'Please.'

'I hear you at night, you know. Creeping down the stairs, rummaging in the kitchen, vomiting in your bathroom. Don't think I don't know.' She suddenly turned to me. 'And don't think I don't know who to blame. Whenever I look at you, Tara, I think of Auschwitz.'

'Oh God,' said Lucinda, turning to leave.

'Shall I tell her?' Mrs Miller drew closer to me. I could smell the booze and cigarettes on her stale breath. 'We all want you to go. Lucinda was practically in tears over it the other night. I rue the day I ever let you stay. You're like some cuckoo in the nest. If—'

'Stop it!' screamed Lucinda. 'Tara, it's not true . . .' she began with all the sincerity of a used-car salesman.

I walked very slowly out of the house, went to ballet and then telephoned my mother. I left the following day, returning home to my triumphant father. For the second time I ended up taking my exams in a centre. I had failed again.

Cindy and I arrived in Guildford about three hours after leaving London. As we entered the clinic and walked past all the physical and mental tragedies present, I felt my insides begin to crawl. It was ironic that I, covered in scars and no stranger to hospital wards, found disability revolting. We discovered Fran, a contorted wreck, in a wheelchair. Lucinda suggested we wheel him into the garden. I don't think she was any more comfortable in the clinic than I was. We pushed Fran down a ramp and stood shivering in the crisp air. Cindy put his chair brakes on and then straightened up. She looked terribly tired and small. She wasn't really getting away with her bulimia any more. Her whole face seemed swollen and her skin had a dry, scaley look.

'Blurgahfucmah,' said Fran, forcing Cindy and me to acknowledge his presence.

'What?' I leant closer to Fran, trying to understand his incomprehensible mumblings. But unfortunately the nearer I got the more he spat in my face. Fran drooled and twitched and spasmed and Cindy and I lit fags.

'He doesn't look much like you,' I said finally. The only resemblance Fran and Cindy seemed to share was their anaemic paleness.

'WemeIwanmewanah.'

'What?' I asked Lucinda.

'He wants a fag.'

Cindy said not to bother, but I decided it couldn't do any harm. I leant forward to give Fran a cig and he suddenly managed to spasm a hand up my skirt. Cindy pulled me back and Fran then ate the fag and started spitting tobacco at us. I tried to wipe some tobacco strands off his face and with another miraculous spasm he grabbed my left breast.

'Christ, Fran!' Lucinda screamed at him. Fran looked mournfully down at the grass and started twitching in a hurt manner.

'Try that again and I'll deck you,' I said to him. He began whining.

'Don't bother,' said Lucinda, looking away from her brother. 'He doesn't understand.'

I wasn't convinced. It seemed to me that Fran understood far too much. He was like Dave Hardcore trapped in a spastic's body.

'It's like Mother says, there's nothing there. He doesn't even know who I am.' Lucinda decided she couldn't cope any more and wheeled Fran back inside. 'Bye bro,' she said, and we walked towards the door. Fran spasmed so badly that he fell onto the floor and cut his lip.

'Just go,' said the nurse as we turned back.

We got into the car and I switched on the engine. I thought that Fran knew exactly who Lucinda was and was torn between loving her as a sister and hating her because she could leave and he couldn't. He reminded me of when I was in bed after the knee operations. I'd always become rigid with anger when people exited after visiting, imagining them skipping back to their active lives whilst I lay there in torment. Cindy and I both lit fags and smoked furiously.

'You know what the funny thing is,' she said, turning to take one last glimpse of the home as we neared the end of the drive. 'Fran's clinic looks so much like Second Chance.'

'I should have visited you,' I apologized. With an enormous effort I managed to get the car into fourth gear. It was obviously on the way out. 'But thank God you're better now.'

'Oh, not you, too,' said Lucinda, staring angrily at me.

'What?'

'I can see it on your face: "You're so lucky. Think about all the poor, starving lesbian Ethiopian cripples." You're just like bloody Nina.' Lucinda put on a whiny accent. ' "How can you do this to your body when you're so lucky not to be like Fran?" '

'But I wasn't thinking that at all,' I protested. 'I'm the last person to Christy Brown someone else. No, I was just thinking that . . . I don't know. How I s'pose other people would look at me and think that I was a self-indulgent, self-pitying whiny cow. And they'd probably be right. But it's, like, I know there are loads of people worse off than me but how's that s'posed to make me feel any better?'

Lucinda relaxed in her seat. 'Thank God. I thought that you were going to be like everyone else. Jesus, my throat's killing me.' She started rummaging through her bag for some cough medicine and I saw some crumpled CVs fall out.

'?'

'They were talking at a meeting the other day about how a lot of getting well is starting to think about others rather than just obsessing about yourself all the time. And the doc's starting to get funny about signing my sick notes.'

'So?'

Lucinda swigged her cough medicine. 'I've applied to join some theatre group working with special needs kids. I'd be their movement worker or something. Oh, stop looking at me like that.'

'Like what?'

'Like you're about to launch into songs of praise. It's only cos I've got nothing to do and the pay's not that bad, and maybe it would help stop me bingeing.'

'Cindy!' I exclaimed. 'You're actually thinking of doing something normal, something *good*.'

Lucinda tried to avoid my gaze, but ended up collapsing into giggles. 'I know. Don't tell anyone, though. It would ruin my self-obsessed image.' I continued looking at her in amazement. Lucinda had never done anything selfless in her life. Jinty always said she'd never heard Lucinda utter a sentence without the word 'I' in it. 'Oh shut up, I'm going to read.'

Lucinda put back her seat and settled down with a copy of *The Joy of Fish*. She looked very beautiful, despite the swollen glands on the side of her face.

13. Another Funeral

My father died.

I'd been vaguely aware that he was undergoing another coronary bypass, but I hadn't taken it terribly seriously. Unfortunately, Pa croaked it under the knife. There'd be an autopsy and then he'd be buried in a week's time. Jinty had already gone home to look after Ma.

'We never communicated,' said Jinty, crying down the phone to me.

'Maybe you never had anything to communicate,' I said reasonably.

'You're just so much help, Tara. When are you coming down?'

'I'll come for the big day.'

'Not before?'

I made a lot of excuses about the pressures of work and

college and wondered if I should take an onion-scented handkerchief to the funeral so as I could pretend to cry.

I called up friends who had known my family to see if any of them would attend the service with me.

'I've got a child,' said Sarah.

'I've got an eating disorder,' said Lucinda.

'Oh God! (followed by insane hysteria and floods of tears): my old boyfriend Rupert's mother when I asked him.

'I've had a nervous breakdown,' said Cassie. I'd not known. 'Why've you been ignoring me?'

The truth was that after New Year's Eve I'd decided that Cassie and the Bolivian Posse were a bunch of no-hopers and that I was signing my own death warrant by hanging around with them. Or maybe more, that the difference between them and me was that I had aspirations and they didn't. I envied Cassie and her new-found reckless E abuse but I knew it wasn't an option for me. If I started using seriously again then that would have been the end for my dancing; if indeed my dancing wasn't already finished. But I went round to visit Cass anyway, mainly because I was curious to see what someone having a nervous breakdown would look like. Actually, Cass looked remarkably well for someone on Invalidity Benefit and was wearing a new poodle-type jersey.

'All right?' I said.

'I've had a nervous breakdown, remember?'

'Right. How's it going?'

'It's really heavy, actually,' she said, sipping some foul herbal tea. 'E's re-wired my brain, you know. The doc's trying to get me referred to a top E specialist in Notting Hill Gate. Apparently I've got all the classic symptoms of E syndrome: lethargy, panic attacks, feeling like you're going mad, hopelessness.'

'But you've always been like that.'

'Thanks a lot,' she said, and started crying. 'You don't know what it's been like. I've had to give up college.' Cassie had never been to college even when she was there. 'I can't do anything.' Cassie never had done anything. 'You just wait. All that E's totally fucked us up.'

'But we always were fucked up.'

At this point Cass became hysterical and asked me to leave. Driving home, I felt a bit bad. I guess I was jealous of Cassie. I'd put in the work (drug abuse, artiness, hopeless relationships), I'd done the background reading (*The Dice Man*, *Trainspotting*, *Naked Lunch*). By rights, her nervous breakdown was mine.

In the end, Lilly agreed to go to the funeral with me. She even treated me to dinner the evening before the service, despite the fact she'd just been sacked again. Lil was having trouble continuing working whilst pursuing her new career as an eco-warrior. She'd just returned from some road protest where she'd dressed as a pantomine cow and hung from trees.

'I remember how it was when none of my friends went to Mum's funeral,' she said, stroking her newly shaven head.

'Yeah.' I felt like there was a limit to the amount of guilt even I could take.

Sadly, Lilly was fooled by my claim that I needed to be alone and after dinner I took a cab back by myself. By accident, I hazarded upon an illegal kebab shop and somehow ended up buying three bottles of wine and sixty cigarettes.

I stayed up all night, getting drunker and drunker whilst composing a dance entitled *No-one Understands*. In between stumbles, I occasionally passed out and then woke up to drink more. Daylight arrived and I vaguely heard my phone ringing and my answerphone recording increasingly desperate-sounding messages. I was sick. That horrendous vomiting – kneeling over the lavatory, contorted with pain, begging God to kill you. Then the doorbell started ringing. I ran my face under the tap. I tried hiding beneath the duvet and playing hip-hop. The bell wouldn't stop. I clambered into a T-shirt and somehow made it downstairs.

'Tara!' said Lilly breathlessly as I opened the door. 'It's twelve. I've been ringing for ages. We've missed—'

I did an enormous burp. 'I'm bored of funerals,' I said, and walked away. Lilly followed me inside. I expected her to start screaming at me but instead she ran me a bath. As I lay, comatose, in the water, I listened to Lilly's muffled whispers. 'She's in no state . . . Jinty, I know, I'm sorry . . . you should see it here . . .'

I staggered out of the bath, left Lilly emptying ashtrays and passed out.

Lil drove me down to Sussex that evening. I lay in the back of the car groaning whilst she chatted about taking her driving test. By the time we arrived, it was pitch-black and raining. Jinty opened the door.

'Lilly,' she said, hugging Lilly. She ignored me and I followed the two of them into the kitchen.

'Where's Ma?' I asked, lighting a fag.

'Do you have to smoke?' Jinty snapped. 'She's in bed, actually. It's been a tiring and distressing day for those of us that could be bothered to make Pa's funeral.'

'She's drunk, then?'

'You can bloody talk . . . *How could you not come?*' Jinty started crying and sat down at the table.

'I don't know,' I admitted, looking around the kitchen. I

couldn't seem to recognize it. 'I honestly did intend to come, but . . .'

'You *intended* to come? Like you always intend to send me a birthday card but I never actually receive one? It's not what you intend to do, it's what you actually *do* do.'

'Don't fucking lecture me, I—'

'Why don't you sit down, Tara?' interrupted Lilly. 'I'll make us all some tea.'

I looked at Jinty, red-faced and still crying. I sat down opposite her, my body collapsing into a chair. She stared at me, shaking her head. 'Come on Jinty . . .' I wished beyond anything that I'd never come back. 'What was the point of me being there?'

'He was our father.'

'Christ, Jinty, he sexually abused you.'

'You only remember the bad times.'

'He was a cunt.'

'Don't say that word.' Jinty wiped her nose on her sleeve. 'He made mistakes. He was a human being.'

'He was a cunt. I forgive nothing.'

For some reason an image of the Fred West children flashed through my mind. I'd seen an interview on telly with two of his kids. Knowing all the appalling crimes their father had committed, accepting all the awful things he'd done to them, they still said that they loved him. He was their father.

'I want to go to bed,' I said.

We had tea and went upstairs. Lilly was given a bedroom and I started to go up to my old room but the hall light didn't work. My courage deserted me.

'Jinty,' I whispered five minutes later, knocking on my sister's door.

'Go away.'

'I can't. The hall light's broken.'

'You're not *still* afraid of the dark?' There was a sigh and the sound of a duvet being thrown off. Jinty came out into the hall, rubbing her eyes. 'OK, let's go.'

We went upstairs and I opened my old door and switched on the light. There was a bed, a cupboard and a chest of drawers. Every trace of me had been eliminated. The only signs of my presence were the tiny splattered bare patches on the wall from where Blu-tack had been removed.

'Maybe I'll sleep in Ama's room.'

Three years was a long time. It was only normal that they'd clean out my room. We went next door.

'Oh God,' I said, switching on Ama's light.

The room was exactly the same as when Ama had left Sussex and gone down to London to live with me: out-of-date posters on the wall and discarded make-up lying on a table. I had assumed, when I'd visited home for the last time for Ama's funeral, that my parents were simply too distressed to clear out her possessions. Instead, they had turned Ama's bedroom into some kind of grotesque shrine.

'God, that woman's sickness knows no bounds,' I said.

'It wasn't Ma, you know,' said Jinty. 'Even she wanted to clean the stuff out but Pa wouldn't let her. He liked to sit in here.'

'Pa? Liked to sit in here?'

'Yes. I could hear him going up the stairs at night. He used to keep a copy of *Jane Eyre* under the duvet.'

'Daddy sat in my dead sister's bedroom reading *Jane Eyre*? Why didn't you tell me?'

'You never wanted to know anything.'

I looked at the room. I wondered if anyone had changed

the sheets since Ama had died; if they still smelt of her. Don't be stupid.

'Jinty, I . . . I can't remember her.'

Jinty took my arm. 'You can sleep on the floor in my room.'

I dreamt of hunting. When Pa and I used to hunt together. He'd taken me out on a leading-rein when I was four. I'd never been like the other little girls at the back, plodding politely on their pony-club hacks. I rode fifteen-handers by the time I was seven.

'I can't do it,' I'd say. And before I knew it Pa would have given the horse a belt and I'd be over the other side of the fence. And if I fell off he'd hold my horse for me and I'd try not to cry with the shock.

'Yes, yes, marvellous, darling.' Even then I'd known that Ma wasn't terribly interested in Pa's and my hunting exploits. And Ama secretly thought hunting was cruel and longed to be one of the fearsome antis. If I mistreated my horses, forgot a feed or failed to notice some slight lameness, Pa would beat me. But I understood.

I felt rather chirpy the next morning, mainly because I didn't have a hangover. The house was still quiet and I went for a wander outside, sniffing the damp dew. In the daylight, the grounds looked awful: overgrown yet bare, uncared for. The stable-block had collapsed and weeds grew through the concrete. I went back inside.

'Tara, darling!' exclaimed Ma when I walked into the kitchen. I noticed there was damp all over one of the walls. 'You couldn't come yesterday?'

'No, you see, I – I had a car accident.'

'Darling! You're all right?'

For one ghastly moment I thought Ma was going to hug me. 'Oh, yes. Just superficial wounds, you know. Boring.'

Ma smiled and attempted to plug in the kettle. She had terrible shakes. I noted her lipstick and thought of the effort she must have made to apply it. 'What are you going to do today?' she asked, desperate to distract me from her inability to operate the on-off switch on the kettle.

'Oh, my friend Lilly drove me down so maybe we'll go to the cemetery together.'

'Marvellous,' said Ma, giving up with the kettle. 'Shall we have fruit juice rather than tea? I'm on a rather wonderful new health kick.'

Lilly drove me down to our church. I wished I had flowers or something. Pa's grave was all new and muddy and covered in fresh blooms. Beside it, Ama's plot was invisible.

'Is that your sister's grave?' asked Lilly quietly as I peered at the headstone. 'Jinty's mentioned her.'

'You know that suicides couldn't even be buried in church land until recently?' I said after a pause.

'I had to arrange Mum's funeral on the state.' Lilly crouched down on the grass. 'Why did your sister kill herself?'

I shrugged my shoulders. 'She left a note for me: *Sorry. Donate any organs.* I don't really know. I had a row with my parents after the funeral and they called me a murderer. I took all the empty bottles of pills to the hospital.'

'So?'

'They were my pills. And I was a cunt to her.'

Ama had been following in the family footsteps and had just dropped out of uni when she came to stay with me. She'd also just been chucked by her boyfriend: a retard with all the personality of a cabbage. The idea was that Ama would get a job and sort her life out. Instead, she just hung around my flat watching TV and reading psycho-babble books like *Be Your Own Best Friend* and *You MUST Relax*. I hated the way she changed for bed in front of me; I didn't want to see her scars.

'You should have come out with me and Rupert. We went to the worst party.'

'Why should I want to go to the worst party?' Ama wasn't being sarcastic, she was genuinely intrigued.

'It was a laugh.'

I went and changed in the loo.

'All right.' Ama looked nervously up at me when I returned. 'Your . . . there's blood all over your face.'

'I need a tranq. D'you want one?' I popped a few Diazapans and then found some tissue to do a bit of vague nasal-area wiping. 'Guess what? I signed on with another doctor today. I want you to start keeping a list of all the names I use.'

'OK. Actually, could I have a pill?' Ama smiled sheepishly. 'I'm a bit nervous as I think I've got a job, you know.'

'Really?'

'Yes. I saw a card in the window of a newsagent's advertising for an old lady's companion.'

'Oh God, it would be like that film *Airplane*, with the old woman hanging herself whilst you go on about your problems.' Ama, always tiny and fragile, looked mortified. 'Sorry. So what did she say?'

'Well, I haven't actually called but I'm sure I could get it.'

'Ama, *honestly*.'

'But I was busy today!' She bowed her head. 'I saw a shrink.'

'I don't want to know.' I switched on the radio.

'Could you possibly turn it down a little?' she pleaded.

'No I fucking couldn't.'

I had to keep the radio loud at night in order to muffle the sound of Ama's sobbing.

I looked at Lilly peering at Ama's headstone and I had the most awful feeling: I wished Lilly was dead and my sister was alive. When Ama had been in hospital, I'd tried to make deals with God: give me Ama back and I'll never take drugs again. Maybe I'll become a nun. I could kill both our parents. I'd even give you money.

'Do you believe in heaven?' asked Lilly, looking up at me.

'Oh let's go, I'm cold.'

Ama had been the only one who remembered. Pa had run some sort of investment firm and it had collapsed. In the process of trying to save the company, we'd sold the Fulham house, moved permanently to the country and Pa had suffered his first heart attack. He'd tried to return to work but had developed chronic angina. Ma had gone away for the summer 'to rest' (remembering Pa's comments, like, 'You need to dry out, you stupid bitch,' implied that possibly a treatment centre may have been involved). Jinty was sent to London to stay with a friend.

Ama and I stayed home that summer.

Pa, never without a hip flask, reverted back to his old army days. Two nannies left within a week. Daddy cited our 'indiscipline'.

'I'm going to make men of you,' he said to me, now ten, and Ama, seven. 'The trouble with this country is that it's gone soft. Well, the rot stops here.'

'Yes, sir.'

'At ease.'

Ama and I would then salute Daddy and turn round on our right heels.

The summer developed a pattern. Uniform and mess inspection before breakfast. Marching and then a strategy lecture. Building the bomb shelter in the orchard. Target practice until it was reluctantly abandoned after Ama and I consistently failed to be able to hold a twelve bore. At Ease (Pa had an angina attack and we ate cornflakes). Comradeship exercises (I'd be forced to fling myself off high walls and trust Pa to catch me. Sometimes he would step aside and say, 'Rule Number One: never trust anyone'). Survival Techniques (attempting to catch and skin unwilling rabbits. Pa had eventually to buy some from a pet shop. I killed one but Ama fainted before she could skin it). Visiting butchers' shops ('When you kill, you'll see bones, gristle, blood. Examine this lamb carefully'). Rule Infringement Punishments: Pa makes us choose which area of our body we wish to be burnt with a hot iron. *Alert!* Last one to drop to the floor (and Pa could scream *Alert!* at any time of the day: during breakfast, fitness training, car journeys) gets a beating.

Ma returns. She sees me in the bath and goes quiet. Daddy goes to hospital, and comes back moving in slow motion, his eyes won't focus. He asks us if we're still studying our maps; maps with a suspicious amount of pink due to being a century old. Jinty comes home and is bounced slowly on Pa's knee: 'My slender lovely.' We're still beaten but it's OK now. Off to board. If anyone asks, we've had a lot of riding accidents. But I'd never let anyone see my body. I was too ashamed.

When Lilly and I returned from the cemetery that afternoon, Ma had gone for a siesta (i.e. already paralytic) and Jinty was sitting in Pa's old study. She was staring out of the window and the hazy afternoon light made her look kind of sad. Lilly and she hugged and started crying. I felt a bit left out.

'I answered the phone this afternoon,' said Jinty, wiping her snotty nose with a jersey sleeve. 'I spoke to a bank manager.'

'Bad mistake.'

'They're thinking of repossessing. Everything's mortaged about six times . . .'

'. . . I was wondering if I'd been left anything in the will,' I said. There was a photo of Ama and me on Pa's desk. 'Can you inherit debts?'

'I asked that and actually you can't. And the Citizens Advice Bureau called. They wanted to say thanks for Pa giving loads of financial advice to poor people.'

'That man just gave, gave, gave.'

'There were people from Pa's *school* there yesterday. They all said how decent and honourable he'd been.'

'Funny, I didn't see them around when we went bankrupt.'

Jinty shrugged. 'Lucinda called for you. She said that she'd really intended to come to the funeral but she was ill or something.'

'She always fucking *intends* . . .'

Jinty raised one of her perfectly plucked eyebrows. 'I know.'

Lilly drove me back to London. I wanted to go home but she refused to trust me.

'Ewan's in Wales, you can sleep with me. And anyway there's something I want to show you.' I tried to interrogate Lil on the nature of her surprise but she insisted I wait. I wondered if it had something to do with bondage. Falling out of the car, I was hit by a terrible kind of weariness and barely made it up to her room.

'I know how you feel,' she said to me as I collapsed on her bed. She sat down beside me and tried to take my hand. I was reminded of when I'd been going out with Rupert and he'd attempted to hold my hand in the street. 'I don't do hands,' I'd snapped.

'You've no idea how I feel,' I sighed.

'Check this. I've never told anyone before.'

And strong, sexy, big-boobed Lilly stood on a chair in front of her wardrobe and took some books and papers from off the top.

'What?' I asked, when she threw them down at me.

'Just look.'

The books were mainly medical dictionaries, yet another copy of Louise L. Hay's *You Can Heal Your Life* and loads of pension and health plan forms ('The chance of a serious illness may seem remote, but the harsh facts are that one in four men and one in five women contract a serious disease before the age of sixty-five; that's one adult every forty seconds'). There was even a telephone number for talking to someone about terminal illness. I wondered how Lilly, barely able to read, could understand the material.

'Since Mum died . . .' Lilly sighed and sat down on her bed. 'Oh, give me a fag. I'm convinced I've got lung cancer anyway.' She lit up and took a heavy drag. 'There are just so many things that can go wrong with you. I'm amazed I'm still existing at all. I just want a doctor and a surgeon permanently by my side, ready to cut out any cancer that might sprout.'

'But cancer isn't inherited.'

'Wrong. There's a "strong genetic disposition".'

'That doesn't mean you'll get cancer. I don't mean this rudely, but your mother was a smack-head. It stands to reason she'd get ill.'

'You don't understand.' Lilly shook her head. 'She fought

till the end. She wouldn't let go. Even when she was in a coma she fought. The doctor said to me, "Our greatest fear is that we are torturing our patients." I don't want to be tortured.'

'Lilly . . .'

'I can't tell Ewan; I can't tell anyone. I think I'm going mad.'

I moved closer to Lilly and very slowly, very deliberately, put my arm around her. 'We really aren't them, I think,' I said.

'This is going to sound really lame,' said Lilly, 'but would you take a look at this mole on my shoulder?' She pulled her jersey to the side. 'You need to check to see if it's slightly raised or bleeding or too dark or a funny shape or just a bit weird.'

'Looks fine to me.'

'I can take it. Go on, tell me, it's malignant, isn't it? Don't hold back.'

'Lilly,' I said, trying not to laugh, 'it's fine. It's a mole.'

Lilly took another deep drag of her cigarette. 'Don't you ever worry about dying, Tara?'

'No, not really. It's more like I have a fear of life.'

Lilly put her head in her hands. 'I'm pregnant again.'

I remembered Sarah once saying that if us lot had given birth to all the babies we'd conceived, we could have filled several kindergartens.

'I mean, I've always really really tried not to feel sorry for myself, or feel like a victim, but basically I've been sacked, orphaned and gone up the spout in the space of about six months. It all seems like, unfair.'

'I know.'

* * *

I remembered Jinty at Ama's funeral. She'd been crying and saying how terrible it was that Ama would never have children and I'd snapped that this was one of the most fatuous statements I'd ever heard. I'd thought of Sarah's first termination. At first she hadn't even known she was preggers and thought she was just having bad period pains. Then we were at a club one night and she'd collapsed and we'd had to go to the hospital in an ambulance. The doctor told Sarah she had an ectopic pregnancy and was suffering internal bleeding.

'Don't save the baby!' she'd screamed as they'd tried to find a vein to put her drip-needle into.

I remembered watching Sarah going into surgery and feeling that I wanted to cry, but that I'd spent so long trying not to that I didn't know how.

14. Night on Disco Mountain

I sat chain-smoking in Sarah's sitting-room with a phone at
my side, the TV and the stereo on and a knife hidden up one
of my sleeves. My obsession with noise and blocking out any
creaks or groans was such that I'd earlier been forced to drug
Coco who, strangely, had been unable to sleep with *Saturday
Night Fever* blaring out full volume. I couldn't bear silence;
wind disturbing a blade of grass three miles away was enough
to convince me that a serial killer was under the sofa. I'd even
called the Samaritans at one stage. It wasn't that Sarah's new
flat in Battersea was that frightening. I'd been all right at
first, nosing around the pad (she'd moved out of her Ma's
because she required more sexual freedom) and browsing
through her fave book *Ambition*. But then I'd foolishly
filched some of her spliff and turned the TV on. I'd been
doing some dance notation whilst idly viewing *Crimewatch*

when I suddenly saw someone I used to know. He was wanted in connection with a murder. It was funny, I'd barely spoken to him, only seen him a couple of times years before, yet I recognized him instantly. You never forget a drop. My body went ice cold. I always thought that the longer time went on without anyone questioning me, the safer I was. Why should they come back for me after all these years? But I realized then that I'd somehow assumed that because I wasn't in that world any more, it didn't exist; deals were no longer done, plea-bargains no longer accepted. But it was still there and I was still a part of it. I would become safer as the years went by, but I would never be safe.

Trying to fuddle my mind, I smoked and drank more. I worried that the police were watching, that babysitters were always murdered in movies. Sarah was supposed to have 'popped out for a quick drink' with her new personal trainer, Bucky Leo. She'd been wearing one of those backless dresses you can't get a bra under and, due to pregnancy leaving her with tits that looked like two deflated balloons, I'd spent an hour lifting and separating them with Sellotape. And now she was hours late. Maybe she'd just skipped the country. Or been involved in a hideous car crash. Oh God.

At about one o'clock, when I heard the sound of the door being opened, I took no chances and hid behind the sofa.

'Ta . . .' Sarah opened the sitting-room door. 'Sorry I'm late darling, but . . . what the fuck?' I peered up from behind the sofa. It didn't look good: the discarded brandy, the knife in my hand, the overflowing ashtrays, the Rizla, the empty bottle of baby soother. 'I don't fucking believe it, for once in my life I trusted you . . .'

I stood up ('standing' in the wider sense of the word). 'I can explain,' I said, realizing I couldn't.

'You're paralytic! Looking after my child! And—' She saw the baby soother bottle.

'She wouldn't stop crying.' I tried to climb over the sofa but fell flat on my face.

'You didn't . . . not the entire bottle. You're only supposed to give them a couple of teaspoons.' Sarah ran next door and I pulled myself up onto the sofa, putting my head in my hands. I'd killed Coco. Court. Prison. Child killers got hell inside. After a few minutes, Sarah returned looking slightly calmer.

'I think she's all right – no bloody thanks to you.' Sarah sat down opposite me and lit a menthol. 'I was such an idiot to trust you.'

'You didn't trust me,' I said, tears forming in my eyes. 'I was just the only one who'd babysit for you for free.'

'Oh please, don't cry, I can't cope with it. I've just had the most incurably boring night of my life with Bucky Leo and his one amazing brain cell. He even called me a special lady.'

'A no-go, then?'

'Not necessarily. I need to get some action to get me in the swing of things again. And he has one mighty fine body.' Sarah stood up and took off her dress, drunkenly trying to remove the Sellotape. 'Oh sod it,' she said, staggering slightly, 'I'm starving. Let's do some coke.'

Sarah opened her Hoover and pulled out an enormous bag of cocaine. Now half naked, you wouldn't have known she'd just had a baby (apart from the Sellotape and the stretch marks). She'd lost two stone on her radical new nasal diet, the coke provided by her former boyfriend Jonny. Tired of poverty, Sarah had threatened to tell Jonny's father about his son's anal habits. Jonny had countered by threatening to tell everyone that Sarah had been a prosser. But he was too afraid of losing the clubs to risk calling Sarah's bluff. He'd presented her with the entire Chanel No 5 Body Collection to ensure her of his understanding.

'I still can't believe you got away with it,' I said jealously as Sarah started cutting up lines with a Mothercare discount card.

'I know, but what else could I do? Work?' Sarah took a disgusted snort. 'You know what convinced him? I told him I'd tell his father that he got into bed one night and I'd seen spunk running out of his arse.' I had a line and looked up to see Sarah staring critically at my obviously repulsive face. 'Have you thought about fake tan?' There was no doubt: Sarah was back on form. I had an awful feeling that I actually preferred her when she was depressed. When she was together she always made me feel like I had something on my nose.

I woke up convinced that someone was holding a bad party in my head. I breathed out and the disgusting stench of a bottle of brandy and forty fags hit me. Staggering out of Sarah's bed, I fell over onto my bad knee. Straightening up, I saw Sarah lying quietly with Coco in her arms. I supposed Coco must have woken up in the night and Sarah had slipped her into bed. They made a touching, some might say nauseating, sight. I padded into Sarah's bathroom. Even in my hopeless state I noticed that she now had Chanel deodorant. I leafed a toothbrush and started attacking my sewer of a mouth. I thought about having a shower but decided I was too ill and pulled on one of Sarah's pregnancy tracksuits. As I walked into the hall I was confronted by a mirror. I viewed a tiny pale figure enveloped in ridiculously oversized clothing, her bleached brown hair pulled into a shabby bun revealing a plain round face. I ventured closer to the pathetic creature: blackheads on the chin, shadows so dark under the eyes that it looked as if she'd been punched, little crow's feet, the beginnings of frown lines between the eyebrows. This was no spring chicken. I'd lost the 'bounce' I'd once had; the ability to stay up all night and, yeah, not look good in the morning but not look as if I needed emergency medical treatment. I was too old for this.

Arriving late at college, I missed ballet, struggled through contemporary and then collapsed in a hallway, desperate to get some sleep. Just as I had arranged my bag as a pillow, Caroline came up and kicked my thigh.

'Lazybones! Come on, get up and I'll buy you a coffee.'

'Oh.' All I wanted to do was sleep. 'OK.' I got up and followed Caro down the hall. Caro had just returned to college after taking a few terms off because of a back injury and general disillusionment with dance. She was a changed person from the pining, ex-boyfriend-obsessed wimp I'd once known; now she was strutting around college in black polo-necked leotards and pearl earrings. She was just doing the odd class at Laban to get back in shape before she returned for proper after Easter. What disgusted me the most was that after a year off Caro was actually stronger than me. Whilst my knee was now developing a hilarious sea-sick swinging motion and I was being further crippled by extortionate physio bills, Caro could still hold her legs in one-hundred-and-eighty degree extensions for five minutes or so.

'I'm so debauched,' she told me over cappuccinos. 'You know I'm a racist and yet there I was last night, sucking this nigger's cock.'

I idly scrawled 'charmer' in table-grease.

'But, honestly, I've been seeing Luke for six months so I'm *so* bored of his cock.' This was the other change in Caro: she had become a voracious man-eater. 'Have you seen any genital action recently, Tara?'

'I haven't even masturbated since Christmas.'

I supposed that I should have been taking tips from Jinty. She'd recently discovered where her clitoris was after a vaginal session with her counsellor. She told me over the phone that she'd had to self-examine with a mirror. I said I was too depressed to listen but she'd countered that I wasn't depressed, I was *re*pressed. Jinty was now writing poems to her genital area and Pa had become 'irrelevant' to her. The only flaw in her sexual liberation was Ben who, when Jinty told him of her explorations, called her a 'lesbian freak'.

'I couldn't give a toss,' she said. 'Idiot's just jealous because I never have sex with him . . . but really, Tara, you should do a workshop too. You know, Tasmin sends pictures of her vagina on Christmas cards.'

But I still couldn't be persuaded to start practising Sex for One. I supposed I was mainly too drunk or too tired and anyway I was crap at it. Besides, I'd read this book which had said that apparently the Chinese view masturbation as mating with ghosts. So if I wanked I was probably having sex with Dave Hardcore or something.

'I dumped Luke last night,' continued Caro whilst smoothing down her chignon.

'What, seriously?' My roast potatoes and peas arrived and I struggled to eat them without chucking.

'Yeah, it was always the same – let's go Dutch, can you lend me a fiver? A girl needs flowers, treats. You know, he never ever bought me a glass of champagne.'

'Outrageous.'

'I know.' Caro sipped her Diet Coke. 'In fact, Luke's why

I reckon I've put on weight. All that cheap food and poor wine.' This was the one hold I had over Caro: she was fatter than me. Caro yawned. 'I'm bored. Let's go get pissed at mine.'

'But . . .' I was exhausted, hungover, had jazz that afternoon, was totally skint. 'Fuck it.' I gave up on my food and went with Caro to pick up some booze.

I justified my now almost permanent inebriation by the fact that my knee ligaments were shot again. I could barely make it upstairs, let alone do fast jazz routines in class. My growing hysteria obviously necessitated constant drunkenness. How could I be expected to face all this again? But as Caro and I left Thresher I remembered how, after my first operation, I'd used to crip on crutches down the offie for my morning fix. I was never sure if alcohol had been the only thing that had saved me from killing myself during that bleak time, or if the boozing had actually prevented me from getting better. Jinty said my recurring knee problems were my fault and a result of me not loving myself and that I had to let go and stop punishing my body. I'd have been quite willing to go along with this theory, hippieish or not, if it could have somehow allowed me to get better. But I wondered if it was just Jinty's way of turning me into a case history for a self-help book. I supposed that anything would have been an improvement on the total sense of hopelessness I now felt. But I didn't honestly believe that I had any control over my body any more.

Caro and I cavorted for the rest of the day. We quaffed vodka, had backbend contests and slurred passionately about how devoted we were to dance. I did try to make an attempt to stop: about six hours after we'd started our binge, Caro asked me if I wanted another drink and I told her I couldn't face any more vodka.

'I'll mix you a cocktail, then.' She then went into the kitchen and, grinning maniacally, tottered back and handed me a glass.

'You don't fool me,' I slurred. 'That's no "cocktail". That's a glass of vodka with two halves of strawberry in it.' I drank it anyway. It would have been rude not to. Then the two of us decided to explore 'emotional aspects of dance'. I made Caro lie half naked on the floor and let me climb on top of her thighs to prove the 'profound effect of one person standing on another's body'. Caro experimented with a lot of stationary, horizontal 'movements'. Then I fell over whilst deconstructing headstands and started blubbing. Caro said she was tired and wanted to go to bed. Stupefied with booze, I joined Caro, collapsing beside her prostrate, snoring figure.

It had been so long since I'd slept rather than collapsed. I lay in bed with the room spinning slowly round (and thank God slowly, since that meant I wasn't going to puke) wondering what next. The old chronic insomnia – terrible-nightmares-when-I-did-get-fucked-enough-to-pass-out lark was off again. I would wake up at night shaking and covered with sweat, my mouth gasping for a terrified breath. They wouldn't even leave me alone in my sleep.

When I groggily reached consciousness the next morning (having already missed my first class) I noticed that every part of my body seemed to stink of something like embalming fluid. It was just like the smell there'd been in the undertakers when I'd gone to see Ama's body. I pulled on yesterday's leotard, which was covered in still-moist tide-marks of BO. I thought of Jinty saying after we'd watched a programme on alcoholics, 'These people and their sordid lives.' Walking to college with Caro, who was bouncing merrily along doing *petit allegro*, I was silently imploding with an invasion of body snatchers. I could feel Ama in my throat, painfully trying to speak ('I've been reading about Greek gods who are like jealous and rush us towards destruction by forces we can't control,'). Pa in my stomach, sucking me in like a particularly deep contraction ('I've only two pieces of advice for you, Tara: never get married and never have children'). Tim in my groin, forcing my pelvis back.

For when I'd told Caro that I hadn't even masturbated since Christmas, I had perhaps been cheeky with the truth. Not that my fingers ever got beyond reaching for Temazas, but I actually had shagged only a week earlier (and I say shag as it wasn't a fuck or a screw but an awful, grotesque shag). I had shagged Tim.

Tim, one of the nicest boys I knew. Well, the only nice boy I knew. Tim, who had always been willing to take over a shift at the bar that I couldn't do. Tim, who I'd known had always carried a wavering flame for me. Tim, who I got completely pissed with on a Friday night after work and had come back to my place with me. Who had tentatively put an arm around my shoulders and I'd thought, Why not? It wasn't that he was ugly or anything. Gerry always said that we forgot how decent-looking Tim was due to his obsessive self-effacement. But Tim was a mind person. He was always trying to make me go to art galleries with him and I was always advising him to take cold showers and go for ten mile runs in the morning. The sex was humiliation personified; the kind of sex you can't think about without cringing and putting your head in your hands. I was feeling so self-conscious that I actually thought of asking Tim to wear a blindfold. And he was so awfully sensitive ('How is that? It doesn't hurt? Are you sure?') and kept on insisting on stroking my scars in an 'understanding' manner. He tried to cuddle up to me afterwards and I just wanted to scream for him to get the fuck off my body.

'So where do we go from here?' he'd said. I'd attempted being casual and smiled and ruffled his hair. I didn't sleep and ran away to college at six that morning, leaving a note saying, *Cheers!!!! See you around!* I forgot it was Saturday. After mooching by the Thames for ages, I returned home, praying Tim wouldn't be there. He wasn't. There was no note except the one I'd left, but Tim had made the bed. I'd never made my bed in my life, assuming that no more could be asked from me than clean sheets. The sight of the neatly placed duvet and plumped pillows sort of broke my heart. I cowered in late for work that evening, dreading some kind of fornication inquisition, but Tim never mentioned our night of passionlessness, except to say, 'I know, relax.'

He wouldn't talk to me now and I missed him. I'd told no-one about our tryst. Everyone else would think it funny but it hadn't been, really.

Realizing that I was still drunk from the night before, it was with a heavy heart that I walked into Tonty's advanced ballet class after popping some Duromine in the loos. The hangovers now meant that it was impossible for me to dance without taking speed (which I got down the Weight Off! slimming clinic with Sarah). Tonty, who always taught in tight leather trousers, spent class prancing spitefully around insulting everyone whilst giving fiendishly difficult combinations to distract us from our 'drab and miserable lives'. I gripped the *barre* and tried to force my battered body into first position. I was in so much pain in so many forms that I could barely differentiate between my increasingly epic hangover, last night's sordid cuts and bruises, a cheeky bunion on my left foot and a slight but promisingly serious swelling on my right hip. Of course, there was no denying the special torment that was my right knee. It wasn't that the knee was actually too physically painful – I could deal with that – but it was more that I was horribly conscious of the damage being done every time my knee started to give way on pliés, sub-luxed in *tendus* and flirted with dislocation on *rondes de jambes*. By *frappés*, it was so swollen I was having problems bending my leg at all.

'Be careful not to overtire yourself, Tara,' Tonty quipped hilariously as I sat down beside the piano. I knew I should get some ice to help ease the swelling but it was too much effort. I couldn't believe it was happening all over again and, smelling the alcohol steaming off me, that I'd been idiotic enough to get drunk the night before. I had no control and no self-control. Involuntary tears of pain, hungoverness and self-pity began to drip down my face. I turned and, trying to distract myself from myself, started reading *Exchanges: Life After Dance*. After class, I walked out of the studio and found a note for me on the noticeboard. My head of year wanted to see me 'urgently' to 'discuss' my non-attendance at class and my scholarship. Not again. I seemed to lurch from crisis to disaster to nightmare scenario. Where were the fun bits? When did I make the great breakthrough they always had in the movies?

'Stand on your head, angel,' said Tonty as I passed him in the corridor.

I went back to the dustbin I called home and, not even bothering to take my clothes off, lay down for a couple of hours before going to physio. Debbie greeted me like a long-lost enemy.

'Tara. Undress over there, OK?' As I took my now obscenely festering tights off, it struck me that I'd probably stripped more for the medical profession than I had for sex.

Debbie examined my absurd right leg and, knowing how much I must have smelt, I felt totally humiliated. Debbie sighed. I knew a sigh was a bad sign at physio.

'What exams do you have next term?'

'Ballet, contemporary, jazz, dance history.'

'One theoretical then!' she said brightly.

I tried desperately not to cry as Debbie told me to put my clothes back on and that we 'had to talk'.

'It's not working, is it, Tara?'

I looked down at the floor and bit my lower lip, trying to create some more pain to distract me from all the other pain.

'I think you need to try something else.'

I could feel the snot building up in my nose.

'I hear "Butcher" Harvey is doing some fascinating things with ligaments.'

All I could think was, All my worst fears have happened.

'Of course, there's teaching.'

I remembered Cassie once saying that if there was a door marked 'death', she'd walk through it. It was all the effort of suicide that she couldn't be bothered with.

'Sonia – you know, the morning physio – has read this rather inspiring book. She thought it might help our hopeless, I mean difficult, cases. It's by Louise L. . . . L. . . .'

'Louise L. Hay, *You Can Heal Your Life*. I've read it.'

Somehow, I made it into work that evening. I dragged my stool to the entrance and dragged my body onto the stool. All I wanted to do was to go home and get into bed (which was funny as since my first operation I'd always viewed bed as a torture chamber). I suppose it was because being door-chick was That Bad, actually worse than working the bar (which Kevin refused to let me return to). Punters would see me sitting down, drinking and smoking, and go, 'I'd love your job, love!' And I'd have to restrain myself from violence. Oh, I had it all as door-chick: fabulous wages, short, convenient hours, a stimulating environment, respect from management. A job with prospects, a job with a future. In fact the only good thing about chicking at the Escape was that I actually had a perverse form of job security. There were few people around with the lack of self-respect and capacity for boredom that I possessed. I sometimes tried to shame myself out of job-hatred by thinking about unemployed people in the North, but I just ended up envying them. To add to the fun, I worked with a bouncer, Traces (so named because he'd once been done for drink driving and they'd tested him for drugs and found traces of every narcotic substance known to man in his blood) who was probably the biggest cunt I'd ever met. Sexist, racist, homophobic, he wouldn't even admit mixed-race people, 'Cos they'd only be beaten up. By me.' At first, Traces and I had traded sexual secrets in our more tedious moments. The trouble was that all moments on the door were tedious and within two nights we'd out-perved each other. Now we never spoke and made no pretence of getting on.

'Fuck off,' he'd say to me when he arrived.

'Your mother sucks cocks to support her crack habit,' I'd reply.

I no longer even bothered to jest off Traces' 'jovial' remarks to the customers. Now when he said, 'You two are all right. The fat one pays double,' I'd just shrug and agree.

Besides, it wasn't as if we were running a popular venue. Two people waiting for a cab outside was viewed as a queue. The criteria for entry (besides not being a 'sooty') were simple: the ability to pay and the ability to walk. And even these basic prerequisites were sometimes waived ('No money?

OK, I'll ave the ring and the watch,' or, 'Just carry im in, mate').

As I was whiling away my hours biting off all the skin around my nails, Seb, my merchant-banker-recovering-alcoholic friend, turned up at the door. He was carrying five bottles of Kaliber, chain-smoking Silk Cut Ultra Low and twitching in an insane manner. Seb and I had been quite pally recently. Bankrupt, I'd been reduced to going round his flat for dinner a couple of evenings a week. Seb never cooked due to being rich, so we always got the 'dine-in' service. I'd tell Seb to order me a baked potato and, miraculously, fried chicken and mayonnaise and chips would arrive. Seb had become obsessed with making everyone else as porky as himself since putting on two stone as a result of his Kaliber habit. Seb's flat was literally stacked with alcohol-free lager. Full and empty crates lay everywhere. He was even having it for breakfast.

'But at least I'm not doing shots for breakfast,' he'd said. 'I guess that's better, isn't it? I shouldn't worry but I think more about alcohol now than I did when I was drinking.'

I kissed Seb and sighed inwardly, resigning myself to another of his two-hour monologues about his not-drinking problem.

'Deutschland,' he said, opening a can.

'Sit here and watch the door for me,' I said quickly, seeing that Traces was being distracted by chatting up some disco-doggie. I limped downstairs to get a vodka and cranberry off Gerry. I'd read that cranberry was good for the kidneys so now I always drank it with vodders.

'Cheers,' I said to Gerry as she sneakily smoked a spliff under the counter. 'You all right?'

'I think I'm going mad,' Gerry sighed. Light from the bar hit her tired face and revealed teeth yellowing from puffing.

'It's like I go through this pain barrier every three months thinking, I can't go in, I can't stand it no more, but I do come in, I do stand it. I just don't know how much longer I can work here without totally losing it.'

I saw Kevin emerging through the back door and slunk quickly upstairs. Outside, there seemed to be some sort of ruck developing over someone wanting to bring in a kebab.

'Now, I'm not a violent man, Traces was saying to the boy with the doner. I backed away from the window, determined not to witness the act of unimaginable savagery that always followed this statement.

After the ambulance left and Traces was taken away to be interviewed by the police, I emerged from the stock-room to find Seb boring someone.

'It's not that I want to drink. I don't want to drink. But I do . . . Tara, where've you been?' The punter saw his chance and made a lucky escape. 'Your manager's been looking everywhere for you. There's been trouble. Your doorman had to hit someone who tried to stab him.' I hoped that Traces had planted the knife unsuccessfully this time. 'He said that this chap was attempting to set up a drugs network in the club.'

'God, that ape has no shame.' Actually it was Traces who controlled the drugs network in the Escape. After only two months on the door, Traces was operating every scam possible and even licensed club bag-thieves.

'Your manager said I could be the doorman for the rest of the evening. What a laugh!'

'Terrific.' Unbelievably, I actually wished Traces was back. If Seb told me one more time about his unrequited love for alcohol, I couldn't be held responsible for my actions. 'What the hell are you doing here anyway?' I snapped, finding politeness increasingly difficult.

'I couldn't relax so I went walking round the Edgware Road and you'll never guess what, but I met this chap from school.'

'Fascinating.'

'We got talking and it turned out that he's become a drug dealer. I bought four ecstasy tablets off him and he gave me free guest passes to a club called Disco Mountain.'

'But Seb, you don't take E.'

'Exactly. I think it's about time I did. I can't go on with this Kaliber obsession. I've had to hire a skip for the crates and I'm up to fourteen stone. And ecstasy makes you lose weight, doesn't it? So why don't we go down afterwards?'

'Seb, I'm sure this is a bad idea.'

I'd barely slept for three days and my body felt as if a rhinoceros had been tap dancing on it. Besides, Seb was patently insane; a government health warning waiting to happen. But I hadn't been clubbing or done disco pills since the last New Year's Eve disaster. I deserved some fun. It would be an act of madness. Maybe just this once. No, Seb was bound to crack up and I looked like a tramp . . .

Seb and I arrived outside Disco Mountain. I left my stuff in his car and we walked remarkably slowly to the entrance, hideously conscious of our shameful appearances. Ambling to the door, I felt like the whole queue was ogling me and wondered how such ugliness was possible in an age of plastic surgery. Luckily, we were sorted with our guest passes and we slumped in alongside the glam youngsters. I wasted no time and robbed two pills off Seb.

'It's the only way forward,' I said as I washed them down with a stray drink I'd found.

'I won't go mad and get brain damaged, will I?' asked Seb, looking at his E. 'I couldn't cope with being a vegetable, no way.' I shrugged my shoulders and Seb closed his eyes and put the pill in his mouth. I felt guilty that I was leading Seb astray. But then he'd been boring me for weeks; I was owed, big time. And it wasn't as if I was offered free E often. Well, ever, actually. And I wanted, just once, to go out and have a reasonable night. It didn't even have to be good, just a change from the normal going-home-and-wanting-to-shoot-myself variety would do.

The two of us slunk into a corner and vaguely attempted to dance. Repetitive beats for repetitive lives; the BPM was so fast that people seemed to be moving in slow motion. I became increasingly convinced that the entire club was laughing at me and eventually freaked and ran away to the Ladies'. I sat on the lav for a while and took a look at my knee, which was now chronically swollen. After having a little cry I splashed my face with cold water. I mooched back to the corner but Seb wasn't there, so starting to come up, I bopped on my own for a while. After about twenty minutes, he still didn't appear. I spent the next hour trying to find him, even getting someone to call out his name in the Men's for me. There was no way he was still in the club. The fucker had pissed off and my keys and money were in his car. I tried to calm down. He'd probably gone fruity and nipped home in a fit of panic. He'd be back when he realized that he had my things. Half an hour later, Seb still hadn't returned. I was starting to freak and could smell a disgusting scared stench oozing out of my armpits. I got some change off a bloke after telling him I needed to call a friend who had disappeared. He looked at me patronizingly as if to say, 'I can see why.' Seb's mobile was switched off and his answerphone was on at home. I left a hysterical message begging him to come and get me.

Resigning myself to waiting, I sat down on a bench and

sipped a stolen drink. I was worn out with worrying and just hoped I wouldn't run out of fags. My smoking problem was as ridiculous as ever, although not quite as bad as Lucinda's fagging, which was giving her permanent bronchitis. And Cindy had just got yet another part with a physical theatre company playing yet another lesbian.

'Everyone thinks I'm so lucky,' she'd said miserably to me a week before. 'They're all like, "What fun!" The thing no-one understands is that I never enjoy myself.'

As I looked around Disco Mountain, I knew exactly what Lucinda had meant. I didn't belong amongst these happy young things. I too had lost the ability to have fun. If I wasn't in a panic or a crisis, all I could feel was a blank nothingness. All the old ways I'd used to escape – drink, drugs, dance – didn't work any more. The only thing I was getting from the E was a vague sense of boredom.

'I saw a counsellor yesterday,' Cindy had told me. 'I was going on about my starving and bingeing and all, and she just said to me, "Why don't you eat?" And you know what? I didn't have a clue.'

I sat alone in the club and thought, Why do I still dance? Force of habit, maybe. And that if I gave up I'd have to admit how long I'd spent chasing nothing. I couldn't even remember why I'd started. Enjoyment? Something to do? It didn't really matter now.

'I fool myself I have choices,' Lucinda had said, 'but no-one would choose to live like me.'

An hour later, Seb still hadn't shown. I had visions of yet another suicide tragedy wrecking my already wrecked life. I split the club and, despite having no money, grabbed a cab. I decided to head to Sarah's as, due to her blackmailing, she was the most likely person I knew to have cash. Luckily, she was up and agreed to pay the driver. She was in the middle of emptying a bottle of Bacardi after just settling Coco for the third time that night.

'You're fucking lucky you didn't wake her,' Sarah said as she poured me a mug of rum, 'as then I'd have been forced to kill you. Do you want a line, darling?'

I was starting to get those horrible neurotic E-twitches and doubted that I'd be able to sleep again that decade. 'OK.'

We did some shots and fairly enormous lines. Then, between my attempts to contact Seb and Sarah's constant self-obsessed interruptions, I explained about my night at Disco Mountain.

'I've killed him,' I said finally. 'There's no way Seb couldn't have got home by now. He could've checked the club three times over and then popped down to Brighton and he'd still be back. And he can't not hear his answerphone; it's right by his bed.'

'Couldn't he be at a friend's?'

'Seb's lost his few friends, since giving up drinking.'

'Maybe he's gone on a bender then?'

'He's on Antabuse. If he's gone on a bender, he'll be in Casualty. Oh God, I can't deal with another death.' Trying to hold down my panic and my shoulders (which were now ear-level) I made the slow and agonizing round of calls to police stations and hospitals. No sign.

'Oh Jesus, Jesus,' I groaned. 'I can't deal with this. Seb's such a bastard. Even if he did freak, he shouldn't have left me. But I can't say that. Maybe he's admitted himself to a psychiatric unit. Oh God, I'll have to call all the loony bins.'

'No fucking way.' Coco had woken up during my hour of telephoning and Sarah wanted to call Crisis. 'Tara, you're completely bloody paranoid. I've had enough.'

'But my keys are in his car! You can't throw me onto the streets, you know I'm afraid of the dark!'

'Christ, you're such a fucking drama queen.' Sarah got up to boil a bottle for Coco. 'Wait a sec, you did check his car, didn't you?'

'Well, no, but why would he be there?'

'Maybe he left the club and waited for you in the car and then fell asleep.'

'But he'd have left a message at the door.'

'Maybe he was thrown out or something.'

'But . . .' Oh God. I remembered. Disco Mountain was notorious for having bouncers who had an amusing habit of storming the blokes' lavs and jumping over the partitions to check no funny business was going on. Maybe Seb had been taking the other E or he'd been performing some sordid gay sex act . . . Sarah gave me some money, advised me to see a psychiatrist, and I clambered into another cab.

Seb was lying in the back of his BMW, curled up into a ball with his thumb in his mouth. I banged on the windows and kicked the doors with more force than was perhaps strictly necessary. Seb awoke with a start, screamed he knew nothing and then saw me and sulkily leant over and opened the front passenger door.

'I thought you were dead, you cunt!' I shouted, attempting to deck him.

'Enough, woman,' he said, shaking me off and lying down again. 'I've been waiting for you for—' He looked at his watch. 'For five agonizing hours. Were the "tunes" just too good for you to actually even bother to come out and investigate my disappearance? My heart's been racing. I thought I was having a stroke at one point.'

'Well why the fuck didn't you tell me you were leaving?'

'It's pretty hard to leave messages when two meatheads are slapping you around and attempting to throw you in front of the next passing vehicle. They caught me as I was defecating and taking a glance at the other pill. Just taking a glance! So I've been lying here waiting for you to come back to the car. Two sets of Her Majesty's finest have tried to arrest me for sitting in my own BMW.'

I suddenly felt totally exhausted and couldn't be bothered any more. Was I insanely paranoid or had my fears been justifiable? Seb was a suicide risk and general loony but maybe I was more loony than him. I lay down on the front seats, staring at the car ceiling. Maybe I'd been mad all along but no-one had told me. I remembered Ama's and my childhood pact: 'If I go mad, kill me,' Ama had said. 'I'll be grateful, honestly.'

'And you'll do the same for me?'

'I'll shoot you with Pa's twelve bore and then say he did it.'

I hadn't noticed that Ama had lost it when she'd been living with me but then I'd been very self-obsessed. But maybe she hadn't lost it, maybe she'd killed herself because it was the sensible thing to do. Things weren't going to get any better, why fuck around?

I couldn't think of anything else to do but smoke. I sat back in the car seat and lit my God-don't-think-about-it fag of the evening.

'I'm sure there's something symbolic in this disaster,' I said eventually, running my fingers through my greasy hair, 'but I can't think what.'

'Was the club any good?' Seb asked, sitting up.

'I don't know. I guess it could have been.'

'We could try again.'

'No, I give up. I admit it, I'm totally beaten. I'm pretty sure I'm having a nervous breakdown like Cassie.'

'I thought you did ecstasy all the time? How can you be such a mess on two?'

'E syndrome, probably. My brain's been re-wired, I think.'
I was about to take a peak in the rear-view mirror when I
realized the inherent suicide danger in this action. 'How was
your disco pill? Did you have a bad time?'

'No, it was . . . enlightening, actually – in between police
interruptions. I lay in the back listening to a gay modern
opera tape.' Seb smiled in a naughty way. 'I thought about
Jem.'

'Oh God.' Jem: dancer, pornographer, wanker. Yet with
the mention of his name I found myself involuntarily quoting
one of his lines: 'I've been betrayed by dance,' I said. 'It's
ruined my life. Class just teaches me what I can't do. And all
E's ever taught me is what I was missing in life. What's the
point of loving complete strangers when you're completely
alone? And they've both fucked my body.'

'Come on, Tara,' said Seb, patting my shoulder, 'you've got
to be positive. Hey, aren't there disabled dance groups?' The
sight of the ruddy-complexioned, rotund Seb giving me E
talk made me want to throw.

'You don't understand.' I remembered when I'd been living
with Ama and she'd claimed that I only had two sentences of
conversation: 'You don't understand,' and, 'You're wrong.'

'I know you haven't got any qualifications or any semblance
of intellectual achievement,' Seb continued, 'but there are
other things you can do.'

'You're wrong. I can't do anything else. Anyway, it's like
that crap old Euro-screamer, you know, if I can't have you, I
don't want nobody.'

'You and your disco philosophy . . .' Seb grinned. 'I do love
you, you know Ta.'

'Oh please, no.'

*　　*　　*

Were there no limits to my torments? Seb climbed over the seat and drove me home. He said taking the E had opened his mind. He knew he was gay now. Whilst lying in the car he'd even thought about taking up yoga and possibly doing some meditation sessions. Swimming with dolphins was an option. Things were going to be different now. He didn't need booze or extreme right-wing politics. He needed love. I needed a gun. I couldn't take any more shit. My E days were over, my dancing was finished. I clawed my way out of a disgusting 'hugging session' with Seb and went up to my flat. There was no fucking way I wasn't going to sleep. I took six Temazas with some of the 'emergency' vodka I kept under my bed and then smoked a spliff. I could feel the drugs fighting in my body: coke and E keeping me up, booze and nicotine making me feel sick and spliff and sleeping pills trying to take me down. I added some Co-Proximal to the equation and thought the battle was won when I rapidly began to coma-out on the floor. The next thing I knew, I felt my body convulsing and vomit violently projecting out of my mouth. I rolled over onto my front and felt carpet and sick against my face. I had been lying on my back. I knew I was very lucky not to have choked on my puke and died, but all I could think was that I couldn't even take an accidental overdose in an interesting way.

15. Cars, Drugs and Babies

I felt like I was running a battered women's refuge. Barely an evening went by without Lilly turning up on my doorstep wearing tatty cardigans and rainbow-coloured facial markings.

'He's done it this time,' she'd say, staggering up the stairs whilst swigging from a plastic bottle of cider. 'I'll take him for everything he's got.'

'But he hasn't got anything,' I'd say, nervously closing my flat door. Ewan was still unemployed and spent all his time boozing, beating up Lilly or going down the Thames and spouting on about how much he missed the sea.

'Yeah, but you see he does have . . . spirituality. You see, no-one knows what Ewan's really like. He talks to me about small fish and the stars at night.' This didn't seem to prevent Ewan from decking Lilly when she was pregnant. 'Is the offie still open? I've got really bad stomach pains and I've almost finished the bottle.'

I'd then troop back to the off licence and pick us up some more cheap cider. I did worry that it couldn't be healthy for Lilly to drink so much in her condition, but I wasn't about to try and stop her. Let's face it, I couldn't even stop myself.

It was sad to see how quickly Lilly's relationship had developed into farce. Handsome, Welsh Ewan, who'd given up everything he had (which even then was admittedly not very much) to come to London to be with his loved one. Who used to hug Lilly in pubs and scream, 'I love this woman, me!' They'd been so happy, fucking, taking trips, living in squalor. But then Lilly had become an eco-warrior, she'd been sacked again and found out she was pregnant. She got another pub job. Ewan started drinking heavily and would lurk around the bar haranguing any customers who dared to speak to or even look at Lilly. She got the shove after Ewan snooker-cued a bloke for winking at her. With no money and nothing to do, they started rucking. I soon got used to turning up at Lilly's to find her door kicked in, the windows smashed and Lilly's few clothes in shreds. Don't get me wrong, Lilly was no victim – she'd beaten up Peanuts when he dumped her and she wasn't shy with her fists. But even Lilly's strength and height wouldn't help her against a hard, six-foot-two Welshman. And from the stories Lilly told me it was apparent that Ewan wasn't just a drunk, but was actually psychotic. He'd started holding Lilly prisoner in their bedsit, convinced she was having serial affairs (even with *me*). He'd sometimes turn up at my place screaming with rage and threatening to break in. Luckily my neighbours were nosy sods and the police would cart him away before any damage was done. What I found so difficult to understand was why Lilly kept on going back to Ewan. Time and time again she'd swear it was all over, she was never going back, and the next thing I knew she was telephoning me saying she'd worked it out with him and they were trying again. The whole scenario was driving me mad (especially as I was sworn to secrecy) and whenever I heard the doorbell ring with a hysterical sound I'd flirt with pretending to be out. But I always answered in the end. Where else could Lilly go? She had no relatives and had lost most of her squatter friends over the years. I thought of all the things I'd have wanted if I was having a baby – a husband, a house, money, support, some kind of bribe – and pictured Lilly penniless in her bedsit. I supposed it was understandable why Lilly kept going back to Ewan; she didn't really have anything else.

I didn't have much more. I was still struggling back to health after my all-time nadir of the previous term. I'd gone on some new anti-depressants and started weight-training to gain muscle to support my dodgy knee. I'd also had a steroid injection put in the joint. I knew the steroid was likely to make things worse in the long term, but I'd worry about that later. Not that any of this seemed to have done my dancing much good. Tonty had noticed my newly muscled physique and had accused me of going to Paris over Easter and studying at the Quasimodo school of ballet. A choreographer came to college and put me with the dregs in the repertory second-cast chorus. He said I seemed unmotivated in the extreme and that I should seriously question whether I wanted a career in dance. To my surprise, I was unconcerned. The pills I was using seemed to have taken the edge off everything, putting a milky-white film over my life.

Despite my vacuousness, even I could see that matters were escalating between Lilly and Ewan. As Lilly's belly grew larger, so did her bruises. She escaped to my flat one night, not realizing that I'd invited Jinty round to discuss Home

Matters. Jinty had just been telling me that Ma was having to sell the house as it was about to be repossessed. I brought Lilly upstairs. Jinty hadn't seen Lilly for a while and was unable to cover up her shock at Lilly's appearance. I supposed because I saw Lilly so often I hadn't noticed how much she'd deteriorated. It wasn't just the yellowing bruise on her jaw and the deep scratches down one side of her face. Her clothes were scruffy and unwashed and her shaved head was matted with grease.

'Lilly, what on earth's happened?' asked Jinty. Lilly gave me a desperate look.

'Lil got mugged last week,' I said quickly. 'She's been in shock ever since.'

'What happened? Are you—'

'Leave it, Jints,' I said, 'Lilly doesn't want to talk about it at the moment.' To her credit, Jinty left it, obviously realizing something was up.

'You look well,' said Lilly, sitting down, lighting a fag and opening a bottle of cider.

I saw Jinty about to say something and then swallow her remark.

'Thanks,' said Jinty. She did look good, the bitch. She'd had a new power haircut and was carrying a mobile phone. She'd managed to get the phone off Ben by doing a flow chart demonstrating how his lack of emotional and financial support was leading to a communication gap between them. The phone was a symbol of their love. 'How's being pregnant?'

'All right.' Lilly looked sadly down at the floor and my heart almost broke. Lil had always been deeply maternal and was the sort of person who used to follow pregnant women round shops. She said having a child would be like having a little mate.

'It's not too late to get rid of it,' said Jinty.

'But I want the baby.' Lilly handed me the cider bottle.

'But do you want to be a single parent living in a hard-to-let flat in a council block?'

'I've got Ewan.'

Jinty raised her eyebrows at me. As far as I knew she hadn't heard about the beatings but she still viewed Ewan as a shiftless Welsh layabout.

'How's Ben?' I asked Jinty, desperate to get her off the subject.

'Oh, the idiot. He's a very sad and repressed individual.' She bit some hair between her teeth. 'You know, ever since I came to terms with my sexuality and wanted to express it, he doesn't want to have sex any more. I practically had to force myself on him last night. And then when I tried to give him a blow-job he said he couldn't bear to see me humiliate myself like that. He's just *so* unadventurous in bed. I tried to put my fingers up his bottom and he was having none of it and called me a pervert. And yet when I wouldn't have sex with him that was all he went on about. Idiot.' Jinty showed us a book she was reading called *If it Hurts, It isn't Love*.

'I'd better go,' said Lilly, slowly rising to her feet.

'Don't go,' I begged, dreading time alone with my sister.

'I might as well.' Lil sighed and put her smelly old cardigan back on. She felt in her pockets and then looked up at me. 'Tara, can you, can you lend me a couple of quid? My giro's late. I'll pay you back as soon as—'

'Of course, Lil, don't worry.'

Lilly was the proudest person I knew. Despite her numerous financial crises, she had never once borrowed money off me. I could barely guess how much asking had cost her.

* * *

The next time I saw Lilly was two days later. She had scalds all over her arm from where Ewan had thrown boiling water at her.

'Lilly, this looks *awful*,' I said, gingerly applying antiseptic cream.

'You should see Ewan,' said Lilly stoically. 'I threw a chair at his face.'

'Lil.' I put the top back on the cream. 'You've got to leave him, you know that.'

'I know, he's a cunt.'

'No, I mean not just say you'll leave him but actually leave him.'

'Are you calling me a liar?'

I shook my head and necked some cider.

'I hit him, too.'

'But Lilly, he's a bloke and you're a girl. I know you think you're a man but . . . you're *pregnant*. He could hurt your baby.'

'All couples argue.'

'But they don't all deck each other.'

'They do.'

'Do they? No, I mean, they don't. They talk things through and see counsellors.'

'Oh, and you're so experienced with long-term commitment?'

'Oh Lil, I'm not trying to . . .' I sighed. 'Let's go to bed. Top-to-toe, OK?'

Lilly passed out and as usual I stayed awake chain-smoking. I couldn't let this go on. For one my drinking was as bad as ever now I was joining Lilly on her cider-benders. Also, what was I waiting for before I took action? Until Lilly was permanently maimed? Lilly herself obviously wasn't going to do anything, I think because her whole relationship with Ewan was tied up with her mother's death. Lilly's mother: one of the most truly unattractive people I had ever met. Mean, selfish, violent, cruel. And yet Lilly had loved her. Maybe she honestly thought that that was how all mothers behaved: stubbing their fags out on you and nicking your stuff to sell for heroin. I remembered what Jinty had said to me after Lilly left. That Ma was not just selling the house but was going to live in a commune in Wiltshire. My mother – Queen's secretarial college graduate, lifetime devotee of Liberty's, housewife lush – had become a hippie. She'd even asked to borrow some of Jinty's ambient whale tapes.

'And she's cut back on the booze,' Jinty had said.

'Alcoholics can be very cunning,' I'd said knowledgeably.

'No, she's actually functioning now. Still a total pisshead to be sure but she didn't even pass out when I went to see her. Since Pa died she doesn't seem to need it so much.'

I looked at Lilly lying in bed with her scabby right arm spread across the duvet. I remembered Pa screaming for Ama and me to get downstairs. I'd begged her to go down first as he didn't beat her as badly as he beat me. Knowing what had to be done, I lit another cigarette and reached for the phone.

'CJ?'

I'd first met CJ at Nippers topless cocktail bar. I'd gone over to him and a group of his loud-mouthed associates, trying to persuade them to buy our ridiculously overpriced and disgusting 'champagne'.

'Five bottles, love,' a quiet, chain-smoking bloke had said. I could have kissed him. Unlike the other girls, who made their money through 'extras', I relied on the percentage of takings we received from flogging drinks. I walked back with a tray, trying to hide my breasts behind the bottles.

'Sit down,' CJ had said after I'd spilled half the champagne when one bloke had made a comment about two peas on an ironing board.

'Sorry,' I blushed.

'Forgotten,' he said, waving his hand. 'You're new ere, aren't yer?'

'Yes. I've only been working two weeks.'

'Joying it?'

I shrugged my shoulders and folded my arms over my chest. 'I want to go back to dance college and a friend of mine Sarah said you could make good tips.'

'But she didn't tell yer what you ad to do for tips.'

'No,' I said, shaking my head. I knew I wouldn't last the week so it seemed pointless pretending.

'CJ,' he said, offering his hand.

'Lulu,' I shifted one arm to cover both tits.

He grinned and lit another cigarette. 'And yer real name?'

I said nothing and he grinned even more. 'I was watching yer last night. You don't belong ere, classy bird like you. You're quiet too, don't give away much.' I must have grimaced as he burst out laughing. 'S all right, love, I'm not tryin to chat yers up. I'm thinkin we could do business. D'you drive?'

'Why?' I asked. CJ slapped his thigh.

'Yer perfect, gel. Want any toot?'

I looked around the seedy room full of fat, laughing men and over-made-up girls. Lilly was in the corner giving simultaneous hand-jobs to two blokes. Her arm movements made her look like she was ski-ing. I took a sip of my champagne, which was flat and tasted of pear drops.

'Look, I'm not going to do anything with you.'

'Lionel!' CJ snapped his fingers. 'Packet for the lady.' I was handed a gram of cocaine. CJ then pressed his card into my hand. 'Call me. All you ave to do for me is drive and keep yer mouth shut. You've got me word on that.'

I left Lilly in bed and went to meet CJ. He kept odd hours; one of the disadvantages of his profession. I pulled up outside the sauna in Gospel Oak, scene of many of our conferences (CJ liked it there as it was one of the few places he was able to stop smoking without actually being unconscious). I'd always been the only girl in the sauna and would sit sweltering in a king-sized towel whilst he gave me my instructions.

'All right?' said a quiet voice. I saw CJ, dressed in a white tracksuit and standing beside a Mercedes. I parked my car and got out. 'Still got the motor, then?' He laughed, kissing me on the cheek.

My car had been my first present from CJ. After CJ and his associates had left Nippers, some city idiots had arrived. They threw champagne on my chest and then tried to lick it off. I resigned. I sat in the cab home cursing men and was about to throw away CJ's card. Something stopped me. After days of debating, I'd called and he'd asked me to his 'office', a small bare flat in Ealing. He gave me tea and reassured me that he didn't have any cheeky intentions ('I've got more than enough birds. Do me ead in, they do'). He then explained that he needed someone to do deliveries. Someone female, nicely spoken, who had no connection with his firm. He told me straight: 'You'll be droppin and pickin up money and cocaine. I only deal coke. No crack or heroin shit. You'll get a decent cut but if yer done, I don't know yer.'

'Why are you trusting me? You've only met me once.'

'Know a mate of yours, Sarah. She told me you was goin to work at Nippers.'

'She's involved?'

'Fuck, no!' CJ laughed, started coughing and lit another

fag. 'Wouldn't trust er an inch. She thought it was a right laugh, you endin up there.'

Bitch.

'I know yer man Ben as well. Do some drops to im if I'm short of business.'

'Do you know everyone?'

'It's me business.' CJ leant forward. He really had been exceedingly unattractive. He looked like a syphilitic rat and his teeth were brilliant orange. 'As I say I've been looking out for someone. Let's say I ave a business interest in Nippers. I've been avin you watched. Yer quiet lookin, straight-actin, but I ave it on record you do alf a G of wizz a night.' CJ leant back and inhaled hard. 'Call it instinct if yer like. I ave a feelin yer a lot arder than yer look. So what d'ya say?'

'I haven't got a car.'

'You ave now.' He handed me some keys, an envelope of money and a Vehicle Registration Document. 'Look out of the window.'

CJ hadn't changed much over the years. Standing underneath the streetlamp in Gospel Oak, he looked as yellow as ever. I wanted to ask him what had happened to the bloke who hadn't paid up, if I was safe, but I couldn't. We chit-chatted for a minute or so and then got down to business. There was no point in pretending we were going to see one another again. I gave him some details and he nodded quietly, making notes in a small diary.

'I can't pay,' I said eventually. He lit a cigarette and took my hand, taking the opportunity to put a few notes into it.

'Didn't I say to call me whenever yer needed a favour? It's as good as done, Ta. Now, yer go ome and hit the snorebox. Don't want yer tired for yer dance.'

I turned to go.

'Always look for yer whenever I goes up West,' said CJ suddenly. 'Yer know, checkin the shows for yer name.'

I smiled and got back into the car he had given me.

It was a long drive back to Fulham but the streets sped past as there were so few vehicles around. I felt as if I was watching a repeat of an old film. I'd done this journey so many times before, only the difference was that now I didn't have ten thousand pounds' worth of cocaine in the boot. It seemed unbelievable that I'd actually been a drugs courier. That I spent an entire summer driving round London coked out of my head doing drops. That I used to earn several hundred pounds a day. That I'd probably been in every illegal drinking dive in London (the kinds that used to have huge lines of coke running down the side of the bar). If Ama hadn't died, if my knee hadn't messed up . . . who knows? But I was broke and just didn't care. It was a good day when my first waking thought wasn't, I want to die. The money I'd earnt had kept me going through my first year at dance college, had financed my E days in Chingford. But there had been a legacy. For when you're carrying God-knows-what to God-knows-where you tend to get a bit nervous. I sweated so much my car was like a travelling sauna. And CJ was just as paranoid as I was: chain-smoking, pacing, constantly on the phone. He'd already been down for five years and suffered from terrible stomach ulcers. We always spoke in code. I burnt all my addresses, never once spoke to him from my home phone. But the ultimate question always went un-answered: if I did get done, what would I say? I had nightmares not just about the police getting me but also about CJ getting me as well. And although my paranoia was driving me insane, I knew that it also protected me. That CJ had probably chosen me for the job because of my natural paranoid tendencies. I once asked CJ if it was wise for me to drive the same car all the time and he just took a long drag on his B&H and said, 'If they're on to us, it don't matter what car you use.'

I woke before Lilly the next morning and left for college. I did ballet and then met Caro. By the time I arrived back at my flat, I was paralytically drunk and had spent half an hour in the tube trying to hold vomit in my mouth. I threw up and then went to bed for a couple of hours. Eleven o'clock. I opened my new bottle of emergency vodka. Two a.m. The doorbell goes. I bring Lilly upstairs. Ewan's in hospital. She went to the offie and returned home to find him pulverized. In the ambulance he just lay there screaming, 'Who the fuck have you told? That nigger called me an animal.'

'Have this,' I said, sharing some of my vodka with Lilly. I noticed that her hand was shaking. 'Is he OK now?'

'I think so. The doctor said that he looked much worse than he was. He should be out in a week. I just can't believe it.'

'Is Ewan mixed up in a dodgy crowd?'

'Tara, it was a black bloke that did it. Ewan had never even seen a black bloke until he came to London.' Lilly shook her head. 'It must have been Jinty. You told her, didn't you?'

'What?'

'When she saw me the other week. She must have realized what was going on and got Ben to send one of his thugs round.'

'Ben doesn't have any thugs.'

'Stop protecting her. The rozzers came to the hospital and Ewan said he didn't see nothing, didn't have a clue etc.' Because he was too bloody scared of them finding out what he'd been doing to Lilly, I thought. 'But if Ben thinks I'm letting him get away with this he's fucking wrong. I'm going to call them rozzers and tell them to take a sniff round his flat.'

I looked hard at Lilly. She wasn't crying, she didn't sound hysterical, she was serious. 'It wasn't anything to do with Ben.'

Lilly looked up at me. 'How do you . . . Tara?' I could see she wanted me to tell her that it wasn't true. I said nothing. 'I don't believe it. You've betrayed me for the second time.'

'I couldn't stand by,' I pleaded.

'You had no fucking *right*!' screamed Lilly, throwing her glass of vodka at my bedroom wall.

'I never meant it to go this far. I just wanted him given a talking to. But Lilly . . . he's a *monster*. He hurts you.'

'I love him.'

'He's a monster, a drunk, a psychotic.'

Lilly stood up, her whole body trembling with rage. 'I want you to realize, Tara, that the only reason I'm going to let you off this is cos of your dad dying so recently. I mean, maybe you're unhinged or something. Don't you see, you can't go around getting people beat up cos you don't like what they do.'

'Ewan does.'

'I provoke him! I'm just as guilty as he is. It's not all black and white . . . oh, you're drunk, there's no point in talking to you. Just stay the fuck away from me.'

I had now betrayed Lilly for the second time. The first had been just after I'd given up working for CJ. I'd always known that drugs couriering was a job with a short life-span, but my career had been particularly abruptly terminated. I'd made a delivery one day with instructions to pick up payment at the other end. No payment was forthcoming. CJ's phone was engaged so I drove down to his office. When he heard, he jumped in the car and instructed me to drive back to the house where I'd dropped the drugs. He sat in the car twitching and snorting coke off his hand. As we were nearing the house we saw the man who'd refused to pay casually strolling down the street munching a Mars Bar.

'I've ad it with the cunt,' said CJ. ''E's taken one too many fuckin liberties.' CJ jumped out and within seconds the bloke was lying on the pavement. He was puking up blood. CJ looked around the empty road, got back into the car and carefully wiped a knife on his sweatshirt. Then he ripped the stained top off and shoved it under the car seat.

'Sorry you ad to see that, doll.' He was shaking. 'Went a bit far. Make sure yers clean this up, right?'

I received a call the next day to meet CJ in a park. He told me something had arisen and he was going to have to let me go. One thousand pounds. Take care of yourself. If you ever need a favour, call me.

After CJ, I went back to my normal life. I started seeing friends again, moved flat and paid my first term's fees. Only it wasn't that simple. I still didn't sleep, night after night sighing into my pillow and staring at the wall. Whenever I drove, I spent the entire journey with my eyes locked to the rear-view mirror. And I'd picked up a bit of a toot habit. I used to spend a lot of time with Sarah, snorting and shopping. I was going to meet her at a club one night when I got stopped by the police. They searched me and found three grams of coke in my bra. I refused to say anything until I got to the station. Then I told them I was Lilly. She was away travelling at the time. I couldn't see how it would hurt her. I was interviewed, charged, printed, photographed. The police wanted a contact number to confirm my address. I told them there was no phone number in my house. A squad car drove me round to Lilly's squat and watched as I pretended to unlock the door. Actually, the door had no lock, so I just pushed it open. Then I stood inside and leant against the wall, gasping for breath, my heart pounding against my chest, waiting until it was safe for me to leave. The worst of it was that all the time I had been driving round London I'd been carrying around pieces of Lilly's ID that I was supposed to be looking after.

Lucinda called me at four that morning. I was still wide awake and trying to distract myself from thinking about Lilly. 'What're you up to?' she asked.

'Oh, just another quiet night in phoning the Samaritans . . .' At first I'd been composing suicide notes. I was thinking about writing a book called *A Hundred Ways to Say Goodbye*: suicide notes for any occasion. Then I'd started reading the *Sun*. 'Listen to this: *Dear Deidre, my husband, who is thirty, works hard and looks after me. I love him with all my heart – despite his mood swings, drink problem, selfish love-making and the fact that he's slept with two prostitutes . . .* People are so weird.'

'The weirdest.'

'Haven't you got rehearsals tomorrow?'

'I've been sacked. Aren't you at college?'

'Can't sleep.'

I thought, I can't sleep, I can't eat, I can't have sex, I can't do any of the things that constitute normal human existence.

'It's been the worst week of my life,' said Lucinda.

'I know what you mean.'

'Once you debate,' she said slowly, 'it's inevitable. When you wrestle you're in the illness.'

'Have you binged?'

'Seventeen hours.'

'Have you drunk?'

'Fourteen hours.'

There wasn't much else to say, really. 'We always repeat the same shit,' I sighed. 'I'm so bored of myself. It's as if I'm trying to bore myself to death.'

'Maybe you should try Prozac.'

'I'm already on it.'

I still didn't know if CJ had killed that bloke.

16. Your Love

Sarah and I were lying in her sitting-room surrounded by piles of *Vogue*. Coco was in the corner eating an issue and attempting to spit bits at me. She really was a charming baby.

'I mean, *wedding*,' sighed Sarah, lighting another menthol. 'What textures does that word suggest?'

'Sort of nasty polyester fake satin?'

Sarah rolled her eyes. 'You're hopeless. It's lucky no-one will ever marry you. Texturally wise, "wedding" says silk, lace, satin, rubber—'

'Rubber?'

'Possibly. There was a wedding at the Torture Garden and both boys wore rubber.'

'I think rubber's out, Sarah. I mean, the whole point of your wedding is about pretending to be normal.'

'Yes, but if I look too straight Shamus will know something's up.'

'Shamus?'

'Jonny's father. Who I—'

' "Escorted"?'

'I know. I've even told him I'm thinking of converting to Catholicism, and you know I once wanked someone off on an altar.' Sarah smoothed her hair. 'It was quite dull, actually.'

'What's Jonny going to wear?' I was wondering when Sarah was going to offer me some of the coke I knew she was snorting every time she went to the lav. She seemed to have had a permanent 'cold' ever since Coco's birth.

'A morning suit, but he'll wear women's knickers underneath. He wants to make a statement.'

'A statement that no-one can see.'

'That's Jonny.'

To say that Sarah and Jonny's engagement had been a shock is perhaps inadequate. The news had kept Fulham in hysteria for a week. Sarah: ex-escort, human Hoover, who'd run off with a bouncer and then had Jonny's baby. Jonny: nightclub manager, Millwall fanatic, blackmail victim, boyfriend of club assistant Savage. They'd met again at Sarah's last sordid foray at the Torture Garden (where she'd borrowed Seb's cape and gone dressed as a Nazi stormtrooper). Sarah had thought Jonny might attack her over the blackmailing but instead he started drunkenly sobbing on her shoulder. He'd had to break up with Savage. His father was becoming suspicious.

'I can't imagine how he's guessed,' Jonny had wailed.

'Probably Savage's new handlebar moustache.'

Jonny had put his head in his hands and admitted that covering up what he was was becoming harder and harder but if his father found out he was gay, he would disown him.

'Couldn't you make it on your own?' Sarah had tentatively asked.

'What?'

'I know. We only get anywhere off other people's backs.'

'Of off lying on our backs.'

'You're as much of a prostitute as I am.'

'I know.' Jonny had sniffed some amyl. 'Fuck it, let's get married. It'll solve both our problems.'

'OK.'

Romance. Alive and well and living in Fulham. The only bone of contention had been Jonny trying to make Savage best man. Sarah had said she'd compromise and that he could be bridesmaid but eventually it was agreed that Savage would act as greeter. I'd asked Sarah if she was sure about marrying and she'd just shrugged and said, 'What have I got to lose? I just have to last two years and I'll get fifty per cent. At least I don't have to pretend to love him, and Coco gets a father. Anyway, Shamus is buying us a place in Chelsea and we'll both be able to bring home whoever we like.'

'But what if you ever do actually, you know, want to get together with someone one day?'

Sarah snorted with laughter. 'I won't and . . .' Sarah had looked down at her rather gaudy engagement ring. 'Besides, Jonny is my other half. I do love him in a way, I think. What I mean is, he knows what I am and it's OK by him. I told him about my uncle, you know.'

'Sarah . . .' I looked at Sarah's manicured nails and compared them with my own dirty, bitten variety. 'Do you ever think that you'll never be like other people? That you'll never really fall in love and that no-one will ever love you?'

'Are we talking about me or you here?'

Dance college was coming to a finish. We were taught
our phrases for the external examiners. We pinned strange
numbers on our chests. Chairs of people wrote and took
notes. I was the best in my contemporary but the group was
so talentless it didn't count. Tonty said he wanted to remind
us that he was writing our ballet reports the following day
and he still hadn't received any bribes. I was thrown out of
the repertory piece. The official reason was that I didn't know
the material. The unofficial reason was that the choreographer thought me a 'lazy, sulky unco-operative depressive'.
I remembered the joy of starting ballet when I was younger,
ecstatic at finally finding an activity where I felt some kind of
release, where I found my voice. I remembered performing,
coming off stage shaking and sweating and thinking, I'm
good! I forgot I was good! I understood my fundamental
problem with dance: I didn't want to spend my life performing other people's steps, but I didn't have any of my own.

I became the only person in college immune to exam
hysteria. No sobbing in corridors. No frantic late-night
agonizing in sweaty studios. I watched with detachment as
everyone else grew steadily loonier. Personal Investigations
were conducted by the more artistic third years: one bloke
nailing himself to a studio wall, another holding a tea party in
the women's showers, a girl even ending up in the atrium
with a begging tin and sign around her neck saying 'I can't
Dance' whilst a video of her doing ballet played ('In a dance
college environment,' her manifesto read, 'being a lousy
dancer is a major disadvantage . . . to what extent should
we accept ourselves as we are and to what extent should we
struggle for change?'). I stopped struggling. While the other
third years talked of future plans – to audition, to become lap
dancers, to commit kamikaze in Japan – I had no plans apart

from a vague ambition to be an aerobics instructor. So I sat and smoked outside college, watching ambulances as they came and went, thinking, I'm here but I already miss it.

Caro used to sit and smoke with me. She was going to Italy to do some jazz show. It'd already gone a bit wrong after she'd got pissed one night and slept with the rehearsal director. I realized that this was why I liked Caro: despite her pretences, she had an inability to control herself. Also, it was obvious she was developing a drink problem. Unlike everyone else, who went down the pub to get drunk, Caro went down the pub and swore not to get drunk.

'I'm not drinking this week,' she'd say, and then end up drinking in one night what most normal people drank in a week. 'The difference between me and you baby,' she'd slur, 'is that I can control it.'

Then we'd get back to Caro's place and she'd open another bottle of wine, spilling most of it on the floor. 'God, dancing dehydrates me,' she'd moan, and pop six Nurofen.

'Steady on,' I'd warn.

'No, the Nurofen are like the drink. They don't really affect me. Another glass?'

'Just a small one.'

'I spose I might as well drink the rest,' she'd giggle. 'My battle with drink: I give up, you win.'

Then Caro would wake me the following day and we'd clutch our heads and gulp coffee. 'God those Nurofen affected me badly,' she'd groan. 'I think I might have a hair of the dog.'

'But Caro, you can't drink in the morning.'

'Oh, it's almost afternoon, baby.'

*   *   *

It was summer. Fulham smelt like Greece or rather like Athens on a particularly polluted day. Everyone was sporting ridiculous sun-shades and peeling shoulders. There was something in the air; even my sluggish sex drive had raised its ugly and twisted head.

'D'you realize your face contorts every time you look at Tim?' said Gerry to me one sticky night at work. The club was totally dead and I'd given up sitting on the door trying to beg people to come in.

'Probably a tick or something.'

'No, I don't think so.' She lit a spliff under the counter and grinned. 'You've been leering at him all night.'

'Don't be ridiculous.'

'You were practically drooling at one stage. And you've started wearing make-up again.'

'So?'

'I heard you earlier on; telling Tim you were cutting down on the booze and thinking of going to pottery workshops. Pathetic.'

I put my third vodka shot down. I'd been had. 'How could I have been so blind?' I asked Gerry. 'I'm so ashamed.' I realized that I had fancied Tim for ages. Whether it was biology or desperation or just general sadness, I had begun to find him strangely attractive. Even the way he stroked his rat-like goatee had begun to charm rather than irritate me. 'You won't tell anyone?' I begged. 'Oh the embarrassment.' I knew Tim didn't fancy me any more. Since our Shag he had treated me with a mixture of bemusement and disgust. 'Rejected by Tim,' I said, shaking my head. 'Life can degrade me no further.'

Gerry laughed and then started choking on her spliff. 'Relax. I'm not grassing you to no-one.'

'You're not?'

'I couldn't get through the pain barrier again.'

'What?'

'I've had it with this place. I'm leaving to become a trainee estate agent.'

'Fuck,' I said, 'I almost believed you there.'

'I'm being serious. I start Monday.'

'But Gerry . . .' Gerry was an ex-dancer, we'd always worked at the Escape together, what would I do without her? 'You can't. What about me?'

'Selfish to the end, eh?' Gerry passed me the spliff and sprayed a bit of air freshener around. Then she leant on the bar and smiled. 'Thing was, I always reckoned I'd travel, but when I went to Thailand this summer I realized I hated travellers.'

The strange, parallel world of travellers: people who delighted in being mugged, revelled in sleeping in train stations, orgasmed over catching bizarre medieval diseases.

'When we were there, me and Paul went to this camp in the hills to smoke opium. It was the most fucking beautiful place but it fucking stank. I couldn't work it out at first, and then I realized that the stink was shit. The people were so stoned they couldn't be arsed to go to the bog so they just lay there shitting themselves.' Gerry grabbed my hand. 'The way we drink isn't normal, Tara. I don't know whether I drink to work or work to drink. I spliff like fuck but I still can't stop.'

'I'll miss you,' I said miserably.

'No you won't.' Gerry collapsed in laughter. 'You're too fucking self-obsessed to miss anyone.'

Actually, Gerry was wrong. I had been missing someone for a considerable amount of time: my friend Susie from Barkingside. She'd been travelling round Australia for ages until she'd been unable to get another visa. She returned back home (saying no-one laughed like Essex people – well, no-one else had as much to laugh at, did they?) and visited me two weeks later. She looked brown and well fed and was wearing a tattered T-shirt saying *Slappers On Tour*.

'How was it?' I asked when Susie had made herself comfortable on my bed.

'Dangerous people, desperate acts . . . top fun!'

'Did you learn anything?'

'Learn?' Susie looked at me strangely. 'I went there to ave a laugh. See new things, meet different people, ave a lot of sex.' Susie sniffed my sheets. 'Ave these been changed since I left?'

'How many men did you have sex with?'

'Jeez, I d'know, there was women as well . . . d'you count oral sex?'

I shrugged my shoulders.

'Let's say not . . . d'you count if you can't remember their names?' Susie sighed. 'I've got a map at ome.' She watched me as I lit another cigarette. 'You look like a fuckin stick insect. What ave you been up to?'

'Nothing.'

'You must ave done something.'

'No. Really, nothing at all's changed for me.'

Sarah wanted to hold her 'hen' night at somewhere smart, but Jonny's father refused to pay due to the fact that he was paying for everything else. It was with great reluctance that Sarah decided to have her party at the Escape, the self-confessed saddest club in London. She attempted to be fashionable and call it her Goodbye to Slumming party, but she didn't fool me. I was instructed to bring some male fitties but I didn't know any so I invited my merchant wanker Seb in thanks for him getting Jinty an interview at his bank.

Seb told me he had a great surprise for me. He turned up at my flat with Jem.

'I would have called this a stupefaction rather than a surprise,' I said to Seb when Jem went into the bathroom to check his reflection.

'*He* called *Me!*' whispered Seb in my ear.

'He hasn't taken any money off you?' I asked.

'God you're such a cynic, Tara. He said he missed me. We've moved in together. We've decided we're bisexuals who only sleep with men.'

'Really.'

Seb smiled beatifically and handed me an E. 'I don't need to drink now. Love changes everything.'

We walked to Seb's new Porsche and I grabbed Jem and sat him in the back beside me. Seb put his new state-of-the-art CD player on and I quietly snarled to Jem, 'And the real reason?'

'What?'

'Why did you call Seb?'

'I have a lot of feelings for him.'

'What feelings?'

'There's no point in explaining to you, is there petal?'

'Got bored of East Finchley, did you?'

Jem's pretty face contorted as he attempted a sneer. 'Seb's going to Peru with me to start filming the first section of my movie, *Nasal Renegade*. One must make sacrifices for one's creativity. Besides, I make him happy. Look how he cavorts and frolics around me.'

'Fool that he is.'

Jem eyed me nastily. 'I've obtained some new eye cream. You should borrow it. Women go off so quickly, dearie. Besides,' he spoke up again, 'I've decided to start a religion. In many ways, *Nasal Renegade* will be less an adventure movie and more a man's search – a dangerous search – for his self.'

'I see.' I noticed for the first time that both Seb and Jem were dressed in white and that Jem wore beads.

'One must understand,' mused Jem, 'that our problem is that we view our problems as *our* problems when in fact they are *society's* problems.'

'Really.' I wondered if I had enough cigarettes to last the evening.

'Look at you: broke, badly dressed, a victim of your own delinquency; pathetic, really. But, as a dancer, if you had financial and community support . . .'

'The lottery,' I burbled. 'It wouldn't change my life, I'd still sign on . . .'

'WE'VE LOST OUR SENSE OF COMMUNITY!' screamed Seb from the front. I worried that it was a dark, clear night yet Seb was driving with no headlights and the windscreen wipers on.

'You see,' said Jem, leaning closer to me and fingering his chin, 'we've become so caught up in individualism that our very freedom has become a burden.'

I knew then that Jem had read *Being and Nothingness*. We'd done it in Philosophy for Dancers.

'I see Purism as being more based on spirituality than religion. Not God as such; more a mixture of Buddhism, AA and the Freemasons. Of course, not any old pleb could join. Purism would be very much a young, fashionable Soho-based religion.'

'A support group for wankers.'

'People capable of masturbation, yes,' Jem said bitchily. 'The Face are interested, actually.'

I didn't ask if I could join. Jem probably wouldn't let me and besides I looked like an anaemic elephant in white.

We arrived at the club and I thought that amazingly it

seemed to have reached new heights of sordidness. Half the neon sign had been cut out and now read The E Club. Traces was on the door playing with a flick-knife and greeted me with a customary, 'Fuck off.'

'Nice to see you didn't go to too much trouble with your appearance,' he mocked as I walked inside. I did look pretty terrible. I'd put on make-up and a fresh pair of jeans, but my clothes were old and tatty and my hair brittle and straw-like. I was without excuse. Walking down the stairs, I paused for a moment and considered doing an about turn. Hordes of Sarah's Sloaney wankers were there, braying and gorgeous, plus the load of wankers that called themselves my friends. To my surprise, Jem took my arm.

'Come on, petal, let's show the breeders the meaning of style.'

Jem and I went to the bar and ordered Brain Damages for ourselves and Perrier for Seb.

'Frankly,' confided Jem, 'with the amount of disco pills Seb's taking I don't think he'd notice what we gave him to drink.' When we returned, Seb was talking to Cassie, who was obviously pissed and pretending to be collecting ashtrays. After Gerry had left, I got Cassie a job at the club. I knew it was a terrible idea – no-one worked at the Escape long without experiencing liver damage – but Cass was skint and I was lonely at work. Traces took great delight in telling me the names that the other staff called me behind my back (his favourite was 'the mad ballerina'). I was only really kept on as some kind of household pet.

Cassie was leaning on Seb's shoulder and spouting a load of bollocks about how love had changed her life. The last time I'd seen Cass, she'd been covered in eczema and going on about how the blood was staining her sheets. Then Touchy-Feely had said he was in love with her and had started attending a sex addicts' group. Cassie bought some great clothes and started using an ultra-strong steroid cream. Cass was cool now. She'd given up the E and just got drunk instead.

'Tara!' she said, stumbling forward and hugging me.

'Hi,' I said. There was no denying that Cass did look so much better. All that remained of her rampaging facial eczema were a couple of dry, flaky patches. Her eyes shone and even her thin blonde hair looked glossy.

'Touchy and I are going to Glastonbury together.'

'How lovely.'

I wondered if it was such a good idea. The last time Cass had gone to Glastonbury she'd got so stoned that she'd been unable to put up her tent and had spent the night kipping in the drugs counselling section.

'Are you OK?' she asked me.

'Just tired,' I said, sitting down in a chair.

'What's the matter?' she asked, crouching in front of me.

'Nothing . . . it's just, what idiot lives like me, you know?'

'Oh, Ta,' said Cass gently. 'You just need someone to love you. Since Touchy and I have been serious, everything's changed. He accepts me as I am. I thought no-one could do that.'

I looked over at Sarah, who was dressed in rubber with a veil of black mesh over her face. We fool ourselves thinking we choose to live like this. No-one would choose to live like this.

'Sorry,' giggled Cassie as she dropped her drink and it splashed up on my jeans. 'I got thrown out of college yesterday. I forgot to do these essays and then I forgot to get a doctor's note excusing me for not doing them.' She grinned. 'Everyone else is terribly worried but I'm not in the least bothered. Now I've just got practical problems instead of psychological and practical problems.'

Cass was the only bright light in the evening that was doomed before it had even begun. The whole crowd was shrieking with laughter. Not giggles or snorts of laughter, but high-pitched wails. It was like listening to people drowning. I was soon drinking so heavily that I became unable to distinguish anyone. The whole lot of them seemed to merge into some loud, red abstract painting. I couldn't stop ordering Brain Damages and leant against the bar watching Tim.

'Are you OK?' he asked.

'I wish, I wish people would stop asking me if I'm OK.' Actually, my life's in fucking tatters. 'Sorry. How about you?'

'Can't complain. I sold a mobile yesterday.' He smiled and began to take glasses out of the dishwasher and wipe them with a cloth. He was the only barperson who bothered to polish the glasses. How could I have been so blind? I'd liked Tim all along. I saw his eyes wander to the other side of the bar where Cassie was pouring a disastrous pint of lager. He put the cloth down and went over to help her. My heart broke.

I stood – and then swayed – in the corner, sternly drinking my rank cocktail. If I was honest, I'd been drunk for years. My last sober day had probably been when I was having a knee operation and under a general anaesthetic. The slippery slope of alcohol. You set yourself limits. If I . . . then I'd stop. I'd recently started suffering blackouts. They weren't too bad. I'd be at home drinking my emergency vodka and the next day things would be kind of blank. But I remembered when I'd thought that if I had blackouts I'd stop boozing. But then the boundary shifted. As long as I didn't piss myself . . . Every day I'd wake up to see the AA book *Tomorrow I'll be Different* on my bedside table and decide that I wouldn't drink that evening. But by the afternoon I'd forgotten. Lucinda said to me our problem was that we didn't really want to stop; that we set ourselves lives so brutal that they'd have been impossible without escape routes. Lucinda wasn't at the party that evening as she'd started using smack again. John from AA (who'd been her counsellor at Second Chance) had recently been thrown out of the clinic for using and sleeping with patients. He'd telephoned Lucinda and asked her out for a drink. This was suspicious as he knew from their therapy sessions that Lucinda always fucked people when she drank (which was why she didn't drink). She went out with John, got paralytic, slept with him, and somehow split her head open in the process. They were now on some mad heroin binge, locked in Cindy's flat spending day after day chasing. Lucinda had given up. She said that when your own drugs counsellor said you were as mad as a snake and had no hope of ever recovering, you tended to believe them. And that if he too was using again, he who'd known everything about using and recovery, you knew that no amount of self-knowledge would save you.

'It's funny,' she said, 'as when I left Second Chance everyone said I was going too soon and I'd be bingeing by the next day. I said that I had a choice whether to binge or not and John just looked at me and went, "You haven't got any choice." At least I admit it now.'

I thought of my contemporary teacher saying to me, 'Everyone wants to do a solo until they're on the stage alone.' It was funny to think that my dancing really was all over now. I would leave college and probably never do class again. I supposed it was like the ending of a bad marriage: you couldn't even remember why you'd married the person in the first place, yet you didn't know how you'd carry on without them.

*   *   *

Reader, I married him . . . It was Sarah's new line and she repeated it over and over again on the way to Chelsea Register Office. I was squeezed into the car beside Sarah, Coco and Jinty, with Sarah's mother and the driver in front. The summer heat made me itchy and I wished I had worn something cooler. But it was difficult covering up full-body scars with flimsy outfits. Sarah was dressed in a rather obscene white number: short skirt and top barely covering up the stretchmarks on her stomach. Sarah's mother didn't seem terribly happy. She kept looking out of the car window, shaking her head and saying, 'Children having children . . .' Sarah said her mother had early-onset Alzheimer's.

'Reader, I married him,' chortled Sarah. 'Jonny's Pa's worth four mill, y'know. Totally caked, darlings.'

Sarah and Jonny got married. Savage grinned in a sinister fashion. Jonny's pa looked fat and happy. Coco was sick over herself. Ben and Jinty tried to appear couplish and even held hands. Sarah's mother shook. Lilly patted her belly and smiled at Ewan. Cassie looked green and hungover. Touchy stroked Cassie's hair and every so often whispered softly in her ear.

We went outside onto the steps. We'd been instructed not to throw confetti, both by Sarah (it was common) and by the register office (it messed up the steps) but everyone did. I watched the little bits of paper blowing into the smoke-snarled fumes of the King's Road and it reminded me of the snow-filled lands of Narnia.

'You look like you've seen a ghost,' said Jinty, coming up to stand beside me.

'I am a ghost.'

'Oh God, you're all such a bunch of addicts. Ben was throwing coke at Sarah, you know.'

I had one of those lightning-strikes of realization that you read about in novels: *A shot rang out* . . . 'Jinty, I feel like I'm haunting my own life.' I realized that I'd been dead for years. That I'd died with Amaranda. Not just a part of me, but all of me. Ama had admitted what I'd known all along: that we were weak. Whilst other people triumphed over adversity, we withered and floundered, simply existing to repeat our own mistakes. For years I had only controlled my drinking by dancing. Without dance, I was finished.

'Earth calling Planet Tara.' Jinty stared in amusement at me. 'You really have to cut down. Anyway, enough about you. I got the job at Seb's bank. I am officially a graduate trainee merchant banker.'

I looked at Ben being playfully punched by Savage. 'So when are you ending it with Ben?'

Ben was no longer even rich. Ever since Peanuts had got done, Ben's heart hadn't really been in dealing. Then his manky parrot Budweiser had died of a heart attack during roller-skating instructions. Jinty said Ben's whole life was a pathetic charade and that he was so broke that he'd actually been forced to sign on.

'Well . . .' Jinty started biting her hair. 'I've become involved with this chap from Life Dance. Purely sexual, we don't talk.'

'So you're going to dump Ben for him?'

'God no, he lives in Enfield.' Jinty wiped some confetti off her sleeve. 'He gives me orgasms, that's all. But it's time the idiot and I split up. We've fulfilled each other's co-dependent emotional needs and now it's time for me to move on.'

'And coincidentally you can afford your own flat.'

'Jesus, Tara.' Jinty looked at me with genuine frustration

on her face. 'I'm not saying Ben's dosh wasn't helpful, but it was never about that. We only ever worked because of sibling suicide and the fact that he was the one bloke I'd met who disliked sex as much as I did. Now I've come to terms with Pa I can move on.'

'What about Ben?'

'He's a cocaine addict, Tara.' The way Jinty said it, it was as if Ben's addiction meant he couldn't feel anything genuine when I knew that he really did love Jinty. 'Oh God, look at Sarah,' said Jinty in disgust. Sarah had developed a nosebleed. She was stuffing her flowers in her face to try and catch the worst of it. 'She's just ridiculous. She was actually giggling in the ceremony.'

I wondered how Jinty could get over her sexual abuse, whereas Sarah couldn't. When Sarah went off to sign the register I'd felt as if I'd been witnessing someone sign their own death warrant.

I walked down the steps, waiting for the cars to arrive to take us to the Ritz. I watched Lilly and Ewan. She was huge now and was laughing and wiping lipstick off his face. They were moving to Brighton together. Apparently Lilly had said that living in London was turning Ewan into a caged animal so they'd decided to skip town before the baby was born. Ewan had found a fishing job in Sussex and they'd got a flat off the social overlooking the sea. I wondered if they'd be happy and if Ewan would stop decking Lilly. Probably not, but at least they were giving themselves a chance. I was about to go over and join Cassie, who was sitting on the steps holding hands with Touchy, when I suddenly saw a wild-eyed creature running down the street.

'Lucinda!'

Cindy waved and sped towards me, oblivious of the

stares she was getting from the King's Road shoppers.

'Tara, shit,' she heaved, drawing up to me and panting for breath. 'I remembered you'd be here. I had to come and tell you. You know ages ago I wrote to that theatre company and asked for work with special needs kids? The girl they had dropped out. Can you believe it, I've got it!'

'Cindy!'

'And John went back to treatment today. He's gone to some clinic in the Outer Hebrides. He wrote me a poem saying how sorry he was for everything.'

'Cool.'

Lucinda grabbed my arm and stared intently into whatever was left of my eyes. 'Don't you see what this means?'

I shook my head.

'I got the job! Me!'

'What?'

'Don't you understand? I thought I was fucked, it was over, but things have turned around despite me.' Lucinda touched my face. 'It's like . . . you know how it is in class? You go in in the morning and you're totally exhausted and the teacher's throwing all these impossible combinations at you and you think, I just can't do this, no way. But you do. Somehow you're still there at the end of class.'

'But we've both given up dancing,' I murmured.

Lucinda didn't seem to hear me. 'I think we're stronger than we ever realized. Most people are either straights or addicts. We were trying to be both.'

'We failed.'

'You just don't see, do you? It's not as simple as that. Maybe we haven't failed, maybe it's not too late. Tara, *we could be wrong.*'

Lucinda threw back her head and laughed, revealing a mouthful of rotting teeth.